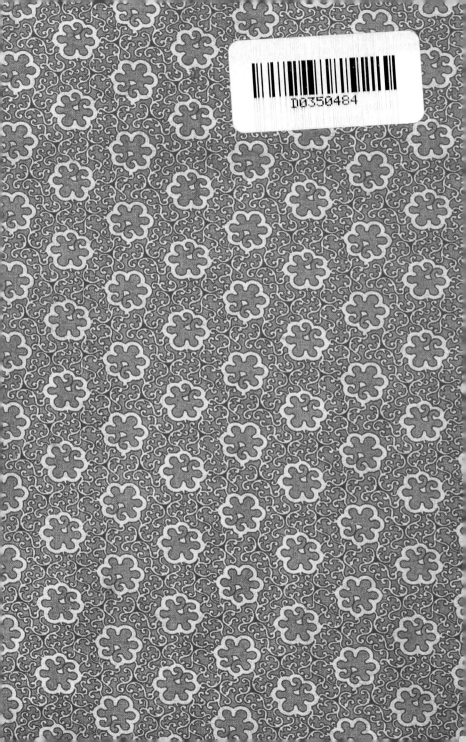

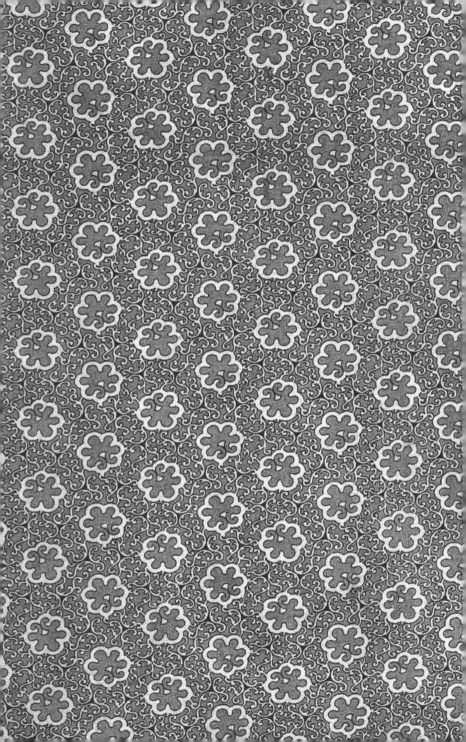

THE

SEPTEMBERS

OF

SHIRAZ

An Imprint of HarperCollins*Publishers*

THE

SEPTEMBERS

OF

SHIRAZ

DISCARD

DALIA SOFER

Designed by Claire Vaccaro

Library of Congress Cataloging-in-Publication Data is available upon request.

ISBN: 978-0-06-113040-3
ISBN-10: 0-06-113040-0

07 08 09 10 11 ID/RRD 10 9 8 7 6

For my parents, Simon and Farah,

my brothers, Joseph and Alfred,

and my sister, Orly

THE

SEPTEMBERS

OF

SHIRAZ

ONE

When Isaac Amin sees two men with rifles walk into his office at half past noon on a warm autumn day in Tehran, his first thought is that he won't be able to join his wife and daughter for lunch, as promised.

"Brother Amin?" the shorter of the men says.

Isaac nods. A few months ago they took his friend Kourosh Nassiri, and just weeks later news got around that Ali the baker had disappeared.

"We're here by orders of the Revolutionary Guards." The smaller man points his rifle directly at Isaac and walks toward him, his steps too long for his legs. "You are under arrest, Brother."

Isaac shuts the inventory notebook before him. He looks down at his desk, at the indifferent items witnessing this event—the scattered files, a metal paperweight, a box of Dunhill cigarettes, a crystal ashtray, and a cup of tea, freshly brewed, two mint leaves floating inside. His calendar is spread open and he stares at it, at today's date, *September 20, 1981,* at the notes scribbled on the page—*call Mr. Nakamura regarding pearls, lunch at home, receive shipment of black opals from Australia around 3:00 PM, pick up shoes from cobbler*—appointments he won't be keeping. On the opposite page is a glossy photo of the Hāfez mausoleum in Shiraz. Under it are the words, "City of Poets and Roses."

"May I see your papers?" Isaac asks.

"Papers?" the man chuckles. "Brother, don't concern yourself with papers."

The other man, silent until now, takes a few steps. "You are Brother Amin, correct?" he asks.

"Yes."

"Then please follow us."

He examines the rifles again, the short man's stubby finger already on the trigger, so he gets up, and with the two men makes his way down his five-story office building, which seems strangely deserted. In the morning he had noticed that only nine of his sixteen employees had come to work, but he had thought nothing of it; people had been unpredictable lately. Now he wonders where they are. Had they known?

As they reach the pavement he senses the sun spreading down his neck and back. He feels calm, almost numb, and he reminds himself he should remain so. A black motorcycle is parked by the curb, next to his own polished, emerald-green Jaguar. The small man smirks at the sleek automobile, then mounts his motorcycle, releases the brake, and ignites the engine. Isaac mounts next, with the second soldier behind him. "Hold on tight," the soldier says. Isaac's arms girdle the small man and the third man rests his hands on Isaac's waist. Sandwiched between the two he feels the bony back of one against his stomach and the belly of the other pushing into his back. The bitter smell of unwashed hair makes him gag. Turning his head to take a breath, he glimpses one of his employees, Morteza, frozen on the sidewalk like a bystander at a funeral procession.

The motorcycle swerves through the narrow spaces between jammed cars. He watches the city glide by, its transformation now so obvious to him: movie posters and shampoo advertisements have been replaced by sweeping murals of clerics; streets once named after kings now claim the revolution as their patron; and once-dapper men and women have become bearded shadows and black veils. The smell of kebab and charcoaled corn, rising from the street vendor's grill, fills the lunch hour. He had often treated himself to a hot skewer of lamb kebab here, sometimes bringing back two dozen for his employees, who would congregate in the kitchen, slide the tender meat off the skewers with slices of bread, and chew loudly. Isaac joined them from time to time, and while he could not allow himself to eat with equal abandon, he would be pleased for having initiated the gathering.

The vendor, fanning his grilled meat, looks at Isaac on the motorcycle, stupefied. Isaac looks back, but his captors pick up speed and he feels dizzy all of a sudden, ready to topple over. He locks his fingers around the driver's girth.

They stop at an unassuming gray building, dismount

the bike, and enter. Greetings are exchanged among the revolutionaries and Isaac is led to a room smelling of sweat and feet. The room is small, maybe one-fifth the size of his living room, with mustard-yellow walls. He is seated on a bench, already filled with about a dozen men. He is squeezed between a middle-aged man and a young boy of sixteen or seventeen.

"I don't know how they keep adding more people on this bench," the man next to him mumbles, as though to himself but loudly enough for Isaac to hear. Isaac notices the man is wearing pajama pants with socks and shoes.

"How long have you been here?" he asks, deciding that the man's hostility has little to do with him.

"I'm not sure," says the man. "They came to my house in the middle of the night. My wife was hysterical. She insisted on making me a cheese sandwich before I left. I don't know what got into her. She cut the cheese, her hands shaking. She even put in some parsley and radishes. As she was about to hand me the sandwich one of the soldiers grabbed it from her, ate it in three or four bites, and said, 'Thanks, Sister. How did you know I was starving?'" Hearing this story makes Isaac feel fortunate; his family at least had been spared a similar scene. "This bench is killing my back," the man continues. "And they won't even let me use the bathroom."

Isaac rests his head against the wall. How odd that he should get arrested today of all days, when he was going to make up his long absences to his wife and daughter by joining them for lunch. For months he had been leaving the house at dawn, when the snow-covered Elburz Mountains slowly unveiled themselves in the red-orange light, and the city shook itself out of sleep, lights in bedrooms and kitchens coming on one after the other, languidly at first, then gaining momentum. And he had been returning from the office long after the supper dishes had been washed and stored away and Shirin had gone to bed. At night, walking up the stairs of his two-story villa, he could already hear the television buzzing, and in the living room he would find Farnaz, in her silk nightgown, cognac in hand, soaking up the chaos of the evening news. The cognac, she said—its stinging vapors, its roundness and warmth—made the news more palatable, and Isaac did not object to this new habit of hers, which, he suspected, made up for his absences. In the living room he would stand next to her, his briefcase an extension of his hand, neither sitting beside her nor ignoring her; standing was all he could manage. They would say little to each other, a few words about the day or Shirin or some explosion somewhere, and he would retire to the bedroom, exhausted, trying to sleep but unable, the television's drone seeping into the darkness. Lying awake in bed he would often think that if she would only shut off the news and come to him, he would remember how to talk to her. But the television, with its images of rioting crowds and burning movie theaters—with its wretched footage of his country coming undone, street by street—had taken his place long before he had learned to find refuge in his work, long even before the cognac had become necessary.

* * *

THREE GUARDS ARRIVE and hand out rice-filled metal bowls. He examines the food; what if it's poisoned? The thought must have occurred to the others, as there isn't a sound in the room. "Eat, you fools!" a guard bellows. "You don't know when your next meal will be coming." Utensils clatter. The rice is dry and tasteless, and undercooked lentils, thrown in like an afterthought, crack between Isaac's teeth. But he is hungry and decides to finish it all.

"Agha—sir!" the man in pajamas cries to one of the guards. "Please. I must go to the bathroom." The guard watches him for a while, then leaves, uninterested. The man coils into himself. He doesn't eat.

Isaac chews and replays the events of that afternoon—how the moment he had seen their shadows in the dim corridor outside his office he had capped his fountain pen and put it down, surrendering before they had even opened their mouths; how absurd everything since that moment feels to him now. For the first time since his arrest he realizes what just happened to him: that his life, if anything is to remain of it, will be different from this day on. That he may never touch his wife again, that he may never see his daughter grow up, that the day he stood at the airport, waving good-bye to his son who was leaving for New York, may have been the last time he sees him. As he considers these things, a hand slides into his. Isaac flinches, turns his head.

"Hello. I'm Ramin," the boy next to him says.

Isaac looks into the boy's wide, dark eyes, and recognizes in them his own terror, which he has been trying to suppress all afternoon. The boy's hand is cold, the fingers like bits of ice.

"How old are you?"

"Sixteen."

Two years younger than his son, Parviz. "Your parents know you're here?"

"My father is dead. And my mother is already in jail. It's been two months."

"They won't keep you long," Isaac says. "You're just a boy."

Ramin nods, takes a deep breath. The reassurance—which Isaac offered out of fatherly instinct rather than actual belief—seems to have calmed him.

"Why do you think they're keeping us here?" the boy continues. "Are they trying to decide which prison to send us to?"

"Keep it down!" A guard's voice pierces the hush that has settled about the room, like dust. "Don't aggravate your case!"

They obey, sit in silence. Isaac imagines Ramin's story. His family could be related to the shah. Or maybe he is one of those hot-blooded communists, protesting the new Islamic regime as they had the old monarchy. Or maybe it's simpler than all that. He could be a Jew, like Isaac, or worse, of the Baha'i faith, believing that all of humanity is one race, and that there is a single religion—that of God.

From his left he hears water trickling onto the floor. "Forgive me," the man who had been sitting next to him says. He is standing in a corner, his back to the others, a yellow puddle forming by his feet and streaming to the middle of the room. A few men shift uncomfortably in their seats. "I can't hold it any longer," he says. "I'm sorry."

Isaac looks at the man—the deep burgundy of his pajama pants, the sheen of his leather shoes—seamless, solid, perfect—hand-stitched no doubt in a dusty atelier in the outskirts of London or Milan. These accessories, hints of the life the man has left behind, make Isaac pity him more. They are all the same here, he realizes, the remnants of the shah's entourage and the powerful businessmen and the communist rebels and the bakers and bazaar vendors and watchmakers. In this room, stripped of their ornaments and belongings, they are nothing more than bodies, each as likely as the next to face a firing squad or to go home, unscathed, with a gripping tale to tell friends and family.

He shuts his eyes, tries not to think about his wife's salty laughter, his son's easy smile, the curlicues of his daughter's hair. When he opens his eyes he sees a man towering above him, his body framed by a light from the lone bulb dangling from the ceiling. "Get up," the man says.

Isaac rises to his feet but his knees, locked into place like rusted doorknobs, make him fall back on the bench. The man remains stern, manila folder under his arm; he offers no help. Isaac tries again, stands up this time. The man removes Isaac's watch and unbuckles his belt; he slides these into the pocket of his green jacket. Then he unties a handkerchief from his wrist and blindfolds Isaac, weaving a double knot in the back of his head and pulling hard on the cloth. Isaac feels his lashes fastened to his face, his castrated eyes submerged in blackness. Already he misses his once effortless capacity to blink—this smallest of movements.

He is led out of the building and onto the street. The

afternoon traffic drowns the sound of his footsteps. Wooden clogs approach him, reminding him of his daughter's footsteps, and as the sound intensifies it brings along a child's voice, "Mama—look! That man. What has he done?" Deprived of his vision, he has forgotten that others can still see. He feels embarrassed, hopes people are not chattering about him by their doorways and windows. The tip of a rifle nudges the small of his back. "Faster!" the man commands. "You think we're going for a stroll?" Isaac picks up the pace.

He is seated in the back of a van, between two men, one of whom smells like cigarette smoke and rose water. As he listens to the engine's shifting roar and the guards' logistical banter—whom should they pick up next, should they stop for gas?—he tries to match voices with faces he had seen earlier, but he realizes that he recalls nothing of his captors. Their clothes had been shabby, that much he can say. And the last one, the one who had blindfolded him, was spadebearded. But faces, they had none.

He thinks of his friend Kourosh Nassiri, whose name he had seen in the newspaper's daily list of the executed one morning as he sipped his tea. He had stared at it, one name among dozens. Farnaz was sitting across from him, polishing her nails. He had looked at her but could not bring himself to tell her what he had just read, because he did not want to upset her, but mostly because he did not wish to witness her grief; he could hardly endure his own. He had left the paper on the table for her and had gone to work. Kourosh's death had made him realize that executions were no longer reserved for the shah's friends, generals, or henchmen; anyone was now eligible, anyone who was not liked or no longer fit in. Stuck in the morning traffic he had wondered how they had killed him—firing squad or hanging were most likely—and his mind continued to produce for him images of his dead friend, no matter how hard he tried to make it stop. It was then that he wondered, for the first time, whether he would be next.

He leans his head back. He knows that this very day could be one of his last; it could also be a day he'll remember years from now, while sipping an espresso in a café or lying awake in bed, in a city still unknown to him but far away from this place. Should he have left the country when the riots were just erupting, as so many had? But where would he have gone? In the two years since the uprisings he has lost much—four employees who fled, his dear friend Kourosh, his car blown to pieces in an explosion in front of Tehran University—luckily his son, who had driven it to school that morning, was not in it—and things less concrete, like his desire to touch his wife, his interest in his daughter's grades, or the memory of places he once meant to visit. All this vanished from his life, and had he not gracefully let go? But it was his thirty-five years of relentless work that he had not been willing to forgo, and the success that he had managed to achieve as a result. It was, also, his belief—very naïve he realizes now—that things gone wrong are eventually set right.

He finds himself praying, the same prayer he would recite as a boy, before going to sleep at night. *Hash-kiveynu Adonai Eloheynu lâ shalom, Vâ ha-amideynu Mal-keynu lâ ha-yim*—"Cause us to lie down, God, our God, in peace, and awaken us to life again, our King." *U-fâ ros aleynu suk-kat shâlomekha, vâ tak-neynu bâ eytzah tovah mil-fanekha, vâ ho-shi-eynu lâ ma-an Shâ mekha*—"Spread over us Your shelter of peace, guide us with Your good counsel. Save us because of Your mercy." When he is done he whispers "Amen," and is surprised that a few sentences—a mere assembly of words—could fill him with such stillness, even if only for the seconds it took him to say them.

After what he estimates to be about forty-five minutes, the steady sound of wheels on asphalt slowly gives way to a kind of rumbling. The gears have been changed several times, he has noticed, from third to second, and now, as they inch their way up a hill, to first.

The van comes to a halt. Isaac hears doors opening and feet hitting the ground. The door slides open and a hand takes hold of his right arm. "Follow me," someone says. He steps out of the van. The air is clean and brisk, the breeze carrying a scent of poplars. They walk several steps then stop. A metal door rattles open. "Be careful," the voice says. "There is a small step."

Inside a hand reaches behind his head and unties the handkerchief. When Isaac opens his eyes he sees a man wearing a black burglar's mask. "I am Brother Mohsen," the man says. "Please follow me."

HE FOLLOWS MOHSEN through a long and narrow corridor. Several men, also masked, walk back and forth, carrying files.

Mohsen leads him down a flight of stairs into a cement basement with no windows, where the air stands heavy, pregnant with the perspiration of the men who breathed it before him. A wooden table is the centerpiece. Two chairs, one of which Isaac is invited to occupy, face each other. Mohsen sits first and spreads the file open.

"So, Brother Amin. What exactly do you do?"

"I'm a gemologist, and a jeweler."

Mohsen's left hand glides cautiously across a piece of paper. "Our records show you travel to Israel quite a bit. Is that correct?"

"Yes."

"What for?"

"Well, sir, I . . ."

"Please call me 'Brother,'" Mohsen interrupts.

This is one of the hardest things to get used to, this business of calling everyone "brother," "sister," "father," "mother." This revolution, like all others, wished to turn the citizens into one big family. Once there had been guillotines for "brothers" who strayed, and later, there were gulags. Who knows what awaits him here?

"I have family in Israel . . . Brother. There are no laws against traveling there, are there?"

"Brother, are you familiar with the Mossad?"

"I've heard of it, yes, Brother. I've read about it." He brings a clammy palm to his forehead and rubs it. Sweat spreads across his chest, his lower back, and around his underarms. He feels dizzy, nauseated; vomit makes its way to his throat then retreats, quickly, leaving behind the foul taste of undigested lentils.

"Brother Mohsen, what is this all about? Am I being accused of something?"

Mohsen's eyes narrow inside the mask's cradle, tiny wrinkles forming on the outer edges.

"I see you like to get right to the point." He shuts the file, places his sturdy hands on the table; his right index finger is amputated at the joint closest to the knuckle. He walks to the door, opens it, and sticking his head out yells, "Hossein-agha, bring me some tea, will you?" As he walks back toward Isaac he mumbles, "This headache is killing me."

This intimate confession by his interrogator calms Isaac. "Look, Brother," he says. "I have nothing to do with government affairs, neither here nor in any other country. I'm a businessman, who happens to be a Jew, that's all."

Mohsen sits back down. "It's not that simple. We're going to have to investigate."

A faint knock introduces a slight man, masked also, holding a tarnished copper tray on which a small glass of tea and a pyramid of sugar cubes rest. The man walks in carefully, tiptoeing almost so as not to interrupt the proceedings, and slides the tray in front of Mohsen. The spicy aroma reaches Isaac's nose from across the table; he stares at the steaming orange liquid through the glass. It has been freshly brewed, he can tell, and the glass, just like the ones he has at home, just like the ones everyone has at home, is the kind they call *kamar-barik*—"slim-waisted," because it curves in the middle like a woman's body. He bought the set with Farnaz on their first trip to Isfahan some twenty-five years earlier, shortly after their wedding. The night the first one chipped, Farnaz stood still by the sink, water running over her hands. He was there, had witnessed it from his seat at the kitchen table. "Oh, no," he had heard her say. "Oh, no." And when he casually told her not to worry, they would get another set, he thought he heard a sniffle but wasn't sure. He was never too sure with Farnaz.

Mohsen places a sugar cube in his mouth then lifts the glass and takes a sip through the opening in his mask. "Brother Amin, you have relatives in the Israeli army."

"Yes. Those relatives are Israeli citizens. Every male Israeli is in the Israeli army."

"Yes, well . . ." He shuffles papers. "Tell me about your wife . . . Farnaz Amin . . . right? What does she do?"

"She's a housewife."

"Really?" Mohsen pulls out a magazine, opens it to a flagged page, and points at the byline with his left index finger, which unlike its right twin, is intact. "So who's this? Let me see . . . I believe it says Farnaz Amin. Is that not your wife?" He slides the magazine across the table.

Isaac stares at the letters swirling on the page, each indistinguishable from the next, until his eyes zero in on the byline, and there it is, in a capricious typeface—his wife's name. "Rendezvous at the Ice Palace" is the title of the article, and he suddenly feels the chill of the ice skating rink, remembers being on the ice with Farnaz as she held young Shirin's hand, gliding to the breathless beat of disco tunes, the three of them trying to catch up with Parviz, who would be showing off like the other teenagers in the middle of the rink, spinning into a pirouette now and then. "She used to write, an article here and there, or a translation . . ."

"And yet you forgot to mention it . . ." Mohsen gulps

down the last of his tea, throws back his head, and places the glass on the tray. Sucking on the leftover sugar cube, he says, "That skating rink was a haven for sin, you realize. And your wife's article was a piece of propaganda for it."

What if Farnaz isn't sitting by the phone, wondering why he is so late for lunch? What if she is facing Mohsen's twin, just on the other side of the courtyard? An acidic liquid rushes from his stomach to the rest of his body, filling in crevices between muscles and bones. He breaks into a sweat, his voice won't come.

"No, Brother, it wasn't what you think," he manages to say. "She just wrote about what was happening around her."

"I see." Mohsen gets up and walks, sneakers swishing against the floor. "And does she still write about 'what is happening around her,' or is that no longer interesting to her?"

"Well, she hasn't written in a long time. That's why I even forgot to mention it. She hasn't been feeling well lately, Brother; she's often ill."

"Oh, how terrible . . . And what would you say is wrong with her?"

"Migraines."

On their last trip to their beach house in the north, she had slept the better part of their ten-day stay, except for the evenings, when her headache would subside along with the sun, and she would emerge from the bedroom, wearing a wool sweater despite the August heat. "Dracula has come out," she would joke, and Shirin, pleased to see her mother, would run to the kitchen to bring her a snack, a bowl of blood-red cherries or white peaches.

"Brother, please tell me. She's safe, isn't she? I mean, she's home, right?"

Mohsen looks back down at the file. "Many factors play against you at the moment. Like I said, we'll have to investigate." He shuts the file, presses his temples with his hands. "Brother Hossein will take you to your cell."

Mohsen disappears and the man who brought in the tea earlier returns. He stands by the door, motioning for Isaac to follow. In the dim hallway Isaac looks down at his wrist, at the empty spot where his watch used to be.

"What time is it?" he asks.

"Brother," says Hossein, "you have to learn not to think about time. It means nothing here."

TWO

The guard, Hossein, stands by the door of the cell, hold-ing a candle to allow Isaac to settle in. Isaac recognizes Ramin, the sixteen-year-old, half asleep on a mattress; so he was brought here, too. Another man sits on the floor, peel-ing a soiled bandage from his feet. Isaac catches a glimpse of the man's swollen toes before the flickering candlelight vanishes and the door slams shut.

"It reeks, I know," the man says. "I'm sorry."

In the dark, Isaac lets his body fall back on an empty mattress; the loose coils bounce a few times before settling. "What happened to your feet?" he asks.

"Lashings," says the man.

The night before him seems very long, as do the many nights that may follow. He unties the laces of his hard leather shoes, removes them, and lies flat on his back. The fullness in his bladder makes him wonder how many hours separate him from dawn, which most likely will be accompanied by a visit to the toilet. He is not sure he can hold out that long; like the man in the pajamas, he may have to just let go. He hears a foot being dragged against the bare cement floor, followed by moans and the squeak of coils. His cellmate must have made it to his mattress, which is adjacent to Isaac's and across from the boy's.

"Ah, my poor foot." The man sighs. "I'm Mehdi, by the way," he whispers in the dark.

"I'm Isaac."

"How is it outside?" Mehdi says.

"Outside? Since when? How long have you been in here?"

"Close to eight months now."

"The situation is the same," he says.

"That's hard to believe," Mehdi mumbles. "It's got to be getting worse, since I'm seeing more and more of my friends here."

Isaac tucks his hands under his head. Someone in the neighboring cell clears his throat every thirty seconds or so. The room spins, an endless black carousel circling around his head.

"I'm here because I'm a *tudeh*—a communist," Mehdi says. "A friend of mine denounced me. I'm almost sure it's him, because I heard he's here, too. We were both professors at the university. They must have beaten my name out of him. They tried to get names out of me too, but I wouldn't give in. Now I look at my feet and I wonder . . . I suppose I shouldn't tell you any of this, but I can't get into any more trouble than I already am." There is restlessness in the man's voice, a controlled urgency.

"So you've been fighting against both governments?" Isaac asks.

"Yes. This regime isn't what we fought for, you know? This is even worse than the old monarchy."

"And the boy? You know anything about him?"

"You mean Ramin? He threw red paint on a mullah."

"Is that all? He is here for throwing paint?"

"His mother is a *tudeh*," Mehdi says. "So they're assuming the boy is, too. They got the mother a couple of months ago. The father they killed about a year ago. And you? What is your crime?"

"I don't know yet," Isaac says.

HE LIES AWAKE, notices a shoebox window high up on the wall, a sapphire sky wrapped around its black bars. The glass is broken, allowing a warm breeze to enter the cell. It's a beautiful night, he realizes—calm, dark, moonless. He tries to sleep but cannot, sees fickle shapes in bright colors, the same kaleidoscopic monsters that would visit him in the dark as a boy, when the voice of his drunken father and the faint whines of his mother would reach him through the locked door of his bedroom. When he shuts his eyes he smells his wife's orange blossom lotion, which she dabs on her face and hands every night. For a moment he thinks he sees her walking toward him, nightgown and all. He whispers goodnight to her, believes somehow that she hears it.

THREE

In the dark Farnaz traces the outlines of the furniture—the curving bedpost where Isaac's striped pajama pants still hang, the half-moon of the alabaster table lamp by her bed, and the sandalwood Buddha, arms stretched toward the sky, a lotus blossom in his hands. Isaac's reading glasses lie in wait on his night table, his magazine still open to an article he must not have finished. Last night she was annoyed with him for reading while she wanted to talk. She had come to bed, way past midnight, her head buzzing from the hours spent watching the news on television. She knew not to unload the latest riots on him; he did not want to hear it.

"They are moving Picasso's *Guernica* from New York to Spain," she said finally, this being the only topic from the day's events to which she thought he might respond.

"Yes?" he said, without taking his eyes off his magazine.

"Apparently Picasso had specified in his will that the

painting could only be taken back to Spain once the country became a republic."

"Well, it's not a republic," he said. "It's a constitutional monarchy."

"It's close enough. That's what the shah wanted to do here. Of course, he was too late." And as soon as she had said this, she knew she had lost him again. He did not want to discuss the failing health of his country, and she insisted, like a careless physician repeating a terminal diagnosis. My dear sir, she seemed to be saying. The cancer has spread. She reaches for his glasses now, and holds them, their metallic earpieces cold against her fingers.

Since yesterday's call from Isaac's brother, Javad, who had heard about the arrest from a friend who had joined the Revolutionary Guards, the phone has not rung once. She thinks of Kourosh Nassiri, how she had seen his name among the list of executed in the paper. She had tried calling Isaac many times that day but he would not take her call; the secretary answered each time, saying Isaac was very busy and would it be all right if he called her back later? But he never called. When he came home that night, looking gray, he put down his briefcase, sat on the sofa, and sobbed. She sat next to him and cried with him. They never spoke of Kourosh Nassiri's execution again.

The dog, a black-furred German shepherd abandoned by Austrian diplomats who had left the country abruptly, gallops back and forth in the garden, howling at the wind. Farnaz wonders if Suzie has detected Isaac's absence, sniffed her way into the void. The day their gardener Abbas brought her in, pleading that they adopt her, Farnaz had resisted the idea. And even as she saw the dog's downcast eyes and smelled its musky fur, wet and disheveled from the morning rain, she shook her head no. She told him she is afraid of dogs, and besides, they are dirty. "They say this dog is very smart and well-behaved; they say it can even open doors," Abbas said. She laughed. "That's all I need! A dog that opens doors." When she snuck another look at the orphaned animal, she saw Isaac patting its head. Soon the two of them were at play in the garden, Isaac throwing a yellow tennis ball—one of Parviz's relics—and the dog running after it, carrying it back in its mouth and dropping it at Isaac's feet. She saw the delight in her husband's eyes and gave in. "Fine," she said. "The dog can stay, but he will not enter the house." A smile spread across Abbas's creased face. "God bless you. And by the way, he's a she. Her name is Suzie."

It amused her to be jealous of this dog, this Austrian-raised Suzie who could make Isaac's eyes laugh in a way she herself had not been able to do in months.

A SHARP PAIN behind her right eye migrates to the nape of her neck and down her back. On the opposite wall, trees peering over the terrace make swaying shadows that most nights manage to put her to sleep. Tonight, as she watches them, she sees a shape hanging from a branch, a shape with flaccid limbs and a limp head. She shuts her eyes and counts to ten, but when she opens them it is still there.

She unlocks the glass door leading to the terrace, hears its rattle as it slides open. A breeze rushes into the bedroom, sending the curtains into an unchoreographed dance. She stumbles through them and steps with her bare feet on the icy marble outside. Leaning against the balustrade, she sees it—a man wrapped in a white sheet, hanging on a low branch of their cherry tree. Isaac? Urine gushes down her legs. She goes back inside, makes her way down the stairs and out to the garden.

When she reaches the damp cloth she runs her hands over it, front then back, finds nothing in its folds but dead air. The housekeeper, Habibeh, probably hung it there after drying the dog and forgot to remove it. She sits on the grass, its wetness seeping through her already-soaked nightgown and into her skin. Feeling a chill settling in her thighs, she goes back in, to her quiet house, which suddenly seems un-necessarily vast—the white limestone facade, the lanterns illuminating the garden path, the shimmering blue of the pool, all posing as elaborate gatekeepers to the unraveling inside.

"FARNAZ-KHANOUM? ARE YOU all right? Shall I bring you some tea? You don't look so good. And why are you sleeping with just a camisole? You'll catch cold . . ."

Farnaz opens her eyes, sees Habibeh standing over her bed. "No, I'm getting up, thank you. I have to go out." Her mouth is dry, a bitter taste trapped in her throat.

"Yes?" Habibeh looks at the bed, at the unruffled side, where Isaac should have been. "Amin-agha never came home?"

"No, Habibeh. They got him." She pushes back the comforter, brings her feet to the floor and stares at them, her toenails painted a pinkish white—like seashells—reminding her of promenades along the beach, where they had been, just weeks ago.

Habibeh rests her hand on Farnaz's shoulder. "Don't worry, khanoum. He is a good man, and he will get out."

"Yes. But wasn't Kourosh a good man? Where is he now?"

"Don't think about that now." Habibeh walks to the windows and pulls open the curtains. The room plunges into a harsh brightness.

"Remember Farnaz-khanoum, that gold silk sari Amin-agha brought me from India? I still have it wrapped in its paper in my closet. From time to time I take it out and run my fingers over it—it's the softest thing I've ever touched. You remember that, khanoum?"

This reminiscence, Farnaz thinks, has the flavor of old stories rehashed at funerals. "Yes, of course I remember," she says.

"It breaks my heart to think of such a good man behind bars." Habibeh shakes her head, taps one hand against the other. In a lowered voice she says, "I've never been the religious type, khanoum, but I will ask Kobra, my half-sister who prays five times a day, to say a few words on agha's behalf. I'd do it myself but I don't think my plea would carry much weight. That's my way of wishing his safe return. *Har Haji yek jour Makeh miravad*—Every pilgrim goes to Mecca his own way."

"Thank you, Habibeh. You are so good to us."

"Now get up, khanoum. Get up. Go do what you have to do." She stands for several seconds, then reaches out to the night table and takes the empty glass of cognac. "This, Farnaz-khanoum, will have to stop."

"I take only one glass, Habibeh, you know that. It calms me down."

"One glass or ten, makes no difference. Not only is it bad for you, it's illegal now." She puts the glass back down and leaves.

Illegal? Yes, drinking alcohol was now on the long list of illicit activities, along with singing, listening to music, going out with uncovered hair. But when did Habibeh become so law-abiding?

Farnaz showers quickly and wears navy slacks, a white turtleneck, and her long black coat—the new government-enforced uniform. Her shapeless reflection in the full-length mirror strips her of the one lure she had possessed before the days of the revolution, when a hip-hugging skirt, a fitted cashmere sweater, and a red smile were enough to get an entire room of a house painted for free, or the most tender meat saved by the butcher. She leans into the mirror and applies powder to conceal the dark crescents under her brown eyes. She twists her long black hair into a bun and covers it with a scarf.

Out in the garden the air is crisp, diffusing the sweet,

clean scent of jasmine. The dog is sprawled by Isaac's old Renault, sniffing a tire. She will take Shirin to school then start looking for Isaac. Last night she told Shirin that her father had gone on an unexpected business trip. "Yes? Just like that?" Shirin said. "Yes, just like that." And when the questions would not stop, Farnaz told her to keep quiet and go to bed. The questions stopped, leaving in their place a muddy silence.

She stands by the iron gate, tea in hand, watching the day unfold—pedestrians walking hurriedly past, cars honking to salvage lost minutes, children bearing the anxious look of the first weeks of school, their backs hunched under massive book bags. A neighbor emerges from her house and hurries down the street. "They brought eggs today!" she yells to Farnaz, and whizzes by. The war with Iraq, already a year old, has made the most mundane items—eggs, cheese, soap—worthy of celebration. Farnaz cannot reconcile the normalcy of the world around her with the collapse of her own. That the city is short by one man this morning makes so little difference—stores still open their doors, schools ring their bells, banks exchange currency, grass-green double-decker buses—men on the bottom, women on top—follow their daily routes.

THE PRISON SQUATS under the afternoon sky—sterile, unsparing, and gray.

"Yes, Sister?" A young man at the gate walks toward her.

He is barely eighteen, with that seriousness of expression peculiar to young people given a grave task for the first time. A cigarette hangs loosely from the side of his mouth.

"I'm looking for my husband, Brother. Can you help me?"

The boy removes the cigarette, exhaling with exaggeration. "Who is your husband?"

"His name is Isaac Amin."

"Yes? Who says he's in this prison?"

"That's what I'm trying to find out, Brother."

The boy takes another drag, looks out in the distance. "Why should I help you?"

"Because my husband is innocent. And because you're a kind, decent person."

"You say he's innocent. Why should I believe you?" He drops the cigarette and crushes it with his foot.

"Brother, I'm just asking you to tell me if he's here. I'm not asking you to release him."

He bites his lower lip, considering her request, then flings his arm in the air. "Ah, to hell with you," he says. " I don't want to help you. And you can't make me do anything I don't want to do, not anymore. Now get lost . . . Sister."

She walks for a long time through the city. Above her, windows and balconies close, shutting out the cool September breeze. Summer is leaving, and with it the buzz of ceiling fans, the smell of wet dust rising through air-conditioning vents, the clink of noontime dishes heard through open windows, the chatter of families passing long, muggy afternoons in courtyards, eating pumpkin seeds and watermelon.

FOUR

The chant of the muezzin fills the cloudless sky above the prison courtyard. *Bismi Allahi alrrahmani alrraheem. Alhamdu illahi rabbi al alameen*—"In the name of Allah, the Beneficent, the Merciful. Praise be to Allah, Lord of the Worlds."

Isaac walks along with a few others toward the prison mosque. He has pursued this path already once today. Now, the sun directly above, he knows it must be noon, time for the second round of prayers. *Alrrahmani alrraheem. Maliki yawmi alddeen*—"The Beneficent, the Merciful. Owner of the Day of Judgment." He stops at a corner shaded by a single poplar. There, clusters of men stand in front of concrete basins, pouring water over their faces, hands, and bare feet in preparation for prayer. He walks to a vacant spot by a basin and removes his shoes and socks. For years he has watched friends, employees, housekeepers perform this ritual of washing for prayer, but somehow he has not retained all of it, does not know which hand pours water over which, which foot must be wiped clean first. "Thee we worship; Thee we ask for help. Show us the straight path."

During the morning prayer Mehdi, who occasionally prays at the mosque to ingratiate himself to his captors, had shown him all the movements, but afterward he had been taken for interrogation and has not returned. Isaac tries to remember his cellmate's lesson; the whole thing is like the memory of a dream trying to surface. "The path of those upon whom Thou hast bestowed favors. Not of those upon whom Thy wrath is brought down, nor of those who go astray." He watches the man next to him gargling water in his mouth and spitting it out, three times. The man turns to Isaac. "What are you waiting for?"

"I've forgotten how it goes," Isaac says, as though he had once known it, as though the procedures have simply evaporated from his mind, like lyrics of a song.

The man cleanses his nose and nostrils three times, then washes his face from ear to ear and forehead to chin. "How does anyone manage to forget this?" he says as he dips his right arm, up to the elbow, into the running water.

"What's all this talk?" a guard yells from behind. Then, noticing Isaac, he says, "Aren't you Brother Amin?"

"Yes."

"Nice gesture, Brother, pretending to be Muslim. But it won't change anything."

"No, sir . . . Brother. I'm not pretending to be anything. I thought everyone has to attend prayers, that's all." This is not entirely true, Isaac knows. Like Mehdi, he had hoped that attending would improve his situation, regardless of his religion. The sun beams directly into his head, dilating the veins on his temples.

"Unless, Brother, you wish to convert."

"Well, I . . . It isn't that simple."

"Then go back to your cell! This incident will be added to your file."

Another guard takes hold of Isaac's arm and drags him across the desolate courtyard. Isaac pictures the men inside the mosque, down on all fours facing Mecca, bodies bowing to the floor and rising again, prayers forming underneath their breaths. He had always been glad that he did not have to partake in this ritual, did not have to drop everything five times a day to pray. Now he wishes he could have stayed with the others—to kneel and rest his forehead on the cool prayer stone.

When they reach his cell he asks for an aspirin and the guard agrees to bring him one. Alone again, he lets his body fall back on his mattress. The sour scent of blood reaches him from across the room, where Mehdi's soiled bandages are piled up. He turns on his side, faces the wall, where someone has inscribed, "I have a bad feeling today. *Allah-o-Akbar*—God is great . . ." He has been captured for about twenty-four hours now. Today's date, September 21, 1981. He would like to link to these numbers an event, concrete and retrievable. The one that emerges is nearly four decades old—the night he made love for the first time, to a girl named Irene McKinley.

He was eighteen years old, and was working in Abadan,

at the petroleum refinery. Every morning he would put on his trousers and starched white shirt, slip his feet into the leather oxfords that had made their way from the trash of the well-to-do villas of southern Abadan to the closets of the modest Khorramshahr port where he lived, and hop on the bicycle that would take him six miles south, to the center of the city where the refinery gurgled.

On his way back in the early afternoon he would pedal through the city aimlessly, postponing as long as possible his return to his quarreling siblings and his unhappy mother, and to the void left by a father with an affinity for liquor. This is how he met Irene, on one of those nomadic afternoons, on the breezy September 21 of 1942. She was in a coffeehouse with a group of American soldiers, stationed with other Allies in Iran to transport supplies to Russia. The only woman in the coffeehouse, she drank tea while the soldiers swilled beers, though from time to time one of them would slide a glass toward her and she would take a sip. Isaac found her not beautiful but attractive, red hair tied back at the nape of her neck, ivory-white freckled skin exposed to the fading sun.

As he entered the coffeehouse a dozen or so men were sipping tea, sugar cubes melting in their mouths as they jabbered. Two of them were playing backgammon, their forceful rolls of dice echoing in the carpetless room. Isaac liked seeing the fair-skinned Americans there, loud and lighthearted, tongues twirling as they spoke. He sat at his regular table by the window overlooking a row of old houses, but instead of his regular tea he ordered a shot of arrack. He felt fluid as he drank it, the chipping teal-colored walls spinning in slow motion, so he ordered another, then a third. He felt everything around him—men, laughter, wooden tables, glimmering glasses, clattering plates, and the girl, the lovely girl with the red hair—blend into a single sensation, a tickling in his stomach, the happiness to be alive, and to be here, in this moment, waiting for the sun to give way to the coolness of the night, when nothing is seen and everything is possible.

He offered to barter a bottle of arrack, which would cost him a few days' salary, for an American military cap. Seeing the effect of the drink on Isaac the Americans found the deal worthy, and already lightened by several rounds of beer, they invited him to their table. Once seated among them he began telling jokes in his broken English. He had never told jokes before, did not know his memory could retain them. The men's laughter gained volume after each punch line, and the girl's smiles, flashed at him sporadically from across the table, fired his momentum. Isaac swilled his arrack. He was grateful to the drink, revered it now more than anything or anyone. He even felt a sudden pang of affection for his drunk father, perhaps for the first time in his life.

He left the coffeehouse with them, American army hat on his head, and along the moonlit streets of Abadan he sang Frank Sinatra's "Shake Down the Stars," which he had recently added to his record collection. When the lyrics escaped him he simulated the sinuous sound of a trumpet, and the girl sang along, her mellow voice curving against the walls of sleepy homes and reverberating in the dark.

They reached the villa-turned-military-station and the

soldiers playfully bade him farewell. The girl looked at him with glassy green eyes. "Stay with me," she said. Isaac was speechless. How was it possible that the girl with the coral-red hair, transplanted at this time to this place thanks to some maniacal despot in Europe, wished to be with him, a lanky boy from Khorramshahr? And what right did she have to be so indiscreet, so chancy, so resolute in her request? "Stay with me," she repeated. Isaac sensed the lightness in his head weighing him down—his limbs, his eyes, most of all his eyes—as though bits of lead were swimming in his blood. He felt an overwhelming desire to sleep.

The memory tickles him now, as though the event had occurred only recently. His headache persists, a steady pounding that refuses to let go of his temples. He ignores it as best he can.

"Get up!" the American girl had said. "You have to leave!" He saw her frantically rummaging through the sheets, producing from the comforter's folds articles of clothing—his trousers, his white shirt now creased and damp, one sock, and his underwear, the sight of which paralyzed him, leaving him lying flat on his back, watching pieces of himself brought together by a stranger's hands. She threw the shirt in his direction.

"You have to go!" she repeated. "It will be daylight soon."

He despised himself at that moment as much as he had marveled at his charms just a few hours earlier. The event he had fantasized about since the onset of puberty had come and gone. He sat up, slid one arm into the shirt's sleeve, then the other. The moist cotton stuck to his back. The smell of his own sweat, blended with her pungent perfume, wafted to his nose. He watched her now as she sat on the edge of the bed, her bare back facing him. When she reached for a carton of cigarettes on the night table, he caught a glimpse of her breasts, as though for the first time. He held the swelling between his legs like a prisoner, wished he could release it.

"I'm sorry," he said. "I am new . . . at this. But I can do better, I promise." He felt ridiculous.

She pulled the sheet up with her free hand to cover herself and turned to him.

"Oh, baby," she said, a cloud of smoke trailing her voice. "Nothing like that. You're not supposed to be here, that's all. You understand that, don't you?"

She explained that she was Lieutenant Holman's secretary, that all day long she shuffled papers dealing with the railroad operation carrying supplies to Russia. He felt better suddenly, could breathe more easily despite the smoke in the room. Yes, he could understand that. Army policy. She was doing good, was helping the global force against the Reich, and he, by putting on his clothes as quickly as possible and vanishing from her quarters, would be doing his bit for the war effort too.

As he dressed he wanted to ask if he could see her again. Instead he said, "How long will your unit be in town?"

"What do you think, this is a circus act?" She laughed. Her voice sounded older to him now, more bitter. "I don't know how long," she said.

He was all dressed except for the sock missing from his left foot. "Can I see you again?" he ventured.

She paused, inhaled, exhaled. "No, that wouldn't be a good idea," she finally said.

He scanned the moonlit room for the sock. He cared less about leaving without it than about her finding it, the hole at the toe howling in daylight. He looked under the bed, wiggled the sheets, ran his fingers over his pants.

"Hey," she said. "What's with the glum face?" She put out the cigarette in a glass; the butt sailed along with a dozen others on the ashen water. She stood, slipped her naked body into a bathrobe. "I tell you what. Let's cut a deal. If you ever come to America, look me up. Irene McKinley, Galveston, Texas."

He nodded, put on his shoes, forgot about the sock—told himself that one day he would forget about the girl too.

But from time to time throughout his life he had thought of her, even though he could no longer recall her face. From that night on he had come to see himself differently, as someone to whom exciting things could happen. Despite her brief appearance in his life, which did not even end on a particularly cheerful note, she had managed to change him. It is to her that he even attributed the fact that, years later, he was able to win over Farnaz.

"HERE," THE GUARD says. "An aspirin." Isaac turns around, stretches out his arm to take the pill, and seeing the guard in his black mask standing over him, he remembers where he is.

FIVE

A draft blows through his window. It's going to be a cold day, Parviz can tell, too cold for late September in Brooklyn. The reassuring warmth of his comforter makes him think of his mother, of the way he used to sneak into her bed when he was a little boy. As soon as the garage gates would rattle open and the determined sound of his father's car would fill the morning, he would leave his own bed and go to hers, where he would find her warm body, still filled with sleep. "The world is going on without us, my Parviz," she would say, half sorry, half relieved. "Don't tell anyone we're such lotus-eaters."

He wishes he could talk to her, but lately no one answers the phone, not even Habibeh. The last time they called him was in late August. It was a sweltering night, and when the phone rang he was chasing a cockroach around his bedroom, cursing and sweating, shoe in hand. He didn't tell them any of this. He told them everything was fine and asked them how they were, and they said fine, everything's fine.

. . .

HE WALKS IN the cool morning, hands in his pocket and coat collar turned up. The university campus is strewn with students perched on steps or clustered on the lawn, but not one has a familiar face. Friendship once came naturally to him. Now he cannot recall how he managed it so effortlessly. His mutation has been insidious, creeping up on him like a disfiguring disease. His proper English—devoid of any slang—is good enough for classes but not for intimacy. And his jokes, when translated, are no longer funny. The world is going on without me, he tells himself.

In class during an architecture slide show he writes a letter to his parents. In the half-dark of the lecture hall he writes that he is doing fine, that school is going well, that his landlord is very nice and takes good care of him. When he is done he looks up. His classmates, half-lit by the projector, are spellbound by the click-click of the transparencies, the professor's monotonous pitch, and the bright images of Californian homes on the screen—the wooden exteriors, the atrium courtyards, the vast expanses of glass overlooking gardens. How clean these homes all seem, how simple and sunny and cheerful, carrying within their uncomplicated lines the promise of docile decades spent in the same town, on the same street, in the same house, but offering no protection against the tedium that accompanies all of that. Looking at the images he realizes that his classmates—congenial and starched and essentially unharmed—are products of such homes.

. . .

In his mailbox, that afternoon, he finds an assortment of bills and a letter from his sister, opened once then sealed with tape. He rips the envelope, quickly scans the note, looking for the phrase "Your uncle and the kids are doing very well," which is the code his parents have set for letting him know that money is being sent. He flips the paper around, holds it up to the yellow-green hue of the fluorescent light, and not finding the phrase, puts the letter in his pocket and descends the stairs to his basement apartment. It occurs to him that he hasn't really read Shirin's note, so preoccupied had he been with the possibility of cash coming his way. Inside the apartment he unfolds the letter, reads it again—this time slowly: "September 8, 1981. Dear Parviz. Started school today. Teachers are nasty. Everything else is okay. I miss you." Underneath she had drawn a red heart—perfect and symmetrical—and signed her name in English, though her "N" was reversed. He smiles, as though to prove to himself and to Shirin that he is glad to receive the letter, with or without news of money.

He takes off his coat and heads to the kitchen. In the refrigerator he finds a bloated carton of milk, long expired. He knows he should dump it but doesn't. Ketchup, mustard, and beer stare back at him from the icy hollow. He grabs a beer, the ketchup, and the bag of molding potato buns on the counter, and settles in front of the television without switching on the lights. He changes channels but finds nothing except waves of static, which he expected, something about "poor reception in the basement." Occasionally a serpentine pattern emerges on the screen—figures distorted as in an amusement park mirror maze—or a sound erupts with no image at all—a sitcom joke followed by a ripple of robotic laughter. Listening to the sitcom he realizes that the same laugh track is used over and over, a man's distinct yelp—not laughter at all—emerging every ten or so seconds. He fills himself with ketchup sandwiches, the sweetness overwhelming, then numbing his taste buds.

Someone knocks on the door, but he ignores it. Then comes his landlord's voice. "I know you are in there, son. Please open."

Had the voice been more rude, less fatherly, he would go on ignoring it. But he gets up and opens the door, not knowing what excuse he will offer this time. In the hallway Zalman Mendelson stands tall in his black suit and Borsalino hat, his red beard resting on his heavy chest. "Good afternoon, my son. How are you?"

"Fine, Mr. Mendelson. And you?"

"Thank God, everything is well. You know of course why I am here."

"Yes, Mr. Mendelson. And I don't have it."

"Well, for two months you haven't paid rent. So what shall we do about it?"

Parviz looks into Mr. Mendelson's blue eyes and wishes he had something to tell him—that money is coming, that he has a plan—but he has nothing.

"You see," Zalman says. "I have six children, and twins on the way. And I am not a rich man. I am renting you the basement because I need the money. So when you don't pay me, you get me into trouble."

"I'm sorry, Mr. Mendelson. My parents haven't sent me money lately. It's not always easy to send money from there."

"All right. I'll give you a few more weeks. Try to come up with something." He walks away, but halfway down the corridor, turns around. "By the way, Parviz, I never asked you. Do you have any place to celebrate the Sabbath?"

"The Sabbath? I don't really celebrate it, Mr. Mendelson."

"You're always welcome at our table, should you change your mind," Zalman says. He stands for a moment, his hands folded before him. When he doesn't receive a response, he walks away.

Parviz takes a sip of beer. It tastes bitter, like aspirin dissolving on one's tongue before being swallowed. He turns off the failing television, walks to his bedroom, and falls back on his bed, onto a mound of wrinkled clothes he is always too hurried or too tired to clean up. It amazes him to think how these things once took care of themselves: clothes thrown on a chair magically hung themselves in the closet the next day; sheets were changed weekly, towels biweekly; carpets were swept, floors sponged, and mirrors wiped—he has no idea how often but often enough that he hadn't once witnessed a dust ball roaming the floor, as he now does— two tiny globes of lint, hair, and dust gliding in the crevice between his bed and the night table, dancing a playful waltz in the mild wind from the open window.

Above him the ceiling creaks, and he imagines the Mendelson children running from room to room, the older ones carrying stews from the kitchen to the dining room, the little ones chasing one another, all in anticipation of the comfort and suffocation of the family dinner. Having spent a rather miserable year in the university dormitory, sharing a room with a pimply boy from Wisconsin who was fond of hockey and who went to the bathroom with the door open, Parviz had thought that getting his own apartment might be less disheartening. But of the many neighborhoods in New York, all of which had seemed equally daunting and unfamiliar to him, he had ended up in this one, thanks to a little notice at his school cafeteria that read "Kind, loving family renting basement room with private entrance to a considerate student." When he arrived at the Mendelsons', he was surprised to find that they were Hassidic Jews, those black-robed orthodox Eastern Europeans that his parents joked about, calling them "those beardies from Poland." One look at Mr. Mendelson's freckled face in the afternoon sun, leaning against the iron railing of his front porch, three children trailing him, and Parviz had thought, No, I cannot live here. But then came the handshake, the laughing blue eyes, the lemonade served by a portly Mrs. Mendelson who said to him, "Call me Rivka, call me Rivka!" and soon he was discussing laundry facilities and garbage disposal.

Yes, the Mendelsons are a kind and loving family, as their ad had said, but they are not his. And besides, there is a moldiness about them, a certain mustiness in their black suits and stockings and wigs. To enter their apartment would be like relegating himself to a ghetto, where the memories of all the wrongs committed against Jews simmer year after year in bulky, indigestible stews.

He tells himself that no matter how lonely he gets, he will not go so far as to persecute himself by sitting at their table, celebrating a day that to him is no different from any other day.

WHEN HE DIALS his parents' number, before going to bed, he is relieved to hear Habibeh's matronly voice. "Habibeh, it's me, Parviz."

"Parviz-agha! *Bah bah*, how nice to hear your voice!"

"How are you?"

"Well." She clears her throat. "Fine."

"Is my mother there?"

"No, Parviz-jan. She's out."

"She's out? It's early morning there, isn't it? What about my father?"

For a while there is no answer and he wonders if the line somehow got disconnected. "Your father," she finally says, "has gone on an unexpected trip and it's not clear when he'll return. Do you understand?"

"Unexpected trip"—the code phrase for trouble. One could not be sure when wires were being tapped, so families, talking across oceans, or just across town, devised their own secret languages. "Yes, I understand."

"But don't worry. It's just a trip and he's bound to return. You'll see . . . And how are you? Are you well?"

"Yes. I'm well."

"Parviz?"

"What?"

"*Ksht*" she says, stomping her foot loudly enough for him to hear. He laughs. That's the sound she used to make when she pretended to engage in karate with him. "Keep up your training," she says. "I'm becoming a black belt and you'll have to compete with me!"

"Yes, yes, I will." He laughs.

When he hangs up he turns on all the lights in his room—the naked bulb on the ceiling, the office lamp on his desk, even the small blue bedside light. He sits on his bed for a while, but unable to tolerate the midnight silence of his room, he leaves.

Outside the air is clean, cleaner than in his basement apartment where humidity swells like steam in a ship's engine room. He walks down the dark street, past sleepy homes with deserted porches, each indistinguishable from the next. His neighbors' chimes tinkle in the wind, creating a fairy tale sound that comforts him.

Beyond his neighborhood he finds a pizza shop still open and enters. He asks himself if it is wise to waste a dollar on a slice and he decides that it is. He sits down and takes slow bites, extending the moment as long as he can. Leaning back in his chair, he examines the murals—uninspired scenes of a Venetian gondola, a Sicilian village, a Mediterranean seascape. On the radio Sinatra sings a mellow song, which he recognizes because his father would play the record in his study on weekends. He remembers entering that study as one would enter a shrine, tiptoeing on the arabesques of the carpet then standing behind his father, waiting for him to feel his presence and turn around. Sometimes he would stand there for as long as five minutes, examining with his six-year-old eyes the paraphernalia on the walls—newspaper clippings with yellow edges, family photographs, greeting cards, and antique swords and daggers hanging like half-moons one beneath the other, from as far back as the time of Cyrus and as recently as the 1920s. The swords intrigued Parviz. The handles—some gilded, others jeweled—made him wonder if they had actually been used by soldiers of the Persian Empire or knights of medieval Europe. That the blades may have once been tainted by the blood of a man, a man now long buried, both thrilled and terrified him. At last his father would turn around and see him there, put an arm around his bony shoulders, open the top drawer of his desk, and pull out a red tin filled with pastel mint candies. To Parviz the mints were magical, and he never asked for them during the week.

THE LAST TIME he saw his father, at the airport on that October morning, was also the first time he saw him cry. "May you be happy, my Parviz," his father had said, his right eye infected, the veins like rivulets spilling red inside it. "Baba-jan, please make sure you see a doctor for that eye," Parviz said. "It's getting worse." His father forced a smile. "Yes, yes. You don't worry about me. Just take care of yourself."

Hugging his father by the gate Parviz felt for the first time a slight curvature in his father's shoulders. "You go on ahead and map out America for us," his father said, tapping him on the back. "Just don't chew too much gum and don't start wearing cowboy hats." He then laughed.

On the plane he leaned his head against the oval window and tried not to cry. "They've sent you off because of the war, yes?" an old woman sitting next to him said. He nodded. The war, the draft, the revolution—all of it. "They did good," she said. "You're the wrong age for this country now. These mullahs will use the last one of you."

Yes, he was the wrong age for his country. But wasn't his father, also, getting to be the wrong age for this country? He thought of his bloodshot eye, of the bend in his back. As the plane finally took off, he watched the city move farther and farther from him—the houses enclosed inside brick court-yards, the miniature cars trapped under smog, and the El-burz Mountains, shrouded in ghostly white, towering over it all. He saw his father driving home, straining with his bad eye. He saw his mother by the kitchen window, looking up at the sky as though expecting to see his plane fly above, as she often did when someone she loved went on a trip. And he saw his little sister, her tongue blue from eating too many candies, color-coordinating her crayons, ready to charge a fee to anyone who wanted to borrow one.

May you be happy, my Parviz.

Baba-jan, I am not happy. Where are you?

SIX

For days her mother's sapphire ring has been missing. "This was the first present your father gave me," her mother said the morning she noticed its absence. She stood by her dresser, looked around at her perfume bottles and her Russian dolls—the smallest one at the edge, nearly falling. She kneeled on the floor, ran her hands over the carpet. By the fourth day, when she was convinced that she would not find the ring, she stood again by the dresser and cried. Afterward, she turned around, to the doorway where Shirin stood. "This was the first present your father gave me," she said, as though she had never said it before.

When the silver teapot disappeared from the dining room console, just two days after the ring, Shirin did not point it out to her mother. The missing ring was causing enough grief, she thought, and besides she feared that she might be the one who was somehow responsible for making these items disappear. She knew she had not taken them, but was there any way to be certain? She could have destroyed them in her sleep, or maybe she just didn't remember taking them; her mind was acting strange lately.

"I hate to think this," her mother told her one morning as she drank her tea, "but I'm starting to think Habibeh took the ring. Who else could it be?" Hearing this accusation further convinced Shirin that she was the culprit herself. "No, it can't be Habibeh," she told her mother. And then, unable to provide an alternative explanation, she said, "It must have fallen somewhere. It will turn up." She hoped, all the while, that the question of the missing teapot would not arise.

SHE THINKS ABOUT the ring as she watches the rope ripple in the air, up then down, each end held by one of her classmates. She jumps, once, twice, three times, bending her knees just in time for the rope to glide under her. The fourth time her feet refuse to leave the ground and she stands there, solid, lifting her body only when it's too late. The other girls yell, "Out! Out! You lose."

She steps aside, the scarf around her head choking her, the fabric rustling against her ears with the slightest movement. She imagines there are tiny elves inside her scarf, crumpling paper against her ears all day long just to irritate her. Just as well that she's out of the game; she's too tired to jump up and down. She walks to the other side of the playground, by the school entrance, where Jamshid the janitor is half asleep in the lunch-hour glare of the sun.

She watches him, a leathery old man, tall and thin, with an uneven beard. She pulls out her uneaten chicken sandwich and hands it to him, then does the same with the banana ripened in her schoolbag since morning. Jamshid snaps out of his afternoon daze and reaches for the goods.

"You're not going to eat these?"

"No. Take them." The departed ring has taken her appetite with it. And then there is the missing teapot. And finally her missing father, gone now for almost two weeks.

Jamshid-agha accepts the food without qualms. "Thank you," he says. "But a girl your age should eat her food. How old are you? Nine, ten?"

"Nine."

"Actually, you're not so young. Nine is old enough to marry. My own wife was only thirteen when I married her."

Walking around the playground, she remembers her mother's comment as the three of them passed by a nearby school one afternoon. "Isn't this a mini Monte Carlo?" she had said. "All these clusters of children devising their own games, each group with its croupier and gamblers. And in the end, you may leave with a few pretty pink chips, but everyone knows there are no real winners. . . ." Her father had laughed at this. Then he said, "No real winners, maybe, but learning a few tricks sure helps."

She watches her classmates, these croupiers and gamblers busy with games—the spin of a bottle, the combat of scissors, paper, stone, the flight of balls overhead, the cascade of glass marbles below. She decides she doesn't want to play these games anymore.

She leans against a wall, slides to the ground, notices candy wrappers by her feet, sailing on the wind's whim. Looking farther out she finds a sea of litter—more candy wrappers, orange and cucumber peels, half-eaten sandwiches, eggshells, even. She never really noticed them before. Above her the sky is a pale blue, without a single cloud—empty— a stark contrast to the playground. Where could it have gone, that ring? Her father had told her all about sapphires, worn by archbishops in the Middle Ages, believed by Buddhists to protect the wearer from illness and disaster, and said by the devout to have been the stone on which the Ten Commandments had been carved. Her mother always called it her good-luck ring. Does this mean she has lost her good luck?

She sees a pair of sneakers approaching her, and she knows it's her friend Leila, because of the Donald Duck sticker on the left shoe. "Why are you sitting on the ground?" Leila says, eating potato chips.

"I'm tired."

Leila sits next to her, offers her the bag of chips. "Me too," she says.

"Do you believe in ghosts?"

"Ghosts? I don't know. My father always says *shahidan zendeand*—martyrs are alive."

"No, I'm serious. Things are disappearing in my house."

"Disappearing? You must have misplaced them."

"Yes, probably." It occurs to her then that her father, too, has simply been misplaced, and that he will one day be returned to his rightful place, in his leather chair in the living room, with his books and cigarettes, sipping the tea that her mother will serve him from the silver teapot, the sapphire ring back on her finger.

SEVEN

I nside the house, perched on the curves of the Niavaran hills, the lights are on. Farnaz stands outside, thinks of the many dinners she and Isaac had attended here. Shahla and Keyvan, Isaac's sister and her husband, were once known for their parties—for the chef they had hired from Paris and the piano concertos they hosted after dinner sometimes, bringing young musicians from Vienna or Berlin or even, occasionally, introducing a budding prodigy from Tehran. She stands by the iron gate and presses the bell.

"Farnaz-khanoum!" the housekeeper says, unlatching the gate. "What a nice surprise! Come in, come in! You scared us. We thought, who could it be at this hour . . ."

"I hope they're not sleeping. I should have called first."

"No, nonsense! Who's sleeping at this hour? It's just, you know, things aren't like they used to be. Everybody's a little jumpy. How's Amin-agha?"

"Who is it, Massoumeh?" Shahla yells from the doorway.

"It's Farnaz-khanoum!"

When they reach the door Shahla says, "You came alone, Farnaz-jan? Where's Isaac?"

"I need to talk to you."

THEY WALK INSIDE, where it is bright and warm. Keyvan, sitting in the living room with his signature cup of black coffee, looks up from his book. A music of soft strings— Mozart—fills the room.

"*Bah bah*, look who's here," he says, shutting the book. He gets up and takes her hand to escort her to a chair, the one Shahla is so fond of, sensuous and curved, with the S-shaped cabriole and the vine-printed satin fabric, part of their collection of rococo furniture. Farnaz removes her scarf and sits.

"Where's Isaac?" Keyvan says.

"They got him."

The phrase quiets the room. Mozart's allegro fills the vast space around them.

"When?" Shahla says.

"About two weeks ago. I got a call from your brother, Javad. Apparently someone he knows told him."

"How awful," Shahla gasps. "Why didn't you tell us earlier?"

"I didn't want to get you involved. Once they get someone, friends and family become targets too. I haven't told anyone, not even your parents. How could I tell Baba Hakim and Afshin-khanoum that their son is in jail? But I knew I needed to warn you. You could already be in great danger, Keyvan-jan, given your father's connections to the shah."

"Yes, I know," Keyvan says. "But we can't leave now. My father has asked me to liquidate his houses and belongings before we join him and my mother in Switzerland."

The housekeeper arrives with a silver tray that she places on the coffee table. On it is the familiar tea set, of yellow porcelain with a garden motif—passed down to Keyvan by his great-grandfather, a court painter during the reign of the Qajar king Nasir al-Din Shah. The set was a present from the king to the artist, upon the king's return from Europe. Farnaz looks at the set, and at the plate of sweets accompanying it—browned madeleines, buttered and plump, made more golden by the soft light of the table lamp—and she thinks, here, on this tray, lie the country's aspirations as well as its demise, its desire for cosmopolitanism and its refusal to see itself for what it has become—an empire that has grown smaller with each passing century, its own magnificence displaced by that of other nations. For what is a housekeeper named Massoumeh, born in Orumiyeh, in the province of Azerbaijan, doing preparing madeleines, that most popular of French pastries?

She remembers the coronation of the shah and the empress some fifteen years earlier, in October 1967. She and Isaac had been invited to the ceremony thanks to Keyvan, whose father was a minister in the government. They had stood with the other guests in the Grand Hall of the Golestan Palace, once the home of Qajar kings, and had watched the royal family make its way along the red carpet, under the blinding glitter of so many crystal chandeliers—the shah's sisters and brothers, his young son, his wife, and finally the monarch himself. People smiled and curtsied as the procession passed before them. Farnaz, dressed in her silver satin dress bought in Paris, smiled but could not bring herself to actually curtsy. She looked at Isaac, who whispered in her ear, "So much fanfare! They take themselves for Napoleon and Josephine! Somebody remind them our bazaars are still filled with donkeys. . . ." She was annoyed with him for making her laugh at a time like this, when one was to repay the honor of having been invited to such an event with stateliness and decorum. She was irritated with him, also, for shattering an illusion, for mocking what she secretly found enchanting. Standing in that hall, surrounded by the dizzying sparkle of the hundreds of stones bejeweling the crowns and tiaras, with only a few hundred other privileged guests, she felt a certain pride, for the ceremony taking place before her and for witnessing it. She was pleased that the shah had crowned not only himself but his wife as well—the first time in the country's history that a woman had been named heiress to the throne. Still, she knew that later, when talking with Isaac or with people who had not partaken in the event, she would no doubt criticize the whole affair for its excesses.

"Maybe we should forget about the houses and belongings and just get out now," Keyvan says. He looks pale and thin, his collarbone visible through his cotton sweater—the kind of man, Farnaz thinks, who would not survive prison.

Shahla picks up the teapot and fills the cups. "We can't just leave," she says as she pours. "How will we sustain ourselves—with love?" She extends a cup to Farnaz but looks at her husband, who glances back at her for an instant before turning his gaze to a painting on the wall, of the Qajar king Nasir al-Din Shah, made by his great-grandfather in 1892.

"This painting alone is reason enough to stay," Shahla says. "How can you leave all this family history behind?"

He rubs his forehead, resting his fingers on the large, visible veins on his temples. "But what if they arrest me? How will this painting—and all the pages I've written about it in all those useless art magazines—help me in jail? Or this tea set, or that chandelier, or this stupid eighteenth-century chair—what will they do for me?" His voice rises—dusty and trembling—a voice untrained for such a pitch, and strained because of it.

"Shhh!" Shahla says. "You want the whole neighborhood to hear you?" She sips her tea, then helps herself to a madeleine, which she brings to her mouth slowly and with deliberate calm. "Can you even imagine your father's face when he sees us at his doorstep in Geneva, empty-handed?" She takes a bite out of her cake, cupping her hand under it to catch any crumbs. "These mullahs have no reason to come after us," she says, bringing the matter to her desired conclusion, as she so often did.

"What reason did they have to come after Isaac?" Farnaz asks.

Keyvan stirs his tea absentmindedly. "My only crime is being my father's son," he says, looking down.

Shahla wipes her hands, then reaches for a cigarette and lights it. "Why all the drama, Professor?" She exhales in her husband's direction, freeing her chest of not just smoke but also acrimony. "Who would you be without your father? And your grandfather and your great-grandfather? Stripped of your lineage, what would you have achieved? You think people would care about your opinions on art if it weren't for your last name? If we leave this country without taking care of our belongings, who in Geneva or Paris or Timbuktu will understand who we once were?"

EIGHT

Homayoun . . . Gholampour . . . Habibi . . ." A guard yells out the names as he makes his way up and down the hallway. Since his arrival, Isaac has not heard so many people called at once. From his mattress he glances at Mehdi, who, without looking away from the roach in the corner says, "You'd better get used to it. If you don't hear your name, thank God, if you do hear your name, say a prayer."

There is commotion in the hallway—metal doors, footsteps, the rattling of keys, sighs, and a man screaming, over and over, "Where? Where? Where?"

"That's Gholampour," Mehdi says. "He knew his end was near. He'd been talking about it for the past few weeks."

"How did he know?" Isaac says.

"He just did. One develops a sense for these things. You smell it in your interrogator's breath. You know he's had it with you."

When the roach passes by Ramin's bare foot the boy gets up and follows it, and grabs it with a clean sweep. "Shall we crunch him or let him go?" he says.

"Why don't we save him for later?" Mehdi grunts. "He may be the best meal we get all day."

The thought of the insect's crunchy flesh rubbing against the boy's skin nauseates Isaac. He lies back on his mattress, tells himself that as long as he is alive he must find some kind of preoccupation—maybe he can ask the guards for some books, the Koran even. Roach in hand, Ramin approaches. Isaac sees the pair of brown antennae wiggling back and forth through the top of the boy's fist. "Get that thing away from me!" he yells, his voice angrier than he intended.

The boy walks away and unclasps his fist. The roach tumbles to the floor and runs for cover. "I'm sorry," Ramin says. "Just playing around." He sits on his mattress, hugs a knee to his chest, and cleans the spaces between his toes with his finger. Isaac almost yells at him again for his repugnant manners, but he realizes that he is not the boy's father and has no authority over him. Here they are equals, both of them taking orders from their captors. Moments later Ramin starts singing, a love song that Farnaz also sang, in the shower sometimes, or while doing dishes. His voice, low and clear, surprises Isaac. He had not thought it possible that so beautiful a sound could emerge from a boy like him. He shuts his eyes and listens. If his days were to end in this place, this boy's voice would be the final sound he would want to hear.

Metal clinks outside. The door opens. "Shut up, boy!" a guard yells. "Singing is not allowed." Then looking at Isaac, he says, "Brother Amin, follow me."

Isaac wills himself to sit up. He unrolls his sock and slides a foot into it.

"Brother," the guard says. "No need for such formalities. Forget the shoes and socks and come with me."

He stands, one foot cold against the floor. "Don't worry," Mehdi mumbles. "Sounds routine." When he is out of the cell he hears Mehdi continue, "May God be with you."

BACK IN THE room where he had been interrogated on the first day, about three weeks ago, he sees a masked man behind the table. When he gets closer he knows it is Mohsen, because of the missing right index finger.

"Are you familiar with the Mossad?" Mohsen says before Isaac has a chance to settle into the chair.

Haven't they been through this? He decides to be firm. "No, Brother, I'm not."

"No? Last time you said yes."

"I probably said I've heard of it."

"Are you arguing with me?"

"No, Brother. I'm just clarifying. Maybe there was a misunderstanding . . ."

Mohsen throws the file on the table and stands up. "The misunderstanding, my dear Brother, is that you seem to think this is a game."

"No . . ."

"Explain Israel then!"

"Like I said, I have family there, Brother. I've been there to visit them."

"You listen to me," Mohsen says. "*Shisheye omreto nashkoun*—Don't break the glass of your life. Admit you're a Zionist spy!"

The image of Mehdi's ravaged feet flash in his mind. Is this the beginning of something terrible?

"We'll crush you, don't you believe me? You've lost. So admit it."

"But, Brother, I have no connection to any political organizations. How can I admit to something I haven't done?"

"Do you have witnesses to show that you're not a spy?"

Demented logic. But Isaac does not contest it. If he turns the tables on his interrogator and asks if *he* has any witnesses claiming that he *is* a spy, then he would be worsening the situation. On the other hand, if he says many people would testify that he has no political connections, he would be putting others in danger. "Brother," he says. "I am a simple man. My preoccupations are my work and my family."

"Simple?" Mohsen laughs. "I suppose figuring out all your bank accounts is very simple. Well, I, for one, had trouble following. Transfers from this bank to that bank, withdrawals . . . I say it takes a pretty sophisticated mind to carry out all those transactions."

"Sophisticated in business, yes. But . . ."

"Listen to me!" Mohsen yells. "We'll get it out of you, you know that. Just admit it and get it over with." He leans across the table, his masked face an inch from Isaac's. His left iris is a lighter brown than the right, the whites of his eyes a sickly yellow. "We know everything about you. Even how many cucumbers you consume," he whispers. "News comes to us from outside."

Isaac wonders whether there really is a news-bearer. A neighbor? An employee? It occurs to him that his brother Javad may have also been arrested; with his loose tongue Javad was sure to slip and say something incriminating. His brother-in-law Keyvan may also be in prison, given his father's connections. Surrounded by his daily comforts, Keyvan is a kind man. But he does not have the resources necessary to withstand pain; he would no doubt say whatever it would take to spare himself. And what about Farnaz? If his wife is, in fact, in the women's block, could she have succumbed to coercion? The thought overwhelms him with guilt. He has always believed that the ultimate test of love is the willingness to die for another. He asks himself if he would die for her. He believes that he would. Is he, then, doubting whether she would do the same for him?

"So?" Mohsen presses.

"Brother, I swear . . ."

"How terrible that it should come to this," Mohsen says. From his shirt pocket he retrieves a pack of cigarettes, slips one through the mask between his lips, and throws the pack on the table. "Help yourself," he says to Isaac as the flame of his yellow lighter ignites the tobacco. "We may be here a long time."

Isaac pulls a cigarette from the pack. He brings it to his

mouth, waits a few seconds for Mohsen to offer him a light. When no offer comes he removes the cigarette and places it on the table. He feels stupid.

"What's the matter?" Mohsen exhales.

"I . . . I need a light."

"Well then, Brother, just ask!" He walks toward Isaac, cigarette in mouth. "And I'd like the same from you. When I ask you for something, I'd like to get it without too much difficulty."

Isaac nods, brings the cigarette to his lips again. Is this some kind of game? He has an uneasy feeling but ignores it. Mohsen bends toward him now, his masked face inching closer, and only stops when the orange tip of his cigarette meets Isaac's bare cheek. Isaac lets out a cry. His unlit cigarette topples from his lips to the floor.

Mohsen pulls back and exhales, clouding Isaac with a thick puff of smoke, which burns his cheek, as though a hole had been drilled through it.

"You see what you're forcing me to do, Brother?" Mohsen says. "Admit it, *bi pedar-o-madar*—you bastard, admit you are a spy!" He grabs Isaac's hand and turns it around, burning his palm with the cigarette, which he presses with a child's determination to crush an insect. "You're nothing! You hear me?" He stops, brings another cigarette to his mouth and lights it, rips open Isaac's shirt and presses the cigarette on his chest. Isaac tries to breathe; his body contracts with pain.

A kick in the stomach throws him to the floor. A wad of saliva lands on his right eye but he has no strength to wipe it.

It travels slowly along his face, down the bridge of his nose and through the left eye, landing on the concrete floor.

"In this prison, Brother Amin," Mohsen says, "we are used to getting what we want. Your resistance is pointless."

WHEN HE IS brought back to his cell he finds Mehdi polishing a piece of wood and Ramin sleeping. Mehdi glances sideways, at Isaac's feet. "They let you off easy," he says.

"Yes." Isaac walks to his bed, removes the one sock. He sits on his mattress, listens to Mehdi's sandpaper shaving off the wood. He feels dizzy. Blisters have formed on his right palm, his cheek, and his chest. He lies on his back, carefully, avoiding all contact between the burns and the mattress.

"You should try to get some honey," Mehdi says. "I think Gholampour had some. They let him have it because of his low blood sugar. Now that he's gone, you might as well . . ."

"Honey?"

"Yes. It helps heal the skin after a burn. And it prevents infection."

Isaac brings his hand to his cheek and touches the blister. It is tender and raw, a semiliquid bulb rising from his skin. The thought of a permanent mark on his face saddens him. But he realizes that "permanent" may not be all that long. "Did you get burned here also?" he asks.

"No. They wasted no time with me. They took me straight for the lashings." Mehdi stops polishing and observes his wooden creation—an oval vessel, pointed in the front and hollowed out.

"So what are you making with that piece of wood?" Isaac says.

"I'm trying to make a Dutch clog. Before they arrested me I had promised my little girl I would make one for her and we would paint it together. But I'm not very good."

"No. It looks like a boat."

"I know!" Mehdi looks at the shoe and shakes his head. "It's a piece of shit, isn't it?"

Isaac smiles, but the movement stretches his skin, reminding him of his blister and his pain.

"Ah!" Mehdi throws the shoe on the floor and lies down. "Enough artistic expression for today. I think I'll take a nap."

Isaac turns on his left side, tucking his hand under his ear. He looks at the wooden vessel thrown on the floor—this so-called shoe—and sees, under its asymmetrical, jagged shape, the clean intentions of its maker, and the hope, however faint, that he will be reunited with his daughter. He admires Mehdi's defiance, more so because he thinks himself incapable of it.

The image that returns to his mind repeatedly now is Mohsen holding his hand and turning it around, palm upward, as if about to offer him something. In that brief instant before the burn, the two men, hand in hand, could have passed as friends. He wonders what Farnaz would do if she knew what just happened to him. The last time he saw her she was upset with him. It was the morning of his arrest.

In bed she had spooned his body with her own, wrapping her arm around his stomach. He had flung the arm away. When he turned to her he knew it was too late. For some time he had been pushing her away, in invisible degrees. It had started with the flowers. He used to bring her a bouquet every now and then—lilies or roses, and whenever he found them, white orchids, because they were her favorite. But he had stopped and had not even realized that he had. "Is there a shortage of flowers also, because of the war?" she joked one night as he came home and found her, as usual, in front of the television. "Flowers?" he said. "The country has been destroyed and you're thinking about flowers?" She shut off the television and looked at him. The sudden silence unnerved him. "How can you say this to me?" she said. "I have been watching the destruction scene by scene. Why do you think I kept insisting we leave, when we had the chance, when everyone else was leaving? Well, since it looks like we are staying, we might as well try to have a normal life." She picked up her glass and took a thoughtful sip. "So where are my flowers, my dear husband?"

He could not bring himself to say anything; he did not feel he had enough strength left in him for another argument. He decided that if she could convince him they should go, he would pack up. "Fine," he said, half bluffing. "It's not too late. We can still go. Travel may be restricted but we can run away through Turkey, or Pakistan. So many are doing it. I'll start looking for smugglers." She was startled, pulled her eyes away from him and looked at the floor. She sat quietly for some time like that, looking down, legs crossed, her slipper dangling from her right foot. Then she looked up and scanned the room—the sofa, the corner bar, the rugs, the miniatures. She took it all in before shaking her head no.

"You see?" he said. "You don't want to go any more than I do. How can you part with your stuff—your paintings and your china and your carpets?"

She looked up, fire in her eyes. "Whose fault is it that we didn't ship *my* stuff when we could have? I may not be able to live without my stuff, but you can't live without your status. That, more than anything, terrifies you."

"My *status*? Maybe so. But may I remind you, Madame Amin, that had you not believed that I would one day reach this status, you would never have married me?"

She got up and locked herself in the bathroom, leaving behind her familiar trail of perfume, which gave him a sudden headache. He sat on the sofa and finished her drink. Since the beginning of the riots he had been living in limbo—liquidating assets and sending funds to his Swiss bank accounts on the one hand, but continuing to expand his business on the other. In truth, he had been unable to make a decision. Listening to the sound of running water coming from the bathroom, it occurred to him that his wife's distress might be caused more by the deterioration of their love than that of their country. He promised himself that he would once again do the little things he once did for her—warming her side of the bed while she put on her face cream and brushed her hair, surprising her with a pastry, bringing her flowers. But each night, on his way home, exhaustion would prevent him from making the detour to the flower shop and he would tell himself, "Tomorrow. The flowers can wait until tomorrow."

LYING NOW ON his mattress he thinks of her perfume and wishes he could kiss her. How ridiculous they had both become. He wonders why they let distance grow between them. It wasn't that he didn't love her anymore, or that he no longer found her beautiful. He was still fond of her black hair, her almond-shaped brown eyes, her lips—always slightly parted, as if she was about to speak, but wouldn't. But she had lost something, something that had made him fall in love with her the day he had met her at the teahouse in Shiraz—a certain warmth, gone now, leaving her face beautiful but flat, like one of her prized paintings.

"I'm sorry," he had said to her that morning, believing at first that he was apologizing for flinging her arm away, but realizing, afterward, that he was sorry for so much more. She had nodded. But he knew he was not forgiven. He had promised to come back for lunch. They needed to spend more time together. She had agreed.

He looks up at the ceiling. The room reeks of soiled bandages and sweat. He pictures water streaming down his body, washing him clean.

NINE

Of prisons, she knows little. The Tower of London, the Bastille, Alcatraz—these are places that Farnaz associates most readily with the word. Of course, she knows—has always known—that in her own time and her own city, prisons also exist. But does one ever really think about what goes on in them, these ugly edifices, crowned with barbed wire? She remembers helping Parviz with his history lesson on the storming of the Bastille, telling him about the mob that invaded the Hôtel des Invalides for ammunition and gathered outside the prison, about the fighting that erupted, and about the governor of Paris, a certain Marquis de Launey, who, finding himself impotent in the face of such fury, had opened the gates, and consequently led the way to his own death: only hours later his decapitated head was paraded down the streets on a pike. This last bit had so fascinated Parviz that he would repeat it to everyone—his father, Javad, Shahla, Keyvan, Habibeh—asking them, over and over, if they knew how the Marquis de Launey had ended up like a kebab on a skewer. His listeners would laugh and say, "Yes, yes! Thanks to you, how can we forget?" He tormented his little sister, too, reminding her, from time to time, of the ill-fated governor, and asking her, when she annoyed him, how she would like it if she were to end up like the marquis. "You think that story scares me?" Shirin would say, cupping her tiny hand around her neck.

Driving now to a prison outside Tehran, she thinks of this story, coming to life all around her. For hadn't she witnessed, only months ago, the charred body of a prostitute placed on a stretcher and paraded down the street, surrounded by a chanting, euphoric mob? Having set the woman's body on fire, the mob seemed oblivious to the fact that her limbs, reduced to ashes, were falling off her. And had she not seen photographs of the shah's ministers in a morgue, naked, like mice in a testing laboratory—an experiment gone bad? And here she is, Farnaz Amin, on her way to the country's most renowned prison, looking for her husband. Her visit to the previous prison had not terrified her as much, perhaps because its location in the city center made it seem less remote, making the events taking place inside it less forbidding.

"You're sure you're going the right way, khanoum-Amin?" Habibeh says. She adjusts the black fabric of her chador to better cover her head.

"I'm following the map. Do you feel it's the wrong way?"

"What do I know, khanoum?" She rolls down the window, sticks out her head, and takes a deep breath. "I don't feel so good."

"What's wrong, Habibeh? Shall I stop the car?"

"No, no. Don't stop on my account."

"Maybe I should have come by myself."

"No, khanoum, no! I wanted to come. I drank too many teas this morning, that's all. Five cups, I think. My heart is racing."

The sprawling gray buildings emerge as the car makes its way to the top of the mountain. Gravel shifts under the wheels, stones hitting the sides of the car from time to time. She parks outside the metal gates. Her hands quiver as she pulls the hand break and adjusts her scarf. "You're sure you want to come in with me?"

"I'm sure, khanoum."

"All right. Just remember, if they ask you questions, say the minimum necessary. Don't elaborate."

"Yes, khanoum. You told me already."

She wonders if bringing Habibeh was a wise decision. This morning, as she got dressed, her stomach churned as she pictured herself walking inside the prison, the gates slamming shut behind her. Bending over to tie her shoelaces, her undigested breakfast moved up from her stomach to her throat, and before she could get herself to the bathroom, she was vomiting on the carpet. Habibeh had rushed in, helped her to the bathroom, and cleaned her face swiftly and with urgency—as if this were a sight she could not tolerate. Farnaz had surrendered to Habibeh's towel, and to the brisk hand that poured water over her face—the palms, callused from decades spent washing linen and holding whisk brooms—rough and unpleasant against her skin. Habibeh then kneeled on the carpet and wiped away the yellow-brown stain. "Shall I come with you today, khanoum?" she had said, without looking up, and Farnaz, still bent over the sink, her stomach sending small aftershocks throughout her body, had said, "Yes. Would you?"

Now, having regained her composure, she regrets her decision, born out of a passing moment of weakness. Habibeh's presence, which she had hoped would bring her comfort, now seems to her a liability.

"What do you want?" a guard says. His face, greasy and pockmarked, gleams in the sun. A transistor radio on a small table next to him is broadcasting a sermon. Next to it is a box of sweets, flies hovering above it.

"I am looking for my husband, Brother," Farnaz says. "Would you tell me if he's here?"

"You're wasting your time. We don't give out such information."

"Brother, please. I just want to know if he's alive. For three weeks I've had no news of him."

The man sizes up Farnaz, then looks at Habibeh. "And who's this?"

"I'm a friend," Habibeh offers.

He stands for a moment before unlatching a ring of keys from his belt. "All right. Wait here." He opens the gate and disappears behind it.

"You see, khanoum, it's good that you brought me!" Habibeh says. "He liked the idea that someone like you would have a friend like me."

The second guard watches them as they wait by the

gate, his rifle hanging from his shoulder, his black beard so thick that it darkens the entire southern hemisphere of his face. So much hair, Farnaz thinks—rough, dirty hair growing feverishly on chins and cheeks and necks throughout the country, like noxious weeds. From the radio comes the cleric's sermon, "O God, destroy infidelity and infidels. O God, destroy your enemies, the Zionists." The open lid of the box of sweets flaps in the wind.

The gate opens and the first guard reappears. "Come in," he says. Habibeh nods under her chador, mumbling to herself, "*Basheh, dorost misheh*—It will be all right." The guard leads them to a desk where an official writes their names and the purpose of their visit. A woman then steps forward and runs her hands over Farnaz's body, beginning from the shoulders and working her way down—the arms, the breasts, the waist, the thighs, the calves, the ankles, and the feet, and, at the end, shoving her hand between her legs and leaving it there, pressing her middle finger, slowly, against the fabric of her pants. Farnaz flinches, but when she sees the guard and the official watching her, she loses her voice—forgets, even, that she has one.

A blindfolded man is brought in. He is thrown against the official's table and told to state his name. "Vartan Sofoyan," the man says, and Farnaz, standing next to him, gasps; he is a pianist, and was once a frequent guest at Keyvan and Shahla's parties.

"You know this man?" the guard yells.

"No."

The man stands erect. His long fingers, which she had

once so admired, rest on the desk, anchoring him in his blindness.

"Then why the gasp, Sister Amin?"

"It's the blindfold, Brother. . . . It startled me."

The pianist's shoulders droop slightly. She wonders whether he recognizes her voice. Years ago, when he had just returned from the Vienna Music Academy, Keyvan and Shahla, who had met him at a reception in Tehran's Rudaki Opera House, invited him to one of their dinners, and he had charmed the guests with his renditions of Rachmaninoff and Debussy. He was Armenian, tall and thin—as Farnaz imagined a pianist trained in Vienna should be—and she had been taken with him from the moment she saw him. When he found out that she liked singing, that she had, in fact, taken voice lessons until the age of eighteen, when her father decided that it was no longer appropriate for a young woman to sing in public, he asked her to accompany him as he played Debussy's *"Il pleure dans mon coeur,"* based on a poem by Verlaine. She was familiar with this song, as it was among those she had practiced as a young girl and which she had hummed, outside of her voice class, while preparing her father's breakfast in the morning or brushing her hair at night, wondering what was the point of having a beautiful voice if one was not allowed to share it. *"Il pleure dans mon coeur,"* she began as Vartan played. *"Comme il pleut sur la ville; Quelle est cette langueur Qui pénètre mon coeur?"* Their performance was such a success that it soon became a ritual, and each time, upon seeing her, Vartan would hold her hand in his and say, "So how is my *cantatrice*?" With his long, agile fingers enveloping her own, she would feel an excitement she had not felt since she had first met Isaac in Shiraz, when he would recite poetry to her and enchant her with his growing knowledge of gemstones, making her believe that theirs would be a sparkling life of ghazals and jewels. But as the years had passed the poetry had left their lives, and the stones themselves had been ground into oval cuts or marquise cuts, stars or cabochons, turning her husband into the kind of man who could offer her the rarest luxuries, but little else, and herself into the kind of woman who had come to accept these terms.

A guard wearing a black mask arrives, a file tucked under his arm. As he removes the pianist's blindfold, Farnaz notices that a finger on the guard's right hand is missing. "Brother Sofoyan?" he says. "Follow me." Vartan rubs his eyes and blinks repeatedly. Seeing Farnaz, he nearly says something, but doesn't.

Another man in a black mask drags Farnaz through a dark, narrow corridor, and shoves her inside a windowless room, not much larger than a closet.

"Do you know that man? Vartan Sofoyan?"

"No. I'm here to find my husband."

"Sofoyan was a friend of the royal family. He played for them on many occasions."

"Brother, I really would like to find out where my husband is."

"You know what will happen to him, to this dandy of a pianist? He'll hear his own recordings at his funeral!"

The locked room is lit only by a bulb dangling from

the ceiling. Anything could happen here, anything at all—and who would know about it? How many rooms, like this one, exist inside this prison, this city, this country? Is Isaac in a room like this, maybe just a few steps away from her? She thinks of Vartan, of the years he had spent training in Vienna, of the compositions he hoped to write. What had been the point of it all, if his days are to end here? Is this where it would be written, his magnum opus—*Requiem for Vartan Sofoyan*?

The man opens a file. "You were once a journalist, isn't that correct, Sister?"

If they have a file on her, then most likely Isaac is here. Realizing that he is in this prison is like receiving news of a terminal illness: the waiting is over. "Oh, I wouldn't call myself that," she says. "I wrote once in a while."

"A dabbler, then?"

"I suppose."

"Only those who can afford to be dabblers dabble. Those who have to work, work."

"I could afford it thanks to my husband, who worked very hard."

"Yes," the guard smiles. "Worked very hard at amassing his fortune."

"Brother, the money did not fall from the sky. He earned it!"

"Don't talk to me that way!" He steps closer to her. "I could finish you off right here, do you understand me? Tell me about these articles you wrote."

Was coming here a big mistake? If they imprison her,

what would happen to Shirin? "Brother, they were light pieces," she says, trying to control the tremor in her voice. "Nothing worth mentioning."

"I'm feeling light this morning. Indulge me."

She had written travel articles—on the porcelain in Limoges, the sangria in Seville, the medieval towns in Umbria. She had been to these places with Isaac. Together they had stood in olive groves, basilicas, bell towers. How ordinary it had all seemed to her then, and how wonderful in its ordinariness it seems to her now. "I wrote about foreign places," she says.

"Yes. You touted the virtues of alcohol, and gushed about cathedrals. Your pieces were propaganda for an indecent life."

"Brother, those alcoholic drinks were just specialties of the places we visited, the cathedrals were the historic remnants . . ."

"Yes. And the Ice Palace in Tehran, what kind of historic remnant was that?"

The halo around the light bulb expands, making her see dancing spots of light around her. The room spins. "Brother, why am I being interrogated? I came here of my own accord. I am not charged with anything. Please just tell me if my husband is here."

The guard steps away from her and opens the door. "It's time you understood, Sister Amin, that the days when people like you could demand things from us are over. Now it's our turn. Let's go, Sister."

Standing in the dim room, hearing the pleading voice of a prisoner being questioned somewhere nearby, she feels the prison as a real place—made of concrete and steel, where people wake up, eat, use the toilet, and sleep, their tedious routine interrupted by the terror of interrogations. For most people, she thinks, the notion of death is no more than a wallpaper—present but rarely seen. Prisoners, who have little to distract them, have no choice but to stare at this wallpaper.

They walk through the corridor and back to the prison's entrance. Another guard opens the gate for her. "Your friend is outside," he says.

Habibeh leans on the car, tapping her hand on the hood. They drive away in silence.

"I'm sorry, Habibeh, for dragging you into this," Farnaz says as they approach the city.

"I'm the one who's sorry, khanoum. This visit made me realize that Amin-agha is in real trouble."

"Did they interrogate you also? Did they say anything to you?"

"They told me, khanoum, that they will come to search the house for evidence of wrongdoing. They said that while Amin-agha may have seemed to be a nice man, he was involved in some dirty dealings, that even . . ."

"What dirty dealings?"

"I don't know. They didn't say."

"Anything else?"

Habibeh bites her lower lip, as she often does when she feels unsure of what she is about to say. "They also asked me whether I like being a servant."

"What kind of a question is that? You're not letting these people put ideas in your head, are you, Habibeh?"

"No, of course not. But I don't know, khanoum. My son says there is a lot of injustice that needs to be set right."

"What? Morteza has become a revolutionary now?"

"Well, yes. He has joined the Guards. I didn't want to tell you because I thought you might get upset with me. But when I listen to him, I realize he makes a lot of sense."

"What does he say that makes so much sense?"

"I can't say, khanoum. You won't like hearing it."

"It's all right. Tell me."

"If I tell you, promise you won't get mad."

"I won't."

"He says, why should some people live like kings and the rest like rats? And why should the wealthy, enamored with Europe and the West, dictate how the whole country should dress, talk, live? What if we like our chadors and our Koran? What if we want our own mullahs to rule us, not that saint—what's his name?" She taps her fingers on the dashboard, trying to remember the name. "Morteza told me he is worshipped in Europe . . . I know! Saint Laurent, or something like that . . ."

"Yves Saint Laurent?" Farnaz laughs. "He's not a saint, Habibeh. He's a designer. That's just his name."

Habibeh blushes. She looks out the window. "You see, Farnaz-khnaoum, you belittle me every chance you get."

"I'm not belittling you. But you don't know what you're talking about. You're just repeating some nonsense you heard. This Marxist gibberish has been invoked so often in so many parts of the world. And it failed every time."

"Khanoum, you're doing it again."

How long has this resentment been brewing? Farnaz wonders if Morteza, whom Isaac hired a few years ago as an office manger, had anything to do with her husband's arrest.

"You're entitled to your feelings, Habibeh," she says. "But what I ask of you is that you don't forget the friendship we've shared through all these years—the trips we took, the jokes we laughed at, and most of all, the troubles that we confided in each other."

"No, no, I don't forget." She looks out the window again, the wind flapping her chador against her face. "But khanoum," she says, "am I a friend to you, as Kourosh Nassiri and his wife were? What do I know about you, after all? I may know what you like for breakfast, or how many sugars you take in your tea, or even—excuse me for saying this—the color of your underwear. But what do I really know?" She shakes her head and continues in a lower voice, "No, khanoum. I don't think what we have is friendship. I believe it's tolerance, and habit. Like animals in a forest, we have learned to live with one another."

THEY DRIVE THE rest of the way in silence. As they approach the house Farnaz feels a tightening in her heart, caused not only by her exchange with Habibeh, but also by the irrefutable knowledge that Isaac is in the harshest prison in the country. Parking behind his old Renault—the beat-up car of his youth that he refused to let go of—she realizes that she had not loved him as he deserved to be loved. Over the years she had come to think of him as a formal man—reliable, predictable, and shrewd—qualities she had insisted on before marrying him, but which she later found stifling. What was it that she had wanted from him? Had he remained a poet, in his little sun-drenched apartment in Shiraz, who would have married him? Not her, certainly.

TEN

Parviz's exit out of the subway coincides with the end of studies at the neighborhood yeshiva, and scores of boys and young men in black suits and earlocks congregating outside the red brick building in clusters of twos and threes. He walks past the yeshiva, and past the neighboring houses and shops, where silver wine cups and candelabras catch the afternoon rays behind the glass windows. He passes by his landlord's hat shop, sees Zalman Mendelson steaming a black hat with great care, the vapor rising from his machine in mighty puffs. Mr. Mendelson looks up and motions with his hand to invite him in.

The shop is narrow and warm, rows of black hats stacked one on top of the other on shelves along the walls. He has been avoiding his landlord since their last encounter, even crossing the street whenever he had to pass by the hat shop. Today, distracted by an argument two people were having about the recent assassination of Anwar Sadat, the Egyptian president, he forgot to cross. On hearing the news, a few weeks earlier, Parviz had been startled that a man would be killed for nothing other than his attempt to make peace with his neighbors. So deep a hatred, he realized, could never be rectified with handshakes and treaties.

"Hello, Mr. Mendelson," he says. "I'm sorry but I still don't have it." He feels awkward as he stands in the doorway, his hands in his pockets.

Zalman goes on steaming. "You think I called you in for the rent? No. If I want the money, I come and ask you for it. We said we would wait a few weeks, and a deal's a deal, right? How are things with you, Parviz? You're enjoying school?"

"Sure. It's all right." Parviz examines the shop, the peeling yellow-cream walls, the antique cash register, and the framed photo of the community's lead rabbi—whom they call "Rebbe"—with his black eyes and his full religious beard, frightening any viewer who cares to look long enough. "I guess this is the right neighborhood for a hat shop," he laughs.

"Like a hot dog stand at a ballgame," says Zalman. "We're keeping the hat business alive. In the old days, everyone wore hats. People liked to dress up. Now it's just us. How many men do you know who own a fedora?"

Parviz runs his fingers over the felt hats, feeling the firm cloth and the satin ribbon circling the base. "My father had a fedora," he says. "He bought it with my mother during a trip to Rome. But he hardly ever wore it."

Zalman places the steamed hat on a shelf, takes a new one and starts again. "And your father, how is he now?"

"I don't know. I think he is in prison." Saying it out loud, like this, brings him relief, but also embarrassment. His private pain is opening itself to public sentiments, which will consist of sympathy, no doubt, but also scrutiny—and pity. He does not want to be the boy who garners pity.

Zalman looks up and drops his hand, the steamer's nozzle blowing vapor toward Parviz. The wet warmth, smelling of closed rooms with old radiators huffing in winter, is comforting to him.

"My father, too, had been in jail, before I was born."

"Yes? Where?"

"Leningrad. 1924. He was in the Spalerno prison. That's where the rebbe's father-in-law was also incarcerated." He says this with pride rather than outrage, or sadness even. His blue eyes grow deeper, his chin moves upward, as if the association with the rebbe elevates not only his father's suffering, but also his own.

"What was he charged with, your father?"

"Charged with? My dear Parviz, he was charged with being a Jew. He was charged with not relinquishing his religion when Lenin's state demanded it."

"But it's different with my father. He is not a practicing man. He is not like your father."

"Yes, yes, it's different." Zalman nods. "But in the end, it's the same."

"Did he get out?"

"Eventually. He was exiled to Vladivostok, in Siberia, where he met my mother, Rebecca, the daughter of another exile, Lazar Rosenfeldt. That's where I was born."

On the windowpane is a framed black-and-white photograph of a bearded man, staring into the camera with dark, serious eyes—a look that could be interpreted as triumph, or as hardened grief. "Is that your father, Mr. Mendelson?"

"Yes. This photograph was taken three weeks after I was born, in the winter of 1934. My father never smiled in public because a prison guard had knocked out his teeth. But he was a good man, a learned man, a *bal toyreh*." He gets up with some difficulty and sighs, then disappears in the back of the shop.

Zalman's past vaguely comforts Parviz, making him see his own pain as only a blemish on the faded map of history. Others before him had endured grief, and others after him will, as well.

What had it been like, Parviz wonders, to have grown up with a father who was ashamed of smiling in public? Did the father, over time, forget how to smile altogether? The poses that people assume for photographs often become the poses of their lives, don't they? He thinks of his own grandfather, Baba-Hakim. In group pictures he always sat slightly apart from everyone, gazing upward—at the ceiling or at a tree—anything but the camera lens. His father, on the other hand, stared at the camera with defiance, as though daring it to negate his presence.

Zalman's eldest daughter, Rachel, walks into the shop, carrying a plastic bag in one hand and roses in the other. At sixteen, she is small and thin, with an angular, serious face, and large brown eyes that refuse to make contact with Parviz. *"Tatteleh!"* she says. "I brought you your snack."

"Right on time." Zalman emerges from the back and takes the bag. "There was a lot of *tumul* coming from my stomach!" He unloads the contents—a banana, a yogurt, a slice of bread.

Many times Parviz had tried to introduce himself to Rachel, but she always managed to avoid him, crossing the street or simply looking away if they were already too close.

"Parviz," Zalman says, "I'm sure you've met my daughter Rachel?"

"Not officially, no." Parviz extends his hand but she refuses to take it.

"No hands!" Zalman laughs. "Men and women don't touch. You have so much to learn, my boy."

"Sorry," Parviz stutters.

Rachel nods shyly. "I have to go help Mameh with dinner. Shalom." She disappears from the shop with her roses.

"Shalom, my angel!" Zalman dips his bread in the yogurt and takes a bite. "She is such a good girl, my Rachel. She comes here straight from work and brings me my snack. She hasn't missed a day . . ."

"Work? Doesn't she go to school?"

"She does, she does. But after school she works in a flower shop not far from here, and then, God bless her, she goes home and helps Rivka with dinner and chores. I was opposed to her working outside the home, but she insisted. She's a stubborn one, so what could I do? I know something about stubbornness. At her age, I was even worse. I told her she could do it only if she stayed in this neighborhood. That was our little compromise." He leaves his half-eaten yogurt on the counter, rinses his hands in a small sink, and resumes steaming. "Are you hungry, Parviz? Help yourself to the banana."

"No, thank you." The banana, ripe and spotless, would have been the perfect antidote to his stomach's disquietude, but how can he take it from a man who must feed six children and a pregnant wife, and to whom he is already indebted? Rachel's resourcefulness shames him, making him wonder if his own lethargy is actually indolence. The rise of his debts—to Zalman, to Rivka, who from time to time brings him leftovers, or a slice of cake she has baked, and to Yanki, the local grocer who had allowed him to shop on credit for about a month—has not increased his ability to make an effort. "I cannot go on feeding you for free indefinitely," Yanki had said. "Maybe if you weren't such a *traifener bain*—nonobservant Jew—life would start treating you better." The comment had angered Parviz, but what could he have said to a man who had, after all, fed him for weeks?

Lately he has been waking up every morning believing that after classes he would sit down and organize his life, slice his days into contoured, distinguishable hours—of classes, studying, and working a part-time job. But each day, as the afternoon arrived, fatigue overtook him and he told himself that surely a nap, followed by a cup of tea, would restore his body. Invariably he emerged from the nap even drowsier than before, and, resorting to beer instead of tea, he comforted himself with a single thought: Tomorrow. I will map out my life tomorrow. This is how his wasted hours accumulated, much like his debt, and he found himself impotent in the face of both.

"I have a proposition," Zalman says. "Work for me to pay off the rent. And I'll even give you some pocket money on top of it."

"Work for you? Here in the shop?" The idea sounds ridiculous to him. "I appreciate the offer, Mr. Mendelson," he says, "but I don't think I would be any good as a shop clerk."

"It's a request, my boy." He stops steaming and looks up. "I know you're going through a difficult period, but I can't have you as a houseguest indefinitely. Do you understand?"

He nods. He does understand. But why is it, he wonders, that no one understands his situation? This is not how his life was supposed to turn out. Only two years ago he was debating between an architecture school in Paris and another in Zurich, and his parents were considering buying him an apartment in whichever city he ended up in. That he should now be a burden on others both angers and shames him. "All right, I'll do it," he says.

"I would need you to come three afternoons a week, with no excuses. Does that work?"

"Yes, I suppose."

"Good. Be here next Tuesday."

"I'll be here." He feels hot suddenly, the steam choking him. He cannot stay in the shop a second longer. "Well, good-bye, Mr. Mendelson."

"*Alaichem shalom*—peace be with you!"

• • •

HE WALKS INTO the gray, humid afternoon, where people are carrying on with the day—the woman buying bread from Yanki; the old man walking home, the fringes of his *tallit* peering from the bottom of his jacket a reminder, to himself and to the rest of the world, of who he is. All these people, gathered here from Warsaw and Berlin and Krakow—the residue of a generation—have a private history, a log of losses and longings, the specter of their dead interrupting their days. And yet life goes on here, as elsewhere in the world. Milk must be bought, bread broken, shoes shined, dreams dreamt. Life goes on for him also. His acquiescence to Zalman Mendelson fills him with sadness. It is proof of his fall—from son of a wealthy man to starving shop boy. It is also an affirmation of his desire to survive, which he views as both a necessity and a betrayal—of his past, his family, his father.

ELEVEN

Leila's family seems to live on the floor—the floor is where they eat, sleep, pray. Until recently, housekeepers sat on the floor, people like Shirin and her family sat on sofas, the king sat on a throne. This was once the order of things and it had seemed right. Now the order has been muddled. The king has lost his throne and Shirin is on the floor with Leila. In front of them, on a vinyl tablecloth laid out on the carpet, is a plate of lavash bread and feta cheese, and two cups of tea. This is the meal that Leila's mother most often prepares for them, and Shirin associates this with housekeepers also, because in her house it is Habibeh and Abbas the gardener who usually eat it. She doesn't say this. Instead she sits next to her friend and eats her cheese. She knows that before the revolution she and Leila would not have been friends—they would not even have met. It is only because private schools had closed their doors and the city had reshuffled its students that the two of them happened to find themselves in the same class. Was their friendship, then, a good thing?

"No news from your father?" Leila says.

"No, not yet." She talked to Leila about her father on that afternoon some two weeks ago when neither her mother nor Habibeh had come to pick her up from school. For three hours she had stood in the abandoned playground with the old man Jamshid-agha, the sound of each approaching car filling her with both hope and dread. "Don't worry, she'll come," the old man repeated. Shirin nodded, wanting very much to believe him, but each passing, empty minute negated her mother's arrival, and she began wondering if her mother, too, had disappeared, like the ring, the teapot, and her father. As dusk approached, and the playground darkened, the afternoon light turning red, then gray, she had looked at the old man and cried. Jamshid-agha had stood in front of her, his hands folded before him. Twice he unfolded them and nearly placed them on her shoulder, but both times he retrieved them and locked them again, in resignation. "Come, let's call," he said. They walked back inside the school, through the fluorescent-lit corridors, which, stripped of the chaos of the other children, seemed to her sinister and ghostly—a mausoleum. "The principal should not go home without making sure all the children are picked up," Jamshid-agha mumbled. "What am I to do now?" She realized then that she had become a burden on the old man, that no doubt he had a long way to go in order to get home, that the following day he would be in the principal's office, complaining, that the principal, too, would find out what happened, and soon the whole school would know that her mother had not picked her up that day. When they found the public phone Jamshid-agha searched his pockets for change. He slipped a coin in the slot and let her dial. Her rings went unanswered. She hung up, but the telephone ate up the coin. "Do you have a friend?" the old man said, searching his pockets for more change, and she felt bad about this also—that Jamshid-agha, a janitor in his old age, must part like this with his coins, which were no doubt very dear to him. She promised to pay him back and he said, "You don't worry about that now." She called Leila, who came to pick her up with her mother. In the car, no one said a word. The rumbling of the car's old engine filled the silence. Later in Leila's room, she cried and spoke of her father's disappearance. When her mother finally called Leila's house and arrived, frantic, she kissed and hugged Shirin, in a way she hadn't done in months, then leading her to the car, she said, "Your father isn't on a business trip, like I told you. He is in prison. But don't worry, because prison is now routine." She looked like she was about to cry, but Shirin wasn't sure.

These were the only words spoken between them that night. Later in bed, Shirin thought of her Monopoly game, of that square in the corner with the distraught convict behind bars. In Monopoly, too, prison is routine. Even the best players have to leave everything and jump across the board to that dreaded box, missing a few turns while the game goes on.

* * *

"You think he'll come back, your father?" Leila makes herself a second sandwich.

"I don't know."

"My father says the people who are being taken to prison are sinners. He would know, since he works for the Revolutionary Guards."

"My father is not a sinner."

Since his disappearance Shirin has often tried to remember the last time she saw her father—what he had been wearing, what he had eaten for breakfast, whether he had waved good-bye as he left the kitchen table and walked out. She has come to believe that these final moments may hold in them the answer to his arrest, but she recalls nothing extraordinary about that morning, cannot even remember, for example, whether he had kissed her on her forehead before leaving, as he sometimes did. She has tried, also, to retrace the comings and goings of visitors during the few weeks prior to his departure, hoping to discover a clue to his arrest. The only visitor she remembers is Uncle Javad, who had come one afternoon, staying for just an hour or so. He had had tea and cake in the living room with her mother. He had been unshaven but in good spirits and from time to time Shirin overheard the two of them laughing. "No, I'm done with Fereshteh!" Uncle Javad was saying. "Any woman who tells me my feet smell like a wet mop is getting too bossy and has to go!" Later as he was leaving, he stopped by Shirin's room. "And how is my beautiful girl?" he said. Uncle Javad was known for his collection of beautiful girls and Shirin liked the idea that he found her beautiful, too. He pulled out a paper bag from his pocket and handed it to her. Inside were two hairpins decorated with crystal-studded cherries. She walked to her mirror and pinned them to her hair, one on each side. As she fixed her hair she looked at his reflection, behind hers, and saw in his face a vague sadness. She wondered if it was caused by the shadow cast by his stubble, or if it was something more. "I like the pins very much," she told him, and he said, "I like them on you." People often spoke badly of Uncle Javad—they said he was a charlatan and a womanizer—but Shirin was fond of him.

Leila's mother, Farideh-khanoum, emerges from the kitchen with a wooden crate of apples, which she places on the floor. "Be a good girl, Leila-jan, and take this to the basement. My back is killing me. And while you're down there, sweep the floor a bit, would you?"

Farideh-khanoum is not a bad-looking woman, Shirin notices. Her brown eyes, honey-hued in sunlight, soften the rest of her tired face. But she does not possess the kind of beauty that her own mother does. People often called her mother *magnifique*. "Farnaz-jan, *tu es magnifique!*" they would say in French, the language they used for both praise and condemnation. Women would ask her where she had bought a certain bag, or a pair of shoes, or a silk scarf, and she would smile and say, "Oh, this? I got it in Paris," or "Rome," or "Hong Kong." This pleased Shirin. The remoteness of these places safeguarded her mother's uniqueness and, by association, her own.

She offers to help carry the crate but Leila refuses. They open the squeaky door to the basement and walk down wooden steps. Leila pulls a hanging chain and a small light comes on. It is cool here, and damp. Crates of pears and pomegranates are stacked in one corner, and Leila rests the apples on top. Next to these is a bicycle, with rusty spokes and flat tires. There is an armoire with a broken door, filled with old clothes—pastel-colored skirts and geometric-patterned silk scarves where perfume still lingers. Framed artworks lean against a wall—watercolor landscapes and charcoal drawings. Dusty books are stored in shelves. In a corner, under a stack of old magazines, is a half-open box. Shirin shoves the lid with her foot and sees brownish bottles inside. She pulls one out, and recognizes it, the rectangular bottle with the picture of the walking man dressed in a tailcoat and tall hat. On the label are the words *Johnnie Walker,* in English. "Look, a box full of these bottles!"

Leila takes the bottle and kneels to the floor. "Baba is always talking about how alcohol is forbidden . . ." She puts the bottle back, closes the box, places the magazines back on top, scattering them a bit. "Maybe they don't know about it. Maybe they forgot they had it. Should I tell them?"

"No. Maybe one of them knows about it but doesn't want the other one to find out."

"Yes, you're right. But if having alcohol is a sin, wouldn't I be considered a sinner if I say nothing of it?"

Leila's religiosity always surprises Shirin, but she doesn't contest it. She adds it to the list of differences between them, believes it to be another outcome of living on the floor. "If you withhold information in order to protect someone, God won't punish you," she says.

Leila nods, considering the statement. She picks up the broom and begins sweeping. Shirin pulls an old skirt from the armoire and holds it up against her body. She takes out a few scarves, then a hat. As the shelf empties, she notices dozens of files stacked in the back. She pulls them out and opens one. She reads, *Mahmoud Motamedi. Age: 36. Occupation: journalist. Charge: treason.* Next to the charge is a log: *eight o'clock, no one home; noon, housekeeper says they are traveling; midnight, guards break in, housekeeper gone also. Next attempt: suspect's beach house in Ramsar.*

She opens other files. They are all the same, with different names, ages, and occupations, but similar charges—*royalist, Zionist, advocate of indecency.* What are these files, she wonders. Doesn't *charge* mean doing something wrong, for which one must go to prison? But her father is in prison without having done anything wrong.

She feels cold, as though a winter draft had just blown through the room. She looks over at Leila, who is busy sweeping, dust rising under her broom. She opens one of the files again and examines it more carefully. Here, in these files, are the names of men who, like her father, are destined to vanish. She glances at Leila again and finds her bent over a box of books, trying to sweep the space behind it. It occurs to her that if she were to make one file disappear, she could be saving one man's life. She takes a file randomly and tucks it in her pants, under the long coat of her uniform, then quickly places the hat and scarves back in the closet.

"I think I'll call my mother and tell her to come get me," she says, as casually as she can. "I'm not feeling well."

Leila looks up, her face red from her bent position. "Really? Do you want us to take you home?"

"No, no. I can see you have a lot to do."

"All right. See you tomorrow."

UPSTAIRS AS SHE waits for her mother, she takes the file from under her coat and slips it into her schoolbag. Leila's mother brings her a glass of rosewater. "Sit down, Shirin-jan. Drink this. You look flushed. Do you have a fever?" She places her hand on Shirin's forehead. "You do feel hot . . ."

Shirin brings the glass to her mouth. Her fingers quiver a little and she fears she may drop it. She wonders if Leila's mother can see her heart pounding through her clothes. What if she suspects something?

"You poor child," Farideh-khanoum says. "You're really not well . . ."

When her mother honks she puts down the glass and reaches for her bag, but Farideh-khanoum lifts it first. "I'll carry this to the car, Shirin-jan" she says.

Outside the adults exchange formalities. "Thank you, Farideh-khanoum," her mother says. "I'm sorry if she was a burden . . ."

"No, Amin-khanoum! Please don't mention it." Farideh-khanoum places the schoolbag in the backseat of the car. Then standing upright and facing Shirin's mother, she rubs her hands together, lets them drop to her side, and finally tucks them in the pockets of her skirt. She seems embarrassed, apologetic, almost—reactions that Shirin has seen her mother trigger in many people.

"You're getting sick, Shirin-jan?" her mother says in the car. "We'll go home and I'll fix you a nice soup."

In her room, she opens her bag and pulls out the file. *Ali Reza Rasti, 42. Occupation: professor of philosophy. Charge: advocate of indecency.* She hides the file in the bottom drawer of her desk, under her old notebooks. Is it possible that Ali Reza Rasti will avoid her father's fate?

TWELVE

Once a week the prisoners are allowed to spend an hour outside their cells. Today Isaac sits by the prison mosque with Mehdi and Ramin and a few other men he has met since his arrival, some six weeks ago: Hamid, a low-ranking general from the shah's army; Reza, a young revolutionary who was involved in the capture of the American hostages but ended up in jail, presumably for helping his father, a minister of the shah, escape the country; and old man Muhammad, whom no one knows much about, except that he has three daughters in the women's block—one for being a communist, one for being an adulteress, and the third for being their sister.

"What a day!" says the old man. "So clean you can smell jasmine in the air."

"You have a vivid imagination, Muhammad-agha," Reza says. "All I can smell is Mehdi's stinking foot." Turning to Mehdi he says, "You have to insist they take care of that foot of yours, or else you'll end up with a stump. Look at it, the tip of your toe is almost black."

Mehdi extends his leg, examines his bandaged foot from a distance, and shrugs.

"Wait until it's your turn, agha-Reza," Hamid says. To Isaac this bitter admonition sounds more like a curse than a warning. Hamid has been subject to several interrogations, each accompanied by a round of lashings. His swollen feet bulging from brown plastic slippers are a sorry sight.

"I shouldn't even be here," Reza retorts. "Everyone knows there has been a mistake."

"You and I are from the same stock," Hamid says quietly. "There has been no mistake. Your father and I both served the shah dutifully, did we not? We all know you're the one who helped your father escape."

"Nonsense. My father and I stopped talking a long time ago."

A guard approaches, points his rifle at the group. "Keep it down!" he yells.

The men fall silent. Isaac brushes a hand over the cigarette burns on his chest and face, which throb from time to time. A pigeon flaps its wings overhead and lands a few feet away. It taps its beak on the ground, but finding nothing, takes flight and disappears into the blue sky.

"I hear Fariborz got a carton of Marlboros," Ramin says. "He just had a visit from his wife. He's selling them for fifty tomans."

"Per cigarette?" Mehdi asks.

"Yes."

Isaac smiles at the outrageous fee; prison commerce intrigues him. But what intrigues him even more is the possibility of a family visit, which no one has ever mentioned.

"So there are visitation rights?" he asks.

"What rights?" Hamid says. "It's whoever manages to bribe the guards and slip through the gates. That's your visitation rights."

"Why the interest, Amin-agha?" Reza says. "You think you can continue running your business here?"

Isaac looks out beyond the men, at the horizon rising from the dust. He does not answer.

"You know what your problem is?" Reza continues. "You have no beliefs. As long as you can buy your Italian shoes and your fancy watches and your villas by the sea, you're happy. 'Who cares what kind of regime it is, as long as I make money!' Right? Am I not right, Amin-agha? Isn't that what you're all about?"

Isaac senses the men's eyes on him. He feels hot suddenly. He realizes that to a certain extent Reza is right; he does not have beliefs, at least not the way Reza does. Sure, he can discuss politics for hours, and in fact he often used to, sitting with his friends in his living room, whiskey on the rocks and freshly roasted pistachios fueling the men into the night. But a man like Reza is willing to die for a belief, something Isaac would not do.

"So what?" he says finally. "So what if I wanted a good life? So what if I like hand-stitched shoes and tailored suits and waking up with my wife and children by the sea? Is that a crime? You know what is my belief, agha-Reza? My belief is that life is to be enjoyed. Don't look at me bitterly because things didn't work out the way you'd hoped." In the silence that follows he remembers some Hāfez verses, which he had memorized long ago, when he was a student in Shiraz. He recites them, without further thought. "Give thanks for nights in good company . . ."

The old man's face lights up with recognition. He joins in. "And take the gifts a tranquil heart may bring . . ."

The other men smile; some begin to recite whatever they can remember, throwing in words here and there. "No heart is dark when the kind moon does shine / And grass-grown riverbanks are fair to see."

They finish the verse with gusto, emphasizing "fair to see." There is a moment of silence, then nervous laughter. Even Reza, who did not join the recitation, makes a strange movement with his mouth, which Isaac interprets as a smile.

Back in his cell Isaac thinks of Reza and the thousands of revolutionaries like him—men and women who thought they were part of something big, much bigger than their daily lives—who thought they were changing the course of history. And here they are, having replaced crowns with turbans.

He thinks of the day the shah left, that cold January day nearly two years ago, crowds cheering everywhere, drivers flashing headlights, honking horns, shopkeepers giving away sweets, cab drivers offering free rides, strangers embracing, young women dancing. He had stood on his roof and watched the city, radios and televisions buzzing over clotheslines swaying in the icy air—the woman in the house across from his peeling apples by her kitchen window; the old man leaning on his cane by the street corner, watching in disbelief; the street vendor offering passersby free charcoaled corn; the neighbor's gardener clapping and smiling a toothless smile.

"*Shah raft, Shah raft!*—The shah is gone, the shah is gone!" people cheered.

Later that night he saw the departure on the evening news. The shah at the airport, bony and ill with cancer, with the empress by his side, the two of them forcing smiles.

So this is how it all ends, Isaac thought. Here's the end of the Peacock Throne and its White Revolution—those gilded decades of cultural and economic reforms. Watching the shriveled king on television he thought of the *Darya-e-Noor*—"Sea of Light" diamond, that immaculate, rectangular stone that weighed one hundred eighty-six carats and sparkled on the shah's *kepi* on the day of his coronation. Standing with Farnaz in the Grand Hall of the Golestan Palace, Isaac had been unable to take his eyes off it. If the shah had seemed to him ostentatious, even ridiculous, his stone had not. Unlike this shah, and the many others who had worn it before him, the diamond, perfect in its luster and clarity, had in it something timeless and idyllic, something of the earth from which it came, a durability and purity that no human—or dynasty—could achieve.

Was it not this very durability that the shah wished to emulate, only four years after his coronation, with the celebration of the twenty-five-hundredth anniversary of the Persian Empire—that extravagant affair held over three days in Persepolis? Guests from all over the world—heads of state and other dignitaries—had attended the ceremonies, designed to pay homage to Cyrus, the founder of the Persian Empire, and to Darius, whose magnificent city of Persepolis had once been the symbol of the greatest civilization. Among the stone ruins, just outside Shiraz, the shah had built a tent city for his visitors, inspired by Francis I's camp created in the sixteenth century on France's west coast to receive Henry VIII of England. Calling himself *shahan-shah*—"king of kings," the shah had courted his guests with banquets prepared by Parisian chefs: quail eggs stuffed with caviar, roast peacock—the symbol of the Iranian monarchy—filled with foie gras, Château Lafite Rothschild 1945, Dom Perignon Rosé 1959. The guests, living for three days in the desert, surrounded by ancient ruins, drank and ate, indulging their host's wish to paint himself as an heir to Cyrus. Yet the shah's royal blood was in fact no purer than an estuary: he was the son of a common man who had risen from the military ranks to become king. Placing two wreaths of flowers on the tomb of Cyrus, the shah solemnly recited, "*Kourosh, assoudeh bekhab ke ma bidarim*—Cyrus, rest in peace for we are well awake." In the minute of silence that followed his speech the desert wind blew stronger, swirling the yellow dust in the air and flapping the hems of the women's long dresses, an event that was made much of in newspapers: Had Cyrus's soul responded to the shah? people wondered.

But that was 1971. The guests who had so revered him had long since deserted their host, and the shah, as he fled his country, could not find a place to rest his head. With his suitcase in one hand and his bleak medical prognosis in the other, he had gone to Egypt, Morocco, the Bahamas, Mexico, America, and Panama, finally returning to Egypt—one of the few countries willing to have him die on its soil, which he did, in the summer of 1980. Perceived for decades as the beacon of the Middle East, he was now suddenly viewed as the tyrant who had crushed anyone who dared speak against him. He was, in fact, both of these things. But in those final days, as he lay dying in Cairo, Isaac saw him as neither visionary nor despot, but as a man who had wished both himself and his country to be something they were not.

THIRTEEN

Here they play solitaire and old songs. A 1950s recording spins on the turntable, the singer's voice aggravated by the needle's scratch. Baba-Hakim sits by a window, looking out, absentmindedly tapping his fingers to the music. A half-full glass is on the table in front of him, the tea inside looking cold. Afshin-khanoum, on the sofa, concentrates on her game of solitaire. The house smells of simmered onions and camphor oil.

Farnaz has been here for the entire afternoon, but she has yet to tell them about their son's arrest.

"More tea, Farnaz-jan?" Afshin-khanoum says, shuffling her cards. She does not play these games of solitaire just to pass the time. She plays them to predict the future. Before each game she asks a question, and if the game is resolved successfully, it means that the augury will be positive; if not, then it will be negative. Farnaz remembers how for months after the shah had left the country the old woman had sat on her sofa with her cards, asking, "Will he come back?" And each time a game was completed with success she would clap and say, "The shah will be back; my cards say so!"

"No, thank you, Afshin-khanoum. I had three cups already."

"Then have some cake, *aziz*. You're so thin, thinner than before. Right, Hakim? Doesn't she look thin?"

Baba-Hakim nods, without looking away from the courtyard. He had never been much of a conversationalist; now, old age and doctors' orders that he stay away from cigarettes and alcohol have all but silenced him. He turns his gaze to the room, glances at his tea, then at the locked liquor cabinet. He looks out again. Farnaz remembers the trip to Isfahan, some twenty-five years ago, just a few months after she and Isaac were married. She had not liked the father, then. While she, Isaac, and Afshin-khanoum went sightseeing, he sat in teahouses and smoked water pipes. The tile work on the Darb-e-Imam, the dome of the seventeenth-century Sheikh Lotfolla mosque, left him indifferent. The chimerical name of the palace, Chehel Sotoun—"forty columns," which counts among its columns not only the twenty wooden beams that support its entrance but also their reflection in the pool below, eluded him. And when Isaac joked with him, saying, "Baba-jan, you know the saying '*Isfahan, nesf-e-jahan*—Isfahan, half the world'; Do you know what you're missing?" he smiled and said, "Too bad for me. I guess I'll just have to see the other half." Throughout the trip, he carried in his pocket a metal flask of whiskey, from which apathy, fermented and distilled, tipped into his mouth and filtered through his veins, transforming him into the impassive man that he was. "Hakim is like a baby," Afshin-khanoum would say. "Give him his bottle and he'll leave you alone for a few hours." When Farnaz asked him, one afternoon, why he drank so much, he said, "The amount of drink, Farnaz-jan, must equal the amount of pain. But I'm afraid you won't understand." She had not really understood then.

"I have something to tell you," Farnaz says finally. "Isaac is in prison. I didn't know how to tell you . . ."

Afshin-khanoum puts down her cards and looks up, confused. Baba-Hakim looks away from the window and stares at Farnaz. This may be the first time this husband and wife have ever shared an emotion, Farnaz thinks.

"It's been almost a month and a half."

"Why did you wait so long to tell us?" Afshin-khanoum's eyes are recessed under the weight of her lids. A faint odor of mothballs emerges from her.

"I didn't want to worry you. But now . . . it's been too long. I thought you should know. I also have a favor to ask you. I've been told that most likely the Revolutionary Guards will come to search our house. I was wondering if I could leave Shirin here with you for a few days while I go through all our books and documents and try to get rid of anything that may seem suspicious to them. I don't want her to see me do this. I'm afraid it will alarm her."

"Leave her with us? We can hardly take care of ourselves. Hakim is very ill." Shaking her head she whispers, "So much misfortune . . ." Her face is half lit by the afternoon sun, a few stray hairs dangling from her chin.

"Baba-Hakim, you're ill? What's wrong?"

"My liver, Farnaz-jan, is bad. And my kidneys have become extremely sluggish." His voice belongs to a man who has not spoken in days, maybe weeks. He picks up his worry beads from the table and fingers them. Each bead clacks on the next, following the trajectory of the invisible thread by which it is bound.

These beads, she thinks, will outlive his hands. His wool robe, which he has owned as long as she has known him, and before, will soon be folded and put away in a box, along with his hat, his good shoes, his pocket watch. What had allowed her to tolerate him, on that trip to Isfahan so long ago, was a single sentence. "Please make Isaac happy, Farnaz-jan, because we never did." With this sentence he had made her realize that despite all the things his character lacked, which were many, he possessed at least the capacity to admit who he was: a bad father.

"There are good treatments now for kidney problems," she says. "*Inshallah*—God willing, you'll get better."

He brings his cold tea to his mouth, takes a sip, and returns the glass to the saucer. "No, Farnaz-jan. I will not live long."

Afshin-khanoum looks down at her palms resting on her lap. She takes her black shawl draped on the back of the sofa and wraps it around her shoulders. "I'm sorry, Farnaz-jan, that we can't take Shirin," she says. "This is no place for a child." She caresses the fringes of her scarf, letting them slip, one after the other, through her arthritic fingers. For so long Afshin-khanoum had been defined by what she didn't have, that to take away the little she *did* have—a son who loved her—seems unthinkable. What she didn't have, and this was public knowledge, was the hope, after the birth of Shahla, her third child, of bearing any more children, thanks to the syphilis her husband had offered her after a trip to India, that undying souvenir. She locks her hands on her lap, her head bouncing lightly as she whispers something to herself. She will no doubt withstand the news of her son's disappearance by resorting to solitaire. "Will my son come out alive?" she will ask, hoping that the fifty-two cards will somehow arrange themselves triumphantly, offering her the answer she so needs.

"Yes, Afshin-khanoum, I understand. Well, I should go. Shirin is home alone with Habibeh."

As Farnaz leaves the house and shuts the door behind her, the knocker taps several times against the wood. It is a metal hand, representing the hand of Fatima, the prophet Muhammad's daughter. A neighbor had offered it to Isaac's parents some years ago because the hand is believed to bring good luck to the home's inhabitants. Afshin-khanoum, who was not one to turn down the possibility of better luck, had hung it immediately.

Farnaz walks through the narrow street, framed on both sides by short brick walls, along which is a row of bloody handprints—a common sight, nowadays—the stamp of revolutionaries displaying their sacrifice and their willingness to die. It reminds her of the Ascension mosque in Jerusalem, where they say Jesus left behind a footprint as he went up to heaven.

FOURTEEN

A good structure, like a good man or woman, must have two characteristics: strength and beauty. Parviz first heard this in class, and it seems right to him. For a building to be strong, here the professor quoted John Ruskin, it must accomplish what it was designed to do, and do so efficiently, without an excess of stone, glass, steel. For it to be beautiful, it must reflect its maker's definition of beauty, whatever that definition may be. For only then can it be said that the structure exists honestly.

Shovels, picks, wheelbarrows, winches, ten-ton hydraulic jacks—these were the instruments used to dig seventy-eight feet below the riverbed and build, stone by stone and cable by cable, this Brooklyn Bridge on which he walks. Occasionally, when he has time and the weather permits, he walks across the bridge to Manhattan; it is only once he is back on land that he rides the subway uptown to school. It is a long commute, not the most practical one, but something about the bridge—its combination of suspension and sturdiness—comforts him. A bridge, he thinks, is the only place where uncertainty is permissible, where one can exist with no connection to any land—or any person—but with the reassurance that connection is possible.

Total length of wire in cables: nearly 3,600 miles; number of suspenders: 1,520; total weight of bridge, excluding towers and anchorages: 14,680 tons; number of fatalities during its construction: 20 to 30, including the architect. He first learned these numbers for a test, but unlike a lot of the information that fades once a test has been taken and passed, these figures had stayed with him. Looking out on the water, at the ferries and tugboats passing below the bridge, at the cars rolling on top of it, and the dozens of pedestrians who, like him, are walking toward Manhattan, thinking, no doubt, of the day ahead—the phone calls, the lunches, the possibility of unexpected encounters—he tells himself that the bridge is good, and it is beautiful, and thinking again of Ruskin, he marvels at the knowledge and willpower necessary to build a structure such as this: one must know the weight of each stone, the strength of each wire, the current of the water, in each season. Parviz doesn't think himself capable of such knowledge and willpower.

ZALMAN MENDELSON HAS extended him another invitation, this time for Hanukkah, and Parviz is considering attending. After classes he walks through the streets, passing along the way the pine trees truncated by the thousands and brought to the city for their brief annual holiday function. Already he is anticipating their brutal, inevitable end in the back of garbage trucks, their dry, fallen needles swept from porches and sidewalks. But when he finds himself among throngs of Christmas shoppers, their arms heavy with bags, he feels a lightness in his body, as if he, too, were on his way to the bright boutiques that sell, along with their white scarves and red tins filled with sweets, the promise of winter nights spent with family and friends by living-room fireplaces. He buys some French chocolates for the Mendelsons, spending, against his better judgment, the better portion of his last fifty dollars.

Rachel is leaning on the stoop when he arrives home. He waves hello to her. "A bit cold to be outside, no?"

She wraps her black wool coat tighter around her waist. "It's too hot in the house," she says, looking straight ahead. "I couldn't breathe."

"Yes, those radiators do huff and puff all day."

"I'm not talking about the radiators. I'm talking about people. It's always so crowded around the holidays. It gives me a headache. Not a moment to myself."

Looking at her from below, her body lost inside her coat, her pale skin half lit in the dusk, he finds her rather pretty. He opens the tin and lifts the chocolates up to her. "Please, have one," he says.

She looks inside, then at him, with the same seriousness as before. "It's not kosher," she says. "I can't."

"Chocolate has to be kosher?"

"Yes."

He shuts the tin and reconsiders joining the Mendelsons for dinner. What kind of Jew was he, after all, if he did not even know that one does not bring French chocolates to a Hassidic home? And what kind of Jew was she, for refusing him this small kindness—accepting a gift that he wished to share?

He reads late into the night, first the paper, cover to cover, then pamphlets he received in the mail and intended to throw away, then a forgettable clothing catalog. He lies facedown on his bed, his eyes finally giving up. In his sleep he hears voices rising above him—a chorus of men singing and laughing, doors opening and shutting, the ceiling creaking under dancing footsteps. The sounds pass through him like a dream.

The bang of the front door jolts him, and soon the laughing voices fill the night. He sits up, peeks through the blinds, sees dozens of black pants, the ivory tassels of prayer shawls hanging over them, followed by stockinged legs of women, their shape a mystery in the opaque night. Then come the children, with their dreidels and gold-foiled chocolate coins—the kind *he* should have bought if he had known what he was doing. "Happy Hanukkah!" the voices repeat. But what does it really mean to him, this festival of lights? Does it matter if Judas Maccabee reclaimed the temple of Jerusalem from the Seleucid monarchy? So what if the olive oil that was supposed to last for one day in the temple's menorah miraculously burned for eight? How do these supposed events affect the life of Parviz Amin? And how would celebrating them bring him happiness?

He thinks of his father, imagines the day of his arrest. As he perfected the knot on his tie and ate his eggs, listening to the morning news on the kitchen radio, did he have any premonition that on this day he would disappear from his own life? And when he did disappear, did he believe that, like Judas Maccabee, he would one day reclaim the life that he wished to live?

He sits up on his bed, opens the red tin, and bites into a perfectly round chocolate. The dark ganache melting on his tongue allows him to forget, if only for a few seconds, his complete solitude.

FIFTEEN

A bsence, Shirin thinks, is death's cousin. One day something is there, the next day it isn't. Abracadabra. But she has never liked magic tricks. Magicians make her anxious. So do their assistants. After all, what kind of person would volunteer to be erased? Is there a school somewhere for magicians' assistants? And if so, do students get a degree in *not being*?

What happens to a house full of nonbeings? What if, like her father, she, her mother, and Habibeh would one day disappear also? The house, of course, would not know it. That would be the sad part. The house would continue to exist. Its walls would remain in the same place, the doors ready to be opened and closed. The plates and glasses, too, would stay, even though there would be no one to eat or drink out of them. The chairs would stand still, their laps ready to serve. And the clocks' needles would continue moving forward, and at midnight starting all over again, as though the day that just ended had never been.

This morning she stays in bed and looks out her window, at the wind dusting the sky with the trees' dry leaves. She looks at the branches, pities their nakedness and envies their patience. She watches the pale sunlight trying to break through clouds and failing. She wonders what is the point of it all, this endless cycle.

There was a time when on weekends she would wake up to the smells of eggs, cake, toasted bread. These smells, too, have gone. The house, this morning, smells like nothing. Even a bad smell—dirty socks or rotten eggs—would mean that someone still lives here. Maybe they have all left but she doesn't know it. Is it possible that, like the magician's assistant, they are existing in some other world—a place where they cannot be seen, heard, touched, smelled?

She gets out of bed and walks through the house. Habibeh is gone for the weekend, taking with her the sounds of pots and pans. In the kitchen Shirin opens the refrigerator and takes out the milk, which, she knows, has to be boiled first in case it is spoiled. But she loves cold milk, and who would know if she were to drink straight from the bottle? She brings the bottle to her mouth and sips. A few seconds pass. Nothing happens. She brings the bottle to her mouth and drinks, almost finishing it. And there it is again: nothing.

On her way back to her room she sees that the door to her father's study is closed. Resting her ear against it she hears the shuffling of papers. She opens the door without knocking. Her mother, behind the desk piled high with files, books, and photographs, looks up. "You scared me, Shirin-jan!"

"What are you doing?"

"You see all this?" her mother says. "It has to go." Her hands hover above the desk, palms up, indicating the mess below them.

Normally her mother would have yelled at her for walking into a room without knocking. Today it doesn't seem to matter. "Go where?" Shirin says.

"It has to disappear. You see, people from the new regime may come to search our house. We have to get rid of anything that may look suspicious. Remember how last year you had to tear off the page with the shah's photo from all your books? We have to do the same thing throughout the house—make sure that we have nothing that would prove that we like the old regime."

"Can I help you? I can shred."

"You?" She smiles. "Well, yes, why not? There is so much . . ." The circles under her mother's eyes are darker today. "Oh, your breakfast!" she says. "Are you hungry, Shirin-jan?"

"No, I ate," Shirin lies. She sits next to her mother and rips. They tear up account balances, names and telephone numbers of her father's friends, holiday greeting cards, and photographs—mostly of people she doesn't recognize, or recognizes only after looking at them for a long time. Baba-Hakim was young once, she thinks, even handsome. And Uncle Javad was a skinny boy with messy hair. One photograph, of a young woman—not her mother—in a see-through white dress, taken from the back, makes her stop. The woman is climbing a dune by a beach, a fierce wind whisking her dress and clinging it to her legs. Her hair is wrapped in a sheer scarf tied behind her neck, and she is holding it in place with her left hand, while her right hand swings in midair like a dancer's. She likes that the photograph was taken from the back, that at the moment the shutter snapped, the woman had no idea that she was being captured by a curious eye, probably male, probably her father's. And she is stunned suddenly, to think that this man whom she knows as her father, who wears suits and goes to work and reads the paper, has lived for such a long time before her, has seen so many things she will never see, has known—maybe even loved—so many people she will never know.

There are other photographs, of her parents in the South of France; Keyvan and Shahla sunning by their pool; and her parents' friends Kourosh and Homa, on a ski slope, somewhere. Kourosh, she knows, was killed in prison. What she remembers of him is the nickname "*Aghaye Siyasat*— Mr. Politics.*" He would begin any conversation with "Did you hear of so and so's election?" or "What did you think of such and such assassination?"—things she did not understand but which prompted discussions that continued well into the night, long after she had gone to bed, when she would lie in her dark bedroom and listen to the adults' voices, punctuated by the clink of ice cubes in whiskey glasses. The night she heard of Kourosh's death was the first time she heard her father cry. Lying in her bed behind the closed door she heard the sobbing, which at first she could not believe could come from her father, and then his voice, *"They killed Kourosh, they killed Kourosh. I can't believe it."* Of Kourosh's wife, Homa, she remembers a white mink coat, and that round, perfect mole above her lip. Homa, she knows, had died in a fire. Everyone knows about the fire.

A photograph of herself on the ice-skating rink makes her stop. Where would she begin ripping, in the middle— first tearing it in half and then into pieces, a lock of hair here, a squinting eye there? She leans back and examines the room: the open drawers, the overflowing desk, heaps of paper on the floor. Has her mother gone mad? What will her father think if he returns home and finds his life torn up?

"Are you sure we should do this?" she says.

Her mother drops a paper on the desk. She reaches for a cigarette and brings it to her mouth. "No, I'm not sure," she says.

The cigarettes appear, Shirin knows, whenever things are going badly. They had emerged, for instance, years ago when she was just five or six, when once in a while her mother would take her to the house of a pianist with whom she practiced her singing. For an hour or two Shirin would sit alone in the man's living room, looking at his books, the paintings on the walls, the silver candelabra, the marble floors. What surprised her was a hand puppet of Kermit the Frog on a writing desk, so out of place in that house full of antiques. The puppet was enough to make her like the pianist, and gave her the patience necessary to sit and listen to his piano and to her mother's voice, which, heard through a closed door, would become the voice of a stranger. When the music and singing would die down, she would hear talking and laughter, and she would wonder what private joke had been shared between them. Finally the door would open. "Not too bored?" the pianist would ask Shirin, producing from his pocket a Kinder surprise egg. Shirin would unwrap the egg and eat the chocolate shell. The surprise she would save for later. At night, alone in her bedroom, she would build the toy and add it to her collection on the shelf above her desk, where they all stood, side by side—the zebra, the cat, the warplane, the car—residues of her mother's private life. Because the toys were so tiny, no one ever noticed them, not even Parviz, and it comforted her that so many things, if small enough, or quiet enough, can go unseen. After the sessions with the pianist her mother would be in a lighthearted mood, but her spirits would dive as the night would progress, and by the evening she would be in the living room, reaching for her cigarettes, which, she said, calmed her nerves.

"I'm not sure what's right anymore, Shirin-jan," she says as she exhales, looking out the window and quietly crying. Shirin notices that her mother is still in her pajamas. The polish on her toenails has chipped. Why had she questioned her mother's judgment, like that? She takes that photograph of herself and rips.

SIXTEEN

Isaac watches the dark clouds through the shoebox window, smells the wet morning air. Soon the sky disgorges hail, which taps against the black metal bars. Water enters the cell through the broken window, gathering into a puddle.

A light switches on outside and a pale band appears in the gap under the door, just before it is flung open. "Get up! Let's go. Showers!"

Mehdi places his feet on the floor but his bad foot can no longer support his weight. "Ah!" he moans and falls back on the mattress. "Didn't we just take showers?" he says. "Has it been a week already?" Isaac extends an arm and Mehdi holds on to it, leaning his body against it. Together they drag their way out of the cell. Ramin covers his ear with his hand. "Quiet, some quiet," he mumbles in his sleep. Has the boy forgotten where he is? "Ramin-jan, get up!" Mehdi says, but the boy does not move.

In the hallway they join the flock of prisoners making

their way to the showers. The men disrobe and enter the stalls. Isaac has learned not to look at the naked bodies passing by, at the blistered feet with black nails stepping inside gray puddles on the slimy ceramic floor. He goes into a stall, under the frigid water, and rubs his body and hair quickly with soap. He washes his shirt, his underwear, his socks, knowing that the mildew will remain trapped in them, no matter how hard he scrubs. He steps out of the shower, his clothes on his arm, looking for an empty spot where he can get dressed. Others, like him, are walking and dripping, each man searching for a small space that will offer him a semblance of privacy. Suddenly, in front of him, he sees a familiar face, from long ago.

"Vartan? Vartan Sofoyan?"

The man, naked also, stops, startled. "My God! Isaac Amin!"

They stare at each other for a few seconds. They had never exchanged many words.

"So you're here too . . ." Isaac says. "How long has it been?"

"About two months. I was in a different block. And you, how long?"

"Almost three, I think. It's hard to keep track . . ."

"Yes, I know."

A guard, watching them, approaches. His black rifle seems more threatening here, in the showers, than anywhere else. "You two think this is some sort of a salon?" he yells. "Get your ugly selves dressed and out of my sight."

Isaac and Vartan nod to each other and walk in opposite directions. Minutes later, as he stands in a corner and gets dressed, Isaac replays their interaction. That he had thought neither of his nakedness nor of his dislike for the pianist while they talked surprises him. He imagines the same must have been true for Vartan. Now as he puts on his pants and buttons his wet shirt, his resentment slowly resurfaces, and he feels agitated by the memory of the pianist's tall, naked body.

Through the water's gurgle comes a prisoner's cry, followed by guards' admonitions. In a nearby stall he sees Ramin, his nose bleeding, being stripped by two guards and shoved under the water. The boy's arms form parentheses on his emaciated torso, his hands cupping his genitals, shielding them from view. The water gathering under his feet and swirling into the drain is pink. "That'll teach you!" one of the guards says. "When we say wake up, we mean wake up. This is not the Plaza, you son of a dog."

"I WONDER WHAT they're doing to him," Isaac says to Mehdi when they are back in the cell. "I wish we had dragged him out ourselves."

"Yes. I was so preoccupied with my own foot. And he is such a difficult boy. Actually, he is like so many of my students, arrogant and idealistic. It was infectious for a while, that idealism."

"And you got caught up in it?"

"I don't know. There was a feeling that something was happening, and that we were the ones who were making it happen. We wanted to put an end to the monarchy. We thought we were cheering for democracy. So many different ent groups marched together—the Communists, the Labor Party, the Party of the Masses, you name it. Add to that the religious fundamentalists. What brought us together was our hatred for the shah. But there wasn't much else to keep us together. In the end, we unleashed a monster."

A pair of eyes peers through the opening in the door and a tray of food slides through. Isaac gets up and grabs it. There is cheese, bread, and tea. The two men sit cross-legged on the floor and eat in silence. The rain has stopped but the cell is humid and cold.

"Why are you here, Amin-agha? You still haven't told us much about your life."

"I don't know, but I have two things going against me. I'm a Jew and I lived well under the shah."

"To live well under the shah means you had to shut your eyes and ears. You had to pretend the secret police did not exist."

"Yes, but at least Savak imprisoned and tortured people for one reason—to get information and discourage future subversives. You only got arrested if you actually did something. Awful as it was, the regime had a logic. This government simply wants to destroy human beings, regardless of what they may or may not have done. Its goal is to annihilate. They are after people's souls, Mehdi-agha. It's much more dangerous."

Mehdi nods and sips his tea. "A year ago I would have hated you," he says. "Now I don't know. We have more in common than I would care to admit."

A guard calls for Isaac. The cheese still heavy in his

stomach, Isaac does as he is told. He is taken downstairs, to a different room this time. When he enters he looks for the missing finger on his interrogator's right hand, and finding it, he knows he is dealing with Mohsen again. Some three weeks ago the news that Mohsen had released a prisoner on the spot had spread throughout the prison, making the men more lighthearted, like children anticipating the summer during the final days of school. But when, a week later, he shot another prisoner just as spontaneously as he had released the first, anguish had resettled among the men. Mohsen is a wild card, people said. Who could know how to play him?

"Tell me about your brother—Javad," Mohsen says.

"What would you like to know?"

"What does he do?"

"I am not very close to my brother."

"According to the phone company's records, the two of you speak regularly."

"Yes . . . but our relationship isn't one you'd call intimate. It's merely civil."

"Help me be 'civil' with you, Brother."

"This is the truth, Brother. Javad likes variety. He's always changing jobs. One cannot keep up with him."

"I see. It may interest you to know that he has a new job. Your brother smuggles vodka into the country."

This is news to Isaac. He is not sure he should believe it.

"Islam does not permit alcohol, you know that, right?" Mohsen adds.

"Yes, of course. If my brother is in fact involved in smuggling, I have no knowledge of it."

Mohsen walks behind Isaac, leans into his neck, and whispers, with a humid breath, "You know, I like you for some reason. And I want to help you. But I cannot do it alone. You have to help me. You see, we went over to your brother's residence several times, but he wasn't there. We also checked his so-called office, but apparently he hasn't been there in weeks. Where is he?"

"Brother, I really don't know. How could I? I've been here for three months. Like I said, he's a free spirit. He travels a lot. He's never in one place."

"Bastard! You think you'll get away with it? You come from a family of *taghouti*, of promiscuous sinners. You think you can protect each other?"

"Perhaps there has been some mistake. My brother would not be one to engage in smuggling. He . . ."

"Shut up! The mistake, Brother Amin, is that I have been too lenient with you." He walks away, stares at the view outside his small window—the concrete walls of another prison wing. "I am too tired for you today. I don't even want to see your face. Just know that one day, soon enough, you'll regret your lies and you'll beg me for mercy. But by then, my dear Brother, it will be too late."

When Isaac returns to the cell he finds Ramin on his mattress, cleaning the spaces between his toes. He has grown used to the boy's foul habit and says nothing. He lies on his back. There is a putrid smell in the air, of humidity and urine and blood. He recalls the stifling humidity of Khorramshahr when he was a boy, and how he would pass the summers playing soccer in the street with Javad and a few neighborhood kids, their soles so callused that they would not feel the heat under their bare feet. To cool off, he would often swim in the river with his brother, trying to avoid the black lumps of oil—residue from the refinery—that the water would carry toward them from time to time. The viscous lumps seemed to him like shifting ogres, and he took them as bad omens, though he did not know why. Javad, on the other hand, did not swim away from them, but toward them, trying to capture them in empty pickle jars in order to sell them later. "We'll be oil tycoons," he would tell Isaac. "You have to believe it!" Poor Javad, Isaac thinks, his impractical little brother, whose life so far has been a series of failed get-rich schemes, and whose boyish good looks, now fading, will no longer allow him to charm his way out of trouble. Where is he now?

The muezzin calls for evening prayers. Isaac covers his ears. The sound makes his chest tighten. Lately whenever he hears it, he feels as though he were being buried alive. He turns on his side. Ramin is still preoccupied with his toes.

"Ramin, you're not going to pray?"

"I'm not well," the boy says. "And I can't pretend to be religious anymore."

"I saw what they did to you in the shower this morning," Isaac says, the image of Parviz never far from his mind when talking to Ramin. "You should at least pray here, in the cell. What if a guard comes to check up on you?"

"Amin-agha, are you a religious man?" the boy asks.

Were he not in prison he would have replied that he is not. He has always observed the essential holidays, but he is not a religious man, as such. Now he is not sure. To deny belief terrifies him. In order to hold on to hope, he feels he must believe in something. "I may be becoming one," he finally says.

"Not me. No matter how much I want to believe, I can't. Religion is for the weak, that's what my mother always said."

"I thought this for a long time also," Isaac says. "Now I don't know. It's possible I am just becoming weak."

After a while the boy removes his shirt and begins exercising on the floor. His back is covered with bruises. On his right arm there is a tattoo—tall, beautiful letters, together spelling "Sima."

"Is that your mother's name, tattooed on your arm?" Isaac says.

Ramin stops the exercises, caresses the letters. "Yes, I got the tattoo after they took her to jail."

"It's beautiful."

"So is she," Ramin says.

"Tell me, Ramin, what would you be doing if none of this had happened?"

"I would be traveling. I want to see the world. I want to be a photographer."

It pleases Isaac that the boy speaks in the present—I *want* to be a photographer, not I *wanted*—that all this, his dead father and his jailed mother and his own uncertain fate, is just a transitory phase, a simple interruption.

The door opens and a guard sticks his head in. "What are you doing here boy? Why aren't you praying?"

"I'm sick, Brother," Ramin says.

The guard walks in and lifts him off the floor. "I've had

it with your antics. Sleeping in late, showing up to prayer when you feel like it. Listen to me! This is not some kind of vacation. You're in prison! Do you understand? You are a prisoner! You pray when we tell you to pray."

Ramin looks straight ahead. He doesn't flinch. When the guard lets go of his arm he says, calmly, "Brother, I am not a religious person, but if I were, I'm certain God would forgive me for being ill."

"You are digging your grave with your own hands!" The guard leaves, banging the metal door behind him and rattling his keys for a while before locking it.

"My God, Ramin," Isaac says. "Why tell them you are not a religious person when you know that's the thing they hate to hear most?"

"I speak the truth. That should mean something."

Isaac cannot remember the last time he had such convictions. Even as a boy, and later as a young man, he had been driven less by principles than by his desire to erase the stains on his life—the indifference of his father, the unhappiness of his mother, the rumbling of his stomach, the heat of his city, and the fear that, like his father, he would live an insignificant life.

All this, he had achieved, but the price had been a string of compromises, looped over one another like pearls, creating a life at once beautiful and frail.

He takes deep breaths to calm himself, filling his lungs with the foul air then draining them. The prison, a giant tomb, makes no sound.

SEVENTEEN

When they arrive, on an overcast afternoon in December, Farnaz does not hear the knocks. She stands by the kitchen window, looking at the street below, the homes with closed curtains whose owners have left one by one. The mailman is making his rounds, sliding envelopes through door slits. She imagines their thump as they fall into empty courtyards, letters whose destiny is to never be read.

The knocks grow louder until Farnaz sees them, two men with rifles standing outside her door. She takes a deep breath and walks down. Shirin is standing on top of the stairs, her hand clutching the banister.

"Hurry up!" a man's voice commands. The knocks grow more impatient.

When she reaches the foyer she takes another deep breath and opens the door. She examines the men, one at a time. One, with a bushy black beard and chapped lips, looks disheveled, even dirty, and were it not for his rifle she would have taken him for a laborer. The other, dressed in a military uniform and standing in the back, has a very young face.

"We're here to search the house," the dirty one says.

"Your papers?"

"No papers. We have orders."

She nods and steps aside. They enter without wiping their shoes on the mat. The young soldier acknowledges her with a quick nod. They walk up the stairs, ahead of her. The bearded one starts with her bedroom, the other one goes to Shirin's room, rests his rifle on the child's bed, opens her closet, and begins gutting it, removing the clothes, and throwing them on the floor.

Farnaz takes her daughter's hand and together they walk to her own bedroom, where mounds of clothes are already on the floor. Walking back and forth, the bearded man steps on them with his muddy shoes. He reaches for the tie rack and dismantles it, sending the ties undulating to the floor. "Tell me, did your husband always wear ties?" he says.

"Most of the time, yes," Farnaz says, unsure of the question's significance.

"So he took himself for a *farangui*—a westerner, didn't he?"

"No. He was a businessman. He wore business attire."

"Couldn't he conduct his *business* in ordinary clothes?" He kneels to the floor and runs his hands through the tangled silk.

"I'm not sure what is considered 'ordinary,' Brother. A suit and tie used to be quite ordinary."

"You're wrong. This was 'ordinary' for westernized dandies, not anyone else."

"Brother, is my husband accused of being a dandy? Is that the charge brought against him?" A moment of silence follows and she reproaches herself for having said this.

"How unfortunate that you don't recognize the gravity of your situation." He stands up and moves close to her, so close that his chest touches her breasts. His pungent breath hovers between them. She steps back, notices Shirin on the bed, watching them. Where is Habibeh when she is needed? Had she been here, she could have taken Shirin to the park or for a walk. Why had she decided to visit her family at the last minute? Was her mother really ill, as she had claimed in the morning, or had her revolutionary son warned her about this and she did not want to witness it?

When he is done with Isaac's side of the closet he turns to hers, adding her dresses and sweaters to the pile on the floor. He smiles when he gets to her underwear, retrieving the pieces one by one and holding them in the air just for a moment before throwing them to the floor. He picks up a box of sanitary pads, peeks inside it. He nearly says something but doesn't. Then, noticing a pair of onyx cufflinks in an open box on Isaac's nightstand, he says, "Your husband wore jewelry?"

"That's not jewelry. It's for shirts."

"Show me."

She grabs one of Isaac's shirts from the floor and attaches the cufflink to the sleeve. The last time Isaac wore the shirt with these very cufflinks was two years before, in the early days of the revolution, to a dinner party at their friend Kourosh Nassiri's house. There had been whiskey, pistachios, kebab, Turkish coffee, music, and even opium, all of which allowed the guests to ignore their crumbling country and their fading futures. There, in that room, was the final gathering of the ambassadors to the past. Kourosh had danced and smoked most of the night, barefoot on his silk rug, hands stretched out wide and fingers snapping, coaxing all the women to abandon their husbands and join him for a dance. His wife, Homa, had laughed, herself groggy with more than a few puffs. "Kourosh-jan, what's happening to you?" she would ask, giggling. "Are you leaving me soon?" "No, Homa, don't you know? We're all leaving soon!" he would say, and laugh. After they killed him, their home caught fire, with Homa in it.

Farnaz slides her arm inside the sleeve to give it some shape, and as her hand emerges from the sleeve's end the man says, "Nice . . . very nice . . ." He takes the cufflinks and drops them in his pocket. "It's evidence," he says.

She throws the shirt back on the pile of clothes, where it lies limp and wrinkled. Sitting on the floor and watching him unweave her life, she notices that Shirin is gone. "Brother, I'll be right back. I have to check on my daughter."

"You're not going anywhere. I'm certain your daughter is fine."

"Please. I'll be back in a few minutes. I just . . ."

"Sit, Sister," he says, reaching for his rifle. "Let's not make this more painful than necessary."

She sits back down. Looking at him rummage through her closets, his black eyes bulging with rage, she acknowledges, in a way she has not until now, that things might end terribly. How can this rage, multiplied by millions, be contained, confined, reasoned with? Isaac may not come back after all. She looks at his scattered clothes, his shoes, the fedora they had bought in Rome during that snowstorm—awful reminders of his absence.

"You'd better have a good explanation for this," he says, holding an old military cap. "Did your husband serve in the American military?"

She looks at the cap, weathered and lint-covered. She has always disliked it because Isaac had refused to tell her why it was so special to him, no matter how many times she had asked. That cap symbolized an expired happiness that did not include her—one that could not even be shared with her.

"No, my husband was not in the American military," she says. "That was just a little something an American soldier gave him during the war."

The man keeps the cap as evidence. He has already amassed eleven large bags—books in English, correspondence that Farnaz did not get a chance to rip up, and family photographs she could not bring herself to destroy, including one of Parviz with his classmates at a picnic, his arms around a girl, and one of Isaac in a bathing suit in front of his first car, a used 1954 Renault, laughing at the camera. She had taken that picture during their first trip together. They had spent the night in a motel where the pillowcases displayed the brown rings of unwashed heads and the hallways smelled of urine. She had been upset with him for taking her to a place like that, knowing, all the while, that he could not have done better. For some time after they left the motel she was quiet in the car, looking out the window at the sinuous road down to the sea, wondering why she had married a man whose only belongings were one old suit, a few poetry volumes, and a photograph of his mother. Now that the conjugal contract had been signed, his talent, passion, and potential seemed impotent against the stench of urine. That marriage contract, she also knew, had brought a concrete, definitive end to her own aspirations, making her realize that those long years spent training her voice and studying literature, had, after all, been nothing more than a way to pass the hours while waiting for a husband and beginning her real life.

She rolled down the window. The air smelled of pine. He turned on the radio and Miles Davis's "Bye Bye Blackbird" came on. As the car inched down toward the water the spare, earnest sound of the trumpet calmed her, and by the time they reached the sea she felt tranquil—happy, almost. Was it the sudden shift in altitude that made her so moody? From several thousand feet above sea level they had driven to ninety feet below, and as she breathed the salty air she wondered if being so low and close to water somehow made one more sensible.

They wore their bathing suits and took turns posing for pictures with the car. Looking at him through the camera lens as he laughed and made faces, she felt an overpowering love for him—a love that, since their wedding, she had not felt when looking at him directly. Were these, then, the ingredients necessary for sustained love: salt, water, a prism?

. . .

Shirin reappears. She stands in the doorway, her eyes on the bags of evidence lined against the wall.

"Where were you?" the man asks her.

"I was hungry. I was in the kitchen."

"Yes? And what did you eat?"

"I . . . I ate an apple."

"Brother, please leave her alone," Farnaz says. "She is just a child."

"Tell me, little girl," he says. "Is there mud in your kitchen?"

Shirin's eyes widen. She looks at Farnaz, terrified. There is, in fact, mud on her shoes and on the hems of her pants.

"Shirin-jan," Farnaz says. "You went to the garden to play, right? Tell him that you went out to play. It's all right."

"Yes," she says. "I . . . I went out to play."

The man examines the child for some time with squinted eyes. "Then why did you lie? This child is up to something."

"Brother, please. You are scaring her."

He nods, unconvinced. Shirin sits on the bed, her hands on her lap. Farnaz notices how thin her daughter has become. Has she been eating, sleeping, doing her homework? How will they go on, if Isaac does not return? Can she be a mother, Farnaz asks herself, without being a wife?

Hours later, in the living room, the men cluster all the furniture in one corner and roll up the carpet. They pull out their knives and split open the pillows and sofa cushions, sliding their hands through the slits in the hope of finding more evidence sewn inside. From the tops of shelves and drawers they take down her trinkets—the porcelain creamer, the copper plate, the antique silverware—and park them in a corner of the room as if preparing them for an auction. When she sees her silver teapot, which had been missing for some time, she thanks them for finding it. "Look how happy a piece of silver makes you," the scruffy one says, shaking his head. "There is no cure for your kind."

"I bought this with my husband in Isfahan, right after our wedding," she starts, but stops. How can it be explained, the joy of being in a strange city with a strange man, buying the first items to furnish their communal household—a teapot and twelve glasses? She thinks of all the hours she spent in bazaars and flea markets and antique shops in so many countries, picking these items one by one, considering their color and shape and history, holding them to the light to observe cracks and chips, and wrapping them in towels for the trip back home. A gray-violet glass vase she had bought from a Venetian artisan, now placed on the windowsill, catches the afternoon sunlight and reflects it in disjointed rays on the floor. She remembers so well the day she bought it: a wet and humid May afternoon, vaporetti swinging in the water, tourists stepping onto gondolas, and her walking with Isaac to their seaside hotel, holding a slice of Venice in her little bag. These objects, she had always believed, are infused with the souls of the places from which they came, and of the people who had made or sold them. On long, silent afternoons, when Isaac would be at work and the children at school, she would sit in her sun-filled living room and look at each one—the glass vase, a reminder of Francesca, in Venice; the copper plate, a souvenir of Ismet, in Istanbul; the silver teapot, a keepsake from Firouz, in Isfahan. Living among these objects assured her that hers was a populated world.

"So many things, Sister," the man says. "Why so many?"

THEY SEARCH THE kitchen and the other bedrooms with less fervor. Around midnight, as they are about to leave, they realize that they forgot the garden. They stand by the glass doors and look out into the night. The dog, on the other side of the doors, barks violently.

"Sister, leash that mad dog so we can take a quick look in the garden."

The image of Shirin with her mud-stained shoes and pants appears in her mind. It occurs to her that her daughter would not have simply gone out to play; that she may, in fact, be hiding something. "I'm scared of the dog, Brother," Farnaz says. "She is really my husband's dog. Since he's been gone, the housekeeper takes care of her, and she's not here today. You're welcome to go out there and leash her yourself."

The soldier glances at his colleague, then at his watch. "It's late," he says. "I think we've done enough."

They disappear with their bags of evidence. Farnaz bolts

the door, takes her daughter's hand, and leads her up the stairs. "What were you doing in the garden, Shirin?" she asks once they are in bed.

"Nothing."

"Then why were you so muddy?"

Shirin turns on her side, covering herself, up to the neck, with the blanket. "This blanket smells like Baba," she says quietly.

Farnaz spoons her daughter's small body and shuts her eyes. Huddled like this with Shirin, she remembers the early days of the war, when the terrible thunder of Iraqi bombs falling over a blacked-out Tehran would send the three of them to their hiding place under the stairs—a spot that gave them an illusion of cover but in fact was no safer than any other place in the house. There they would sit with a candle, and as they would wait for the bombs to pass, Isaac would distract them with puppet shows of singing cats and quarreling frogs—shadows of his nimble hands reflected on the opposite wall.

EIGHTEEN

New York loves expanse. It grows upward and spreads its tentacles outward, the island spilling into adjoining lands through its many bridges and tunnels. A person given to idleness, as Parviz has come to think of himself, must move about for the sake of moving, if only to fit into the general scheme of things—an electron obeying the current. Tantamount to movement, he has come to realize, is self-reliance, a fact reflected even in the language: "Take care," a friend may say to another as the two part. In his old life the same two friends would have said to one another, *khodahafez*—"may God protect you."

He finds refuge from the city in Zalman Mendelson's hat shop, spending three afternoons a week steaming identical hats. The task numbs him, half-formed thoughts emerging from his mind like the vapor rising from his steam machine and vanishing just as quickly. Time moves slowly here, like those agonizing hours spent in mind-numbing high school classes, when his young, excitable mind had to castrate all of its instinctual thoughts in order to grasp the rice output in Isfahan, for example, or the pistachio export from Rafsanjan. And yet something has changed in him so gravely that he now actually enjoys these slow, indistinguishable hours, which pass him by, demanding so little of him, no more than fish swimming in an aquarium. He looks at Zalman Mendelson standing at the counter, his accounting books spread open before him, adding and subtracting the profits and losses of his life. He seems a happy man, his round face giving him a generous and benign appearance. And if it weren't for his pale, soapy complexion—no doubt a result of so many years spent in a dim, steamy shop—he would have been the ideal advertisement for the fulfilled life.

"Do you like Brooklyn, Mr. Mendelson?"

Zalman looks up from his book, his glasses sliding down his nose. "Sure. Why wouldn't I like Brooklyn?"

"It's fine, of course. But don't you ever wonder what it would be like to live somewhere else?"

"Why would I wonder about living somewhere else? I live here." Zalman puts down his pen and removes his glasses. "What is this about, my dear boy? What are you trying to say?"

"I don't know. I guess I'm wondering if you ever regret anything."

"Regret anything? Like what?"

"I mean in life. Do you ever wish things could have turned out differently?"

"No, I don't regret," Zalman says. "What should I regret? God has given me a wonderful, healthy family and I thank him every day."

"Yes, sure. But beyond that. Are you sorry, for example, that your father was imprisoned and had to leave Russia? Don't you wonder what your life would have been like if you had lived in Leningrad instead of Brooklyn?"

"Parviz!" He laughs. "You cannot ask questions like these because you will never know the answer. It is all God's will. I cannot question it. Besides, if circumstances were such that my father could have stayed in Leningrad, then he would have never met my mother in Vladivostok and I would have never been born. He would have married someone else and they would have had different children. Things happen for a reason, and only God knows what these reasons are."

A cool breeze announces Rachel, who walks in, looking flushed, the shape of her long, slim arms visible through the sleeves of her sweater. Such lovely, delicate arms should not be wasted on the pious, Parviz thinks. What is the point after all, of having such arms and not being able to embrace those who are taken with them? She places the bag of food on the counter for her father, as she does every afternoon.

"Where is your coat, Rachel?" Zalman asks. "Aren't you cold, walking around like that?"

"I forgot it at the shop."

"You forgot it at the shop? My Rachel, her head always in the clouds . . . Go pick it up, or else you'll have to go to school without a coat tomorrow."

"It's too late now. Mameh needs me to help her with dinner. Dovid and Chana are coming over."

Parviz watches her through the steam. "I can go get it after I'm done here," he offers. "I'll bring it to the house."

She looks at him, for the first time since her arrival. "Thank you," she says. "That would be very kind."

When she leaves a sudden happiness swells in him, along with an anticipation for the evening ahead, which, he knows, will consist of no more than an errand.

"Thank you, Parviz," Zalman says. "Actually, you may enjoy meeting Rachel's boss, Mr. Broukhim. He's Iranian, like you. His wife divorced him after they came to this country, and the poor fellow, old enough to be a grandfather, found himself on the street. She took him for all he was worth, that woman! After thirty years of marriage, she decided she is done with him. Naturally she got custody of their daughter too. He lived in his car for a few months, eating canned beans and tuna. His daughter, about Rachel's age, would sometimes sneak out of the house and bring him food. He came to our community, finally, and we helped him out. Now he is settled here. He has an apartment, a shop, and, God bless him, a dog. He says he is done with women. And who can blame him, after all that?"

THE DOOR CHIMES as he enters the flower shop. A small, mustached man, wearing a tweed jacket, is behind a counter, trimming stems. Parviz introduces himself and they shake hands.

"So you like it here?" Mr. Broukhim says. "What are you studying?"

"Architecture."

"Really? My brother was an architect. Guess what he is doing now? He paints houses." Mr. Broukhim has an easy smile, but weepy eyes. "I tell you. Study something else along with your architecture. One cannot easily transport one country's architectural sensibility to another. People won't take to it."

"Where would I transport it, Mr. Broukhim? I live here now."

"Yes, now you live here. But who knows where you'll end up in a few years? Do you really love this country so much that you can't imagine living anywhere else? Once you leave your own country and start moving around, there is no telling where you'll go next." He disappears into the back, emerges with Rachel's coat, and hands it to Parviz. "Me, I was a doctor. Now, as you can see, I'm in the flower business." He smiles, his palms like an open book circling around him. "But I like to think it's temporary. Between you and me," he whispers, "I don't like these religious beardies. I can't wait to save enough money so I can get out of this neighborhood. But what can I do? They helped me out and now I'm settled here. Well, I don't want to bore you with my problems, Parviz-jan. Give my regards to Rachel and her parents."

"I thought you didn't like the 'beardies.'" Parviz laughs.

"They're the only ones I like! Now go, go!"

* * *

WALKING HOME HE holds the coat against his chest. The sweet, flowery smell that wafts up to his nose surprises him; it is not a scent he would have associated with Rachel. He brings the coat to his face and holds it there for an instant, but seeing Yanki the grocer on the other side of the street he brings it down again.

"*Erev tov!*" Yanki waves hello. "How are things?"

"Fine, thank you. I haven't forgotten about my debt, Yanki. I'll pay you back as soon as I can."

"Sure, sure, you'll pay me back," Yanki says. "*Moshiach* will come before you pay me back!" He turns the corner and disappears.

To the long list of his losses, Parviz adds dignity. In his old life, who would have talked to him as Yanki just did? He thinks of Mr. Broukhim, of his wrinkled face and his tweed jacket, of the gratitude he must once have received from his patients, of the life he must have left behind. Now he has a little flower shop on a little-known street in Brooklyn, and he is learning the difference between violets and African violets.

He walks up the steps to the Mendelsons' and rings the doorbell. He knows that Rachel may send one of her siblings to answer the door. But when the door finally opens she is standing before him.

"Thank you." She smiles as she takes the coat.

"You're welcome. How is that dinner party going?"

"Party?" She laughs. "It's not a party. It's a dinner for a young couple going to London as emissaries tomorrow."

"As 'emissaries'?"

"Yes, you know about our emissaries, don't you? We have thousands of them. They go to foreign countries and help the Jewish communities. They provide kosher food, build schools and synagogues, that sort of thing."

"Sounds like quite an operation. Exporting Judaism."

"No, it's not like that." The smile disappears from her face just as easily as it had appeared. "Well, goodnight. Thanks again for the coat," she says as she shuts the door.

Standing on the stoop, he tucks his gloveless hands in his pockets and looks out onto the dark street. How unyielding is that space between connection and interruption—one false move, one misspoken word, and you find yourself on the wrong side of things.

NINETEEN

Musical chairs in Leila's house means musical cushions. Shirin and the other girls, gathered here for Leila's birthday, lay out pillows and cushions on the floor, while Farideh-khanoum stands by the stereo, in charge of the music. Shirin has always disliked this game, whose purpose, she believes, is to show that in any gathering, there is always one person too many.

On the fourth round she loses her spot. She stands on the periphery with the three other condemned girls and watches the race. Chaos intensifies as seats become scarce, the girls screaming and laughing as they scramble to sit. She looks out the window. A snowstorm was predicted this morning. Large flakes are already coming down, accumulating quickly on trees and rooftops. She remembers how on weekends, in the wintertime, when her father and Parviz were still around, they would go out for lunch to her father's favorite kebab house, or to that Russian restaurant whose chicken

Kiev delivered a flow of melting butter when pricked with a knife. Afterward they would return home, well fed and half asleep, to the lullaby of radiators. Her mother would prepare tea and sing in that feathery voice of hers that made people tell her she should have been a singer. To which she would always reply, "I should have, I should have, I should have been many things. . . ." Her father would sit with a stack of newspapers and catch up on the week's events—the earth-quakes, the assassinations, the stabbings, and robberies. Shirin would curl up on the sofa next to him, comforted by the masculine scent of tobacco, aftershave, and newsprint.

WITH SEVEN GIRLS still in the game, it occurs to her that she has enough time to go to the basement and take more files. Farideh-khanoum is very focused on the game, her finger alternating between the "play" and "pause" buttons. And Leila's father is most likely not at home; if he were, there would not have been any music. But where would she hide the files, since she doesn't have her schoolbag? What if one of the girls sees her? She thinks of that afternoon when the two men had come to search their house, how she had buried that one file, of Ali Reza Rasti, in the garden, next to the cherry tree. She had almost gotten caught, with the mud on her pants. How many times can she get lucky, like that? But she is here, already made irrelevant by the game. Should she not try, at least?

She tiptoes out of the room until she is out of view, then

takes her coat from Leila's room and walks down the creaking stairs to the basement. The stomping of feet above sends her heart racing. She opens the armoire and moves the old clothes. More files have been added to the pile. She takes the top three, wraps her coat around them, and sneaks back up. She shoves the coat—and files—in Leila's closet.

Back in the living room, the competition has intensified between the remaining two players vying for the last seat. The rivals spin, and when the music finally stops the one sitting down is Elaheh, the daughter of the head of a prison. Did Farideh-khanoum ensure Elaheh's victory with her timing? After all, it would not hurt to be on the girl's good side.

Once the birthday song has been sung and the candles blown out, she eats her slice of cake but thinks about the files. How will she retrieve her coat without anyone noticing? What if the whole class finds out? What would Elaheh do if she knew? No doubt she would report back to her father. And the father, what would he do? Drops of vomit form in her throat, with the sour taste of undigested heavy cream. She stops eating. The other girls, already devouring their second and third slices, are planning the next activity. There is talk of hopscotch, Monopoly, the telephone game.

"Shirin-jan, you don't like the cake?" Farideh-khanoum says.

"It's very good. I just . . . I'm not feeling well." Under her sweater, beads of sweat trickle from her chest down to her stomach. She excuses herself and calls her mother to pick her up.

"I'm going to think you are allergic to our house!" Farideh-khanoum laughs. "You get sick every time you come here."

"She's not that much better in school," Elaheh says. "She spends half her life in the infirmary." Because of her new social standing, Elaheh is the most vocal of all the girls, as comfortable with adults as she is with her classmates.

"Yes, Shirin-jan?" Farideh-khanoum says. "Are you that sickly? Well, some children are just like that."

She had been to the infirmary five times in the past two weeks, a fact that had categorized her by her peers, her teachers, and now, Leila's mother, as "sickly." But she doesn't think of herself as a sickly child. What had been troubling her were bouts of nausea, accompanied by sharp stomach pains, and it was only once she was in the infirmary, sipping the tea prepared for her by Soheila-khanoum, the school nurse, that her stomach muscles relaxed and she felt the nausea float away. There, in the hush of the white-walled, sunny room, away from the other children, she would let herself be coddled by the nurse, a kind woman who people said had lost a daughter in one of the revolution's bloodiest riots. "Black Friday" people called the day of that riot. But for Soheila-khanoum, Shirin thought, the blackness must have spilled onto the other days, giving her nothing but black weeks and months. She wondered if Soheila-khanoum got bored or lonely all by herself in that infirmary, the silence a constant reminder of her daughter. She seemed pleased to have a visitor who interrupted that solitude as frequently as Shirin did.

When the girls begin their game of telephone, Shirin retrieves her coat and holds it on her lap, making sure the files are not visible. Waiting for her mother, she watches as each of her classmates whispers a phrase in her neighbor's ear and giggles. The phrase emerges from the lineup, botched.

Her mother honks. She holds the coat in one arm and waves good-bye to her classmates with the other. "Feel better!" some call out and Shirin thanks them, though she wonders if they really mean it.

They drive slowly in the snow, the car skidding every now and then. "I don't have the snow chains on," her mother says. Shirin imagines the car spinning out of control and crashing into a tree. But soon they arrive home, without tragedy.

In her room, she spreads out the files on her desk, and when she sees the name "Javad Amin" scribbled on one, she runs to the bathroom and throws up, finally. As her mother washes her face Shirin looks at her own reflection in the mirror and sees the cherry pins in her hair—Uncle Javad's final gift. She wants to tell her mother about the files, about *his* file, but decides not to. Increasing her mother's grief, she knows, would also increase her chances of dying. Grief terrifies her, because it's invisible.

After a nap and a cup of mint tea she takes the files and buries them in the garden, on top of Ali Reza Rasti's file. "Good luck, Uncle Javad," she says as she covers up his name with soil and snow.

TWENTY

Isaac stares at his hands—the skeletal knuckles, the dark veins, the fingers he has always regarded as too short for his palms. These hands, he thinks, are his connectors to everyone and everything that exists outside of him. He looks at his feet—anonymous, neither beautiful nor ugly—just feet, doing their job, keeping him upright. How much longer will they remain unlashed? The longer he stares at his hands and feet, the more disjointed they seem, and he wonders if he would recognize them were they to be severed, somehow, after an earthquake, for example, or a plane crash, or another random, unforeseen accident. People reside inside their bodies for decades, but they rarely examine these vessels, and all their intricate, dutiful parts. A house is more easily remembered than a body: one can describe the number of rooms, the glass in the windows, the color of the walls, the tiles in the bathroom.

What will happen to his body if he were to die here? Will they shroud him in linen and place him in a wooden casket, as his religion demands, or will they dump him somewhere, in a mass grave perhaps? What will become of his faithful hands and his nameless feet, for which he suddenly feels enormous love? Will a *shomer*—"guardian"—sit by his corpse and recite psalms until he is buried? Will there be seven days of mourning in his house, will mirrors be covered, will his son return? Will anyone say Kaddish for him? He brings his right hand to his mouth and kisses it, resting his lips between two bony knuckles.

"Amin-agha, are you all right?" Ramin says.

"Yes, fine." He is sitting outside with the usual group of prisoners, which now includes Vartan, the pianist, who is not a talkative man, at least not here. Isaac, too, has little to say. These weekly hours of fresh air leave him indifferent. During his first month he would use his hour to breathe as deeply as he could, as if breathing deeper and harder could somehow allow his body to store more oxygen for those remaining one hundred sixty-seven hours of the week. But just as overeating the night before the fast of Yom Kippur does nothing to quell the hunger that inevitably surges during the final hours of that long day of atonement and fasting, so too the deep breaths did little to help him endure those unending days spent in his dank cell. The human body is like that. It needs a constant flow of nourishment, air, and love, to survive. Unlike currency, these things cannot be accumulated. At any given moment, either you have them, or you don't.

"So, Maestro, tell us more about Vienna," Ramin says. The prisoners have nicknamed Vartan "maestro," out of both derision and affection. He has replaced Isaac as the one most picked on by the group.

"I've told you about the city, the cafés, the opera. What else would you like to know?"

"The women," Ramin whispers. "Are they beautiful?"

"Some may find them beautiful. I found them rather plain."

"Forget Vienna," Reza says. "Why don't you tell us about playing music for the shah? What was it like to be the court jester?"

"I was not a court jester. I played at the Rudaki Opera House."

"Agha-Reza, stop putting everyone on trial, will you?" Hamid says. "Maybe if you had gone to the opera house with your father once or twice you wouldn't be the brute that you've turned out to be." Once a minister of the shah, Hamid has gone through more interrogations than the others. But he remains convinced of his innocence and optimistic about his future, probably because he cannot afford to be otherwise.

"You think dressing up and sitting in a room with velvet chairs and crystal chandeliers makes you more cultured, Hamid-agha?" Reza says. "You're just like my father, mean-spirited and arrogant."

"If you think your father is so mean-spirited and arrogant, why did you help him escape?"

"Maestro, did you compose your own music?" Ramin tries to diffuse the tension—the child caught between arguing adults.

"A long time ago I began writing a symphony. But I never finished it."

"To write a whole symphony, you have to be in love," Ramin says. "I'm quite sure that's what you need."

"Perhaps." Vartan glances at Isaac then looks away. Isaac feels a violent anger rising in him. What did it mean, that glance? Was Vartan telling him that he had, in fact, loved Farnaz, or was he merely clarifying that theirs had not been a love story? He realizes that the answer matters little. There had been *something*, maybe no more than a passing affection, but still something, and he will never know exactly what. For now, they are both here, two condemned men sitting side by side. It is even possible that they will die together, their bodies thrown into the same grave, one on top of the other. Who can predict these things?

The guard Hossein stands a few yards away. He is the most lenient of the guards and usually allows the prisoners to talk, if the discussion is innocent enough. He approaches the group, looks around to make sure no other guards are present, and says, in a low voice, "Executions have increased in the past couple of weeks. If you are taken to interrogation this week, I strongly advise each of you to repent."

"Repent?" the old man Muhammad-agha says. This is the first time he has spoken in weeks. "Repent for what, Brother Hossein? For what one doesn't believe, or for what one hasn't done?"

"What's wrong with you, Muhammad-agha?" Hossein says. "If you'd start praying and showing that you are a decent Muslim, a believer, they'd let you go. You're an old man. Why make your final days on this earth more painful than necessary?"

"Because, Brother, my prayers are between me and my God. And in any case, I have nothing to go back to. My wife is dead and my three daughters are in prison."

"We're all goners," Mehdi says as Hossein walks away. "I wish that at least after killing us they would pay our families the blood money."

"Blood money is owed only when a believer accidentally kills another believer," Hamid says. "Our deaths would be neither accidental nor reimbursable."

"Even if our families were to get paid, you, Amin-agha, and your friend the maestro, would be worth half the blood money than the rest of us." Reza smiles. "Are you aware of that?"

Isaac doesn't answer. The blood of a Jew, or a Christian, or any non-Muslim, is not as valuable as that of a Muslim— he knows that of course. But what once seemed to him like one of the many archaic, even amusing, laws of his country suddenly terrifies him. Blood money. An actual tariff placed on people's blood. He looks at Vartan, who is hugging his knees, his torso limp and yielding. What the two of them share, beyond any real or imagined personal history, is a massacre of their forebears—the Jews by the Germans, the Armenians by the Turks—and he wonders if this membership in the club of the slaughtered doesn't create a certain kinship, after all.

"Back in the time of Cyrus and Darius," Hamid says, "our country was just and generous. Everyone was considered equal. We were a great nation, an empire."

"Stop the grandiosity, Hamid-agha!" Mehdi says. "That's our problem in this country. We think we're special because once upon a time we were great. Cyrus. Darius. Persepolis. That was a long time ago! What are we now? Now we are barbarians."

"Not all of us," Hamid says. "Just a couple of years ago, when the revolutionaries tried to bulldoze Persepolis, the governor of Fars and the people of Shiraz prevented them by force. When they wanted to ban our New Year celebrations, no one would have it. These things are important parts of our Zoroastrian past, and we will hold on to them no matter what regime takes over."

"That's enough talk!" Hossein says, holding up his rifle. "Your time is up anyway. Go back to your cells. And remember what I told you."

Walking back to the cell, Isaac wonders whether he could, in fact, repent. Since he is innocent of any crime they may be charging him with, he could repent only for the act of living.

TWENTY-ONE

On the other side of the office gates there is noise and commotion—footsteps, boxes hitting the ground, car doors opening and closing. When Farnaz presses the buzzer, the noises stop and the gates open with a pained rattle. Standing before her is Habibeh's son Morteza, the office manager, his face flushed, wearing a cap with a sharp visor that accentuates his narrow eyes.

"What's happening in there, Morteza?"

"That's nothing." He gestures with his head toward the back of the courtyard. Farnaz tries to sneak a look past his shoulder, but except for a large green truck parked inside she cannot see much. "We're transporting the stones and the equipment to a more secure location to protect them from the revolutionaries. We think they may want to seize them."

"Yes? And how do you know?"

Morteza taps his fingers on the iron gate. "Trust me,

Farnaz-khanoum," he says with a strained voice. "I want to help you."

"I'd like to come in."

"No." He stands before her, arms folded.

"Where are you taking everything?"

"To a safe place. We will let your husband know as soon as he gets out. Now go home. You must have other things to worry about." He steps back and shuts the gate.

How is it that a boy like Morteza, her husband's employee and her housekeeper's son, could talk to her like this? And how could the others gang up on Isaac and rob him of everything? Loyalty is so fragile, like porcelain. One crack, invisible at first to the naked eye, can one day shatter the cup.

She calls Keyvan from a pay phone and he offers to come right over. She knows there isn't much he can do in the face of two dozen men. Still there are times when one needs the illusion of authority. In the old days Keyvan, with one phone call to his father, could have had someone like Morteza imprisoned for life. She waits for him on the sidewalk, wishing for a cigarette. Isaac's Jaguar is still parked outside, as if at any moment he may emerge through the gates and take her out for a quick lunch.

Having lived with him for twenty-five years, she has never imagined her life without him—his presence, like the villa he had built for her, offering her great comfort along with much to fret about. When she met him, so many years ago in Shiraz, she had been studying literature. She saw him for the first time in the lunchtime crowd of a teahouse near the university. He sat alone, sipping his drink, his eyes on his book. Between them was a clear blue pool, terra-cotta vases on its ledge. When he finally looked up and noticed her, she looked away, even though she had planned to smile. The next day she returned to the teahouse, and so did he. Back then she attributed this second encounter to fate; later she learned that he had planned his return in the hope of finding her.

He said, "Is that your parrot up there or is he just following you? I noticed he was here yesterday, also."

Looking up, she saw an emerald parrot with red feathers in the cypress tree above her table. She interpreted the bird's presence as a good omen, and said, "I thought he was your spy, keeping an eye on me."

He introduced himself and told her that he was taking a poetry class at the university for the summer. He said he would have liked to study all year, but his work back in Tehran did not allow him to get away for long. She liked his playful eyes, but it was his confidence that most impressed her. It was only years later that she came to think of that confidence as stubbornness—hardness, even.

When Keyvan arrives, he walks with her to the gate and presses the buzzer. Morteza opens the gate, looking more irritated than before.

"What?"

"What's happening in there?"

"I already explained to Farnaz-khanoum. We're taking the gemstones for safekeeping."

"Where?"

"I have no time for this." He pushes the gate shut but Keyvan holds it open with his arm. "Look, I am asking you to leave, nicely," Morteza says. "This is none of your business. Don't let it get nasty."

Behind him Farnaz can see Isaac's employees—and others she does not recognize—walking back and forth, loading the truck. But it isn't just gems they are taking—it's radios and leather chairs and file cabinets and telephones. She reaches into her purse, grabs a small can of hair spray, and presses the nozzle toward Morteza's face. Morteza cries out and collapses to his knees, vigorously rubbing his eyes with his hands.

When they walk in, all activity stops. The men stand still, some cradling boxes, others holding tables in teams of two, all of them looking down.

"What's going on here?" Farnaz demands. No one answers. The only sound in the courtyard is an occasional curse from Morteza. A few seconds into the silence a man she recognizes as Siamak from accounting resumes carrying a chair toward the truck. Slowly others follow, and commotion continues as if she weren't in the courtyard at all. One man makes his way over to Morteza with a glass of water to wash his eyes.

In the corner by the small fountain, Farhad, a stonecutter, stands idle, one hand resting on his belly, the other holding a cigarette. He looks on calmly, removed from the action. He smiles at Farnaz and looks down. She walks to him, stopping several times in order to avoid collision with the men. "Can you explain this to me, Farhad-agha?"

He takes a long, pensive drag, then empties his lungs with a sigh. "I'm sorry, khanoum. Things have gone awry. I tried to talk sense into them, but there was no use. They said I'm blind to all the exploitation that has been going on for years. They said . . ."

"Exploitation? These people were all unemployed gypsies when Isaac hired them. He took them in, paid for their education, gave them salaries they probably didn't deserve. This is called exploitation?"

"Well, we weren't exactly gypsies, khanoum. We may have lacked education, but we . . ."

"I'm sorry. I didn't mean it like that. Especially not about you. I just don't understand how they can do this, how they can forget everything he did for them."

Farhad takes another drag and shrugs. "That's how it is now," he says. Quietly he adds, "I'm sorry."

Across the courtyard Keyvan is tangled in a conversation with Morteza. "This isn't right," he yells. "He hasn't even had a trial yet."

"Trial?" Morteza laughs. "If you think there is going to be a trial you're going to be very disappointed. In any case, all we are doing here is protecting his assets, but arrogant idiots like you mistake our kindness for thievery."

"Come on, Morteza," Keyvan hisses. "It's clear what this is."

"And what if it is? What are you going to do about it?"

"Morteza," Farnaz interrupts. "Why are you doing this? Was my husband ever bad to you? Did he ever refuse you anything?"

"You see, khanoum," he says, looking at her with eyes still red and teary from the hair spray. "You fail to understand. And I mean this sincerely. This isn't about one man. It is about a collection of men—men who turned their backs to injustice, men who profited from a corrupt government, men who built themselves villas and traveled whenever they pleased to places the likes of me have never even heard of. God has answered the prayers of the weak. God answers the call of the faithful, not of sinners. God . . ."

"Since when are you so 'faithful'? Just a couple of years ago you would show up in your tight jeans and borrow our car to pick up one of your five girlfriends. You think that beard makes you a man of God?" Farnaz realizes that all activity has come to a halt and the men have gathered around, like spectators at a school brawl. "Farnaz-jan, Farnaz-jan— that's enough," Keyvan whispers in her ear, over and over, but she lets his words pass through her. She cannot stop. "And since when is stealing people's possessions the call of God? You are all hypocrites who have suddenly come into power, and you don't know how to handle it."

"Shut up, you dirty Jew!" Morteza thunders. "I tried to be respectful but you won't allow it. So I'll call you by what you are."

There are murmurs around her now—some praising Morteza, a few admonishing him. She turns to the wall to hide her tears. Strings of ivy have crawled down the bricks over the years, like a carpet coming undone. The screeching of desks, the thump of boxes, the aborted single ring of a telephone as it lands in the truck, all buzz behind her in a frenzy. The day has turned cold. Keyvan places his hands on her shoulders. She feels the boniness of his long fingers and is startled by how different they are from Isaac's stronger grip. He leaves them there a long time, and she lets him. He wraps his scarf around her neck and guides her out of the courtyard.

When they arrive home he helps her up the stairs and sits her on the bed. He kneels down, removes her shoes, leans her body against the pillows. He prepares tea for her, offers her an aspirin with a glass of water. He sits beside her and rubs her forehead, and she dozes off, her bed drenched in sunlight.

She wakes up disoriented and cold. The room is dark, predicting the anxiety of a long night to be spent alone. She sits up, hopes to find Keyvan somewhere in the room, but sees no sign of him, except for his scarf still wrapped around her neck.

Behind the closed door of her bedroom, Shirin and Habibeh talk in low voices. She wonders how much Morteza confides in his mother. Is it time to let Habibeh go? But who would care for Shirin? Farnaz doesn't feel capable of doing it by herself—not now. Lying there, listening to her daughter, she sees her own mother, standing by the stove, ordering Farnaz to finish cleaning the house in preparation for Sabbath, or for this or that holiday. She hears her father, remembers how he would stand at the head of the table on the eve of Sabbath, one hand holding the prayer book, the other the cup of wine, reciting the prayers with a sad baritone that hushed everything before him—the sparkling dinnerware waiting to be filled with stew, the crystal glasses expecting wine, and his radio, which remained on whenever he was home, reporting on the war in Europe and the arrival to the throne of the new shah, the so-called "spineless" son of the deposed Reza Shah.

She recalls how after her Friday chores she would accompany her father through narrow unpaved streets to buy sweets. It was on one of these walks, when she was about Shirin's age, that she had told him that her best friend Azar's father was making the hajj—the pilgrimage to Mecca—and that upon his return he would receive the much-coveted title of hajji.

"Baba, will you be taking this pilgrimage also?" she had asked him.

"No, Farnaz-jan," he had said. " We are Jews. Jews don't make the hajj."

"Then how can we become hajjis?"

"We don't."

"That isn't fair. How can we become holy?"

"And since when, may I ask, are you so interested in being holy?"

"I just want to know that I can become it if one day I decide to."

"I see! It's like insurance. All right. I'll tell you how. We can study the Torah. We can become rabbis." Then he had repeated his oft-said line, "The Jews, you know, are the chosen people."

"Chosen by whom?"

"Chosen by God. We are his special people."

"But don't the others think they are chosen also?"

"Every religion has its own beliefs, its own version of what happened."

"If there are so many versions, how can we know which one is true?"

He had looked up, sighing. "If you were born a Jew, then you believe the Jews' version. That's how it works!"

They had walked for a long time without talking, her hand inside his, her ankle twisting every now and then. The answer did not make sense to her. It was like saying, well, if you live in this house, then this is the nicest house on the block. If you live in the next house, then that one is the nicest house.

"Are Jews still Iranians, Baba?"

"Of course. The Jews have been in Iran for a long time—before the time of Cyrus, even. And they lived happily here for centuries, until they were declared *najes*— impure. That's when they lost their businesses, their homes, their belongings. They had to move into the *mahaleh*, a kind of ghetto. And because it was located at the lowest point of Tehran, when it rained all the filth and squalor of the city ended up there."

She imagined living in this gutter, in a one-room house with her parents, the city's excrement flowing into their soup bowls.

"Did you live in the *mahaleh*, Baba?"

"No. By the time I was born the government liked the Jews again."

"How come this government liked the Jews and the other ones didn't?"

"So many questions, Farnaz-jan! So many questions. Come, let's get our sweets and forget about who likes the Jews and who doesn't."

They walked inside the shop, and as her father selected pastries, she caught a glimpse of herself in the back mirror. People always said how pretty she was, how beautiful she would grow up to be. Looking at her reflection, she thought, How do the ghettos and squalor of the Jews concern me? Years later, when her parents emigrated to Israel, she stayed behind. "Why should I leave?" she had said. "This is my country, and I am very happy right here."

But this has become a country of informers, she thinks. To survive, one must either become one—or disappear.

TWENTY-TWO

"What's your favorite flower?" Rachel says.

Parviz has never thought much about flowers. A few come to mind—roses, sunflowers, carnations; none would qualify as his favorite. He remembers the white orchids that his father would bring his mother. "White orchids," he says.

"They're beautiful. I like them, too. But they can be temperamental if you don't give them the care they need—the right amount of sunlight, temperature, and humidity."

"My mother loves orchids. I guess they suit her temperament."

"Are you saying your mother is moody?" She smiles.

He has come to see her on the pretext of buying flowers for a friend. All morning in class he had pictured her watering her plants, making their leaves bow to her with the weight of the droplets. He follows her through the shop now as she shows him the flowers. She seems to have forgiven him for the comment he made when he last saw her—about exporting religion.

"This one," she says, "is a gerbera. With the round face of a sunflower, but more delicate. That one, over there," she says, pointing at a wiry branch with white cotton blooms, "is a gypsophila. The flowers are so light, like fairy dust. But you have to tell me more about your friend. What kind of person is she?"

"My friend," he says, "is reserved, but sweet. I don't know her that well yet."

She looks at him with suspicious eyes. "Red camellias may be a good choice, or white daisies."

Mr. Broukhim, shelving bags of soil, looks up. "Don't go down that road, Parviz-jan!" he calls out. "If I were you, I would buy yellow carnations, or purple hyacinths."

"Don't listen to him." Rachel smiles. "Yellow carnations mean disdain and purple hyacinths are for sorrow."

It fascinates him, this secret language. In a world without words, people could communicate with nothing but plants. There must be a plant to express every emotion—love, joy, solitude, fear, grief, even hope maybe.

He buys the daisies, which Rachel explains convey affection, and when he arrives home he leaves them for her on the stoop, where she always stands. He wonders what it is about her that so appeals to him. She is not an exceptional beauty, nor is she particularly warm. He thinks of the girls he has come to know in class, attractive for the most part, but tiresome because of their forwardness. He thinks of those he had known back home—Mojgan and Nahid, and even Yassi, his girlfriend of two years—how despite their teasing manners they safeguarded their honor, like jewelers awaiting appraisal of their stones—how pure, how precious, how much?

Rachel is unlike all of them. Her religiosity, which not long ago would have repelled him, now offers him something no one else has since his arrival: quietude. Maybe it's because he is incapable of such faith that he has deferred his unanswered prayers to her—being near her ignites in him, somehow, the hope that his father will survive.

THE FOLLOWING AFTERNOON he steams hats with Zalman, his eyes on the door. When, near sundown, she still hasn't come, he finds himself weak and feverish. "Rachel never brought you your snack," he says as casually as he can.

"She called to say she wasn't feeling well," Zalman says. "She went home after school."

"A cold?"

"She didn't say. She just said she wasn't well."

Like a driver who finds himself at a dead-end, Parviz first blames the poor signage, then the poor visibility, and finally his own poor judgment.

TWENTY-THREE

Ramin's mother and old man Muhammad's eldest daughter were killed on the same night. Their names appear in the paper's list of executed, and by the time Isaac and the other prisoners are taken outside for their weekly dose of air, in the early afternoon, the news has spread among the men like the warning of cholera in a damp city. The old man sits on the ground hugging his bony knees, the boy leans against a wall, arms crossed against his chest, glassy-eyed. And so it is, Isaac thinks, that three generations have bonded through death.

"This country has fallen into the hands of savages," Hamid says.

Isaac braces himself for a long tirade from Reza, something about how the country was always in the hands of savages. But it doesn't come. Here, as with any funeral, the men are civil and appropriately somber.

"If they were innocent, then they are martyrs," Reza says. "There is no reason to mourn."

Hamid looks at Reza with his black eyes, but restrains himself.

"My mother is no martyr, she was a communist," Ramin says. "Besides, there is no such thing as a martyr." Then turning to the old man he says, "Muhammad-agha, don't worry. We'll get out of here and show these people what we're made of."

The old man doesn't look up. For a long time he remains quiet. Then in his wrinkled voice, he says, "If the rug of your luck has been woven in black, even the water of Zamzam cannot whiten it."

IN THE CELL, Mehdi is asleep on his mattress, his right foot a swollen mass, the toe now completely black. The unfinished wooden clog is on the floor, upside down. There is a fetid odor in the room. Isaac struggles to sit on the floor beside him. He watches his sunken face, all dry skin and bones, with two yellow lids marooned inside their deep, gray sockets. He puts his palm on Mehdi's forehead.

"Mehdi-jan, have you asked them again about your foot?"

"Yes, just this morning. They won't let me go to the hospital."

The door of the cell opens and a guard shoves Ramin with such force that he lands facedown on his mattress. "You want to end up like your mother, you mule?"

"Brother, is the other guard, Hossein-agha, on duty to-day?" Isaac asks.

"Yes, later. Why?"

"He had suggested a verse from the Koran for me to contemplate, and I wanted to discuss it with him."

"He'll have the night shift," the guard says, eyeing Isaac suspiciously. "If you learn something, why don't you pass it on to this dimwit?" He points to Ramin and leaves.

Ramin tests the soreness of his face with his fingers. "A verse from the Koran, Amin-agha?"

"No, not really. I want to speak to Hossein about Mehdi's foot. He's the only one who may do something about it."

"You're smarter than I am, Amin-agha," the boy says. "Me, I'm a bad liar."

Isaac looks at Ramin, his face still young despite all he has been through, his eyes deep and brown. They made this boy an orphan, he thinks.

He spends the rest of the afternoon on his mattress, waiting for the slit in the door to open. He plans to grab the dinner tray as it glides into the cell, its tarnished metal cold against his hand, and hold it long enough to ask Hossein for help. Something about Hossein, Isaac thinks, suggests a capability for empathy. Unlike the others, his hardness is interrupted, sometimes, by glimmers of kindness, as when he had escorted Isaac to his cell that first night, when he had brought him an aspirin, or when he had informed the prisoners about the increased executions. His warning may have been callous, but it was still a genuine warning and not just a threat—more than anyone else has offered so far.

From his window he watches the shimmering interplay of light and dark, and finally the arrival of dusk—the sad conclusion of another day. So the old man has lost a daughter, Ramin has lost a mother, Mehdi will lose a foot. And he, what has he lost today? Rather, what has he left to lose? He realizes that he must now think of his wife and children not in relation to himself, but as people whom he loves and for whom he wishes a good life. He cannot lose them because he has already done so.

The slit opens. The sickly light from the hallway appears as a yellow rectangle in the door, and the tray slides through. Isaac gets up and grabs it. "Brother Hossein, is that you?"

"Yes."

He pulls in the tray and settles it on the floor, then places his eyes on the opening. Hossein's ash-gray eyes peer at him from the other side.

"Brother, Mehdi will die from his bad foot if something isn't done about it. They may say, So what? but a prisoner should only die of his crime, not of illness."

"Why don't you preoccupy yourself with your own situation? Other people's health problems are none of your business."

"Brother, even I, in my miserable state, cannot just sit here and watch a man die. Please help him."

"I'll see what I can do." His eyes look into Isaac's a few seconds before the metallic slit slams shut.

* * *

HE TRIES TO awaken his cellmates for dinner, but neither responds. Mehdi has passed out, from pain no doubt, and Ramin, sprawled on his mattress, mumbles a few words in his sleep. Isaac sits cross-legged on the floor in front of the tray, alone. There is rice on a tin plate, three very bruised chicken legs, and bread. In theory, he could eat the other men's portions to regain his strength, but he cannot even eat his own. He plucks the meat from the chicken bones and wraps it inside the thin lavash bread. He sits on the mattress next to Ramin, rests the boy's head on his arm, and brings the sandwich to his mouth. Ramin opens his eyes, and seeing Isaac, begins sobbing. "Amin-agha, they really killed my mother!" he cries. Isaac hesitates for a moment before drawing the boy closer, and it occurs to him that he hasn't held his own children like this in years.

Around midnight, the door opens and in come two guards with a stretcher, which in the dark looks like no more than a piece of wood. One man slides his hands under Mehdi's armpits, the other holds on to his ankles, and together they lower him onto the wood, where he lands with a thump. Mehdi shrieks, then mumbles, "Baba, Baba, why did you let them do this to me, why? Baba, Baba . . ." and Isaac thinks, how strange, that no matter how many years a man has lived and what he has seen during those years, in the end he still wants an answer from his father.

"Bijan Yadgar; Behrooz Ghodsi . . ." a guard calls out names. "Jahanshah Soheil, Vartan Sofoyan, Ramin Ameri, Isaac Amin . . ." Hearing his own name Isaac feels the terror hardened inside him over so many months spill through his body like molten rock. He sits still on his mattress, the requiem of keys and locks drowning him. The men carrying the stretcher say, "Get up, both of you! Your names have been called." Ramin opens his eyes then shuts them again, until a guard comes, grabs Isaac by his shirt collar and the boy by his ear, and drags the two into the hallway, where other prisoners are also gathered, among them the pianist.

The men are brought one flight down, into a fluorescent-lit room with chipping walls and blackened linoleum floors, a rusted metal sink, a snaking hose, a black bucket, and reddish-brown stains everywhere. It is cold here, and damp, with an unfamiliar smell, of slaughterhouses and bathrooms and ammonia. Isaac looks at Vartan, who stands stone faced, wringing his hands. Noticing Isaac he bites his lips and shakes his head. Ramin grabs Isaac's arm. "It will be all right, Amin-agha," he says. "It will be all right. You'll see . . . And if not, then surely we'll meet on the other side. Who knows? Since we're innocent, maybe we are martyrs, after all." He smiles, his nervous eyes scanning the room. "Seventy-two virgins may be waiting for each of us . . ."

The men are separated into two groups. At the end of the tally, Issac finds himself on one side of the room with two older fellows whose names he did not catch; Ramin and Vartan face him on the other side with the rest of the men, most of them in their twenties and thirties. The grouping is reminiscent of other selections he has read about, where the able-bodied were kept for labor and the old were parceled to the gas chambers.

The other group is escorted out. Isaac stands with the two men, suppressing a powerful urge to vomit. One of his companions, a tall emaciated man of about sixty with thick glasses, paces the room; the other, a balding man who blinks two or three times per second, mumbles something to himself. The door opens and a guard walks in. "Follow me," he says.

They walk out of the room and out of the building through a back exit. Isaac feels a gush of icy wind on his face as soon as they step into the courtyard, and he trembles, an involuntary tremor that takes hold of his entire body. Their footsteps are heavy and loud in the blue-white light of the moon, and as they walk he hears the emaciated man repeating, "*Allah-o-Akbar, Allah-o-Akbar.*" They walk for what seems to him a very long time. They make lefts and rights, deep inside the prison's belly. When they pass a group of men whom he recognizes as the young men collected earlier, he tries to find Ramin and Vartan, but cannot. "Isaac!" Vartan whispers. Isaac turns around but the guard presses a rifle into his lower back. They continue walking until they reach another building. The guard opens the gate and they are led inside, each man shoved into a separate cell. "You've been assigned to solitary," he says.

Isaac's room is a square large enough to hold a mattress and a sink. As he is thrown inside it he crouches on the floor, trying to stop the tremor running through his wracked body. He knows he was spared this evening.

Lying still on his mattress, he hears a commotion in the courtyard. Then they begin, one after the other, the bullets flying in the air, men shrieking, men pleading, bodies thumping to the ground. Then nothing.

He thinks of Ramin, his death separated from his mother's by no more than a day, and of Vartan, his final audience a firing squad.

TWENTY-FOUR

Five couplets, at the minimum, but no more than twelve usually. The first couplet establishes a rhyme followed by a refrain, a scheme repeated by the second line of each succeeding couplet. Each couplet should stand on its own, but must also be part of the whole. At the end, the poet often invokes himself."

Shirin reads this definition of the ghazal, an ancient poetic form mastered by Hāfez, whose poems her father often recited after dinner, while shaving, or on long drives, when he would break the silence with a verse. Sometimes her mother would join him, turning the poem into a duet.

She skims the pages of her father's old textbook and reads the examples but doesn't understand them. Once after her father had explained a poem to her, something about how time and beauty are both unfaithful, she had asked him, "So what happens at the end, Baba?" and he had said, "There is no end, Shirin-jan. That's the first thing you should learn about ghazals. There is no resolution. Imagine the speaker simply throwing his hands in the air."

Maybe in life, as in a ghazal, there is no resolution. She finds relief in this idea of throwing her arms in the air. Maybe there are no solutions, nothing to be done. She abandons her father's book, along with her own homework, and gets into bed, under the blankets. That it's the middle of the afternoon makes little difference. If there is no real beginning, and no real end, what does time really mean?

The sound of the doorbell snaps her out of her nap. Who could it be? Another unannounced house search? A messenger reporting her father's execution? She gets out of bed and walks to her bedroom door, but doesn't dare to step beyond.

"What a nice surprise," she hears her mother saying. "You're sure you won't come in for tea, Farideh-khanoum? All right, come, Leila-jan. Shirin is doing her homework upstairs."

She walks down and greets Leila. "Is everything all right?" she says once they are alone.

"No," Leila whispers. "My father has been yelling at me and my mother all afternoon. He says some files have been missing from the basement since my birthday."

Shirin tries to speak, but her throat is so dry that her voice won't come. "What files?" she finally mumbles.

"I'm not sure. He said they are files of people who need to be investigated. I told you, didn't I, that my father works with the Revolutionary Guards?"

It occurs to Shirin that the missing file about Uncle

Javad makes her an obvious suspect. Why had she not thought of it before? Isn't it a matter of time before someone digs up the four files in the garden? "Does he know which ones are missing?"

"I don't know. What difference does it make?"

"No difference. I was just asking." Sweat breaks out along her hairline.

"And you know what else?" Leila says. "After he yelled and screamed I saw him drinking from one of those whiskey bottles we found in the basement. And he is always saying how alcohol is forbidden."

"What is he going to do about the files?"

"He wants my mother to find out who took them. We are supposed to interrogate all the girls who were at my party. He says if we don't, he'll do it himself. But he thinks it may be Elaheh."

"Elaheh?"

"Yes. My father doesn't like her father. Baba thinks he should have been the one to get the position that Elaheh's father got as head of the prison. Apparently the two of them got into a big fight over it. Now he thinks Elaheh's father is trying to make him look bad."

"Yes, Elaheh," Shirin says. "Makes sense."

"This is terrible," Leila says. "How am I supposed to interrogate everyone? I'll have no friends left." She sits on the bottom stair, buries her head in her lap. "I never had a birthday party before," she says, looking up again. "I was so excited to have one this year. And all the girls actually came. I couldn't believe it. I guess they didn't come for me.

They came because they know who my father is." She starts walking up the stairs.

"Of course they came for you," Shirin says, consoling her friend but thinking only of herself, and of the trouble she is in.

Leila stops in the middle of the stairs. "You know, before the revolution, my father worked in a morgue. He once told me how he washed the dead people and wrapped them in clean white shrouds before delivering them to their families. He said he got a lot of mangled bodies from prisons, and this really bothered him. Back then, people made fun of him because of his job. Even I was teased at school because of it. Now that he is with the Guards, people respect him. 'I went from being at the bottom of the garbage chute to being at the top,' he says. 'Finally *I* decide who goes down.'"

The image of bodies being thrown down a garbage chute terrifies Shirin. "He really says this?"

"Yes, but please don't repeat it to anyone. I wasn't supposed to talk about it. I just can't believe he is going to ruin everything for me. How am I supposed to interrogate the girls?"

Shirin wonders if she'll be the first one to be questioned. Feeling dizzy, she holds on to the banister.

"At least I don't have to interrogate you," Leila says. "My parents think that with your father already in jail, you wouldn't do something like that. Besides, you're so sickly and frail. . . . My mother also thinks it's Elaheh. 'There is something about that girl I don't like,' she was telling my father. Which is strange, because I'm almost sure she let her win the musical chairs."

"What if Elaheh denies she took them?"

"Of course she'll deny it. Everyone will deny it. I'm supposed to watch for people's reactions. My father showed me a few tricks."

"Like what?"

"For example, if someone can't maintain eye contact with you while you're talking—that's a sign that they may be lying. Or if they wring their hands, or tap their feet . . ."

Shirin makes mental notes. *Maintain eye contact. Do not wring hands, or tap feet . . .*

"I never asked you this," Leila says. "Do you know why your father is in prison?"

"No."

"He didn't work for Savak, did he?"

"What is Savak?"

"It was the shah's secret police. My father talks about it all the time. He says they killed and tortured thousands of people."

"No, not my father."

"But how can you be sure? These guys didn't even tell their own families what they did. That's why it was called a *secret* police. You know, Shirin, I'm starting to realize something: people always say one thing and do another. Take my father. He says alcohol is forbidden, but he drinks. Or my mother, she says she doesn't like Elaheh but she lets her win . . ."

And me, Shirin thinks. I say I didn't take the files, but I did.

*   *   *

THAT NIGHT SHE lies in bed and thinks of her father. If people find out about the files, her father will no doubt be killed. Her mother, too, may be accused and sent to prison.

How could she have believed she would get away with this? She looks at the full moon, bright and low in the sky. She wonders if her father sees it too, from his cell's window.

I am foolish, she thinks. I am nine years old. Do I deserve to reach ten? I have one friend, but as of today I am more afraid of her than of anyone else. All my good friends have gone. I have not seen my brother in two years and I am starting to forget his face. My father, too, is becoming faceless.

She covers herself up to the chin with her blanket, but the chill running through her body doesn't let go.

TWENTY-FIVE

The kitchen simmers in the heat of radiators and the sizzle of onions. The windows sweat from inside, steam slowly rising from the corners and erasing the city. From her chair Farnaz watches Habibeh stirring. "How is your mother doing?" she asks.

"Much better, khanoum, thank you. But the doctor says her sugar is high and she should cut down on sweets. She doesn't listen, of course. Just the other day, on my nephew's birthday, she ate two pieces of cake." She throws a stash of parsley, tomatoes, and peppers into the pot, like confetti. "But let me tell you what a handsome boy he is becoming, my nephew! In a few years he'll make a fine husband for Shirin."

Farnaz smiles. Surely Habibeh knows that a girl like Shirin won't marry the son of a cobbler. This was not a joke she would have made two years ago. "Was Morteza there for the birthday also?" she says.

"No, he doesn't come to these family gatherings. He thinks he has better things to do."

"Yes, like looting," Farnaz whispers in her tea.

"What?"

"He didn't tell you that he looted Isaac's office, he and the other employees?"

"What?" Habibeh rinses her hands and wipes them on her apron. "My Morteza?" she asks, stabbing her chest with her finger.

"Yes. I didn't know how to tell you."

"You must be mistaken, khanoum."

"No, I was there. I saw it. He said they were taking the goods somewhere else for safekeeping, but I know better."

"Yes? You know better? Why is it that you always know better?" Habibeh yells. "How come what you see is always right? Is it possible you choose to see what you want?"

Farnaz looks at Habibeh—her poorly dyed blond hair flattened with oil, the gap between her front teeth, her black skirt stained with indelible sauces and detergents. She imagines briefly what it would be like to live inside Habibeh's body, to look and smell like her, to wear her dappled clothes. "Habibeh," she says. "I saw what I saw."

"Yes, you saw what you saw. You are a kind woman, Farnaz-khanoum. But you are full of contempt. When I tell you maybe my little nephew will one day marry your Shirin, do you think I'm serious? I say such things as a joke. I know that you will never tell me how you really feel, so you say nothing. Or you smile. You know that if you tell me the truth you will sound as arrogant and conceited as that sister-in-law of yours, Shahla-khanoum. You're always making fun of her, but aren't you just like her, deep down? At least she's open about who she is. But you, Farnaz-khanoum, you only hold back."

Farnaz sips her tea, looks out the window, at the patch of white sky still visible through the steam. Everyone holds back, she thinks, in this country where you can get in trouble for looking at someone the wrong way, saying the wrong thing, being the wrong religion. Being two-faced is part of who we are—we say one thing and mean another.

"If that's the way you feel about me, then you're as duplicitous as I am, aren't you, Habibeh? Because I never knew that you find me arrogant and conceited. But all that aside, I am telling you what I saw: I saw your son, with the other employees, taking jewels, paintings, chairs, tables, even telephones. When I confronted him he told me Isaac is paying for the sins of a whole collection of men."

"He said this?" She crosses her arms, a wooden spoon dangling from her hand. "Well maybe he should pay," she says. "Maybe it's time someone paid."

This tea that she is drinking, with spices that calm her nerves, was brewed by a woman for whom Isaac's elimination is a matter of collective retribution. And yet she drinks it, has drunk thousands like it, never considering the potential malignancy of the hands that spooned the leaves and dropped them inside the teapot. How can it all come to this, the decades of shared roofs and bad winters and fleeting summers, of cherries picked from the garden and watermelons carried like children from the bazaar? "Isaac has harmed no one," she says. "Least of all you and your son. He does not need to pay."

Habibeh turns back to the sink and skins the chicken. "I don't know, khanoum. You and Amin-agha have been generous to us. But something was wrong. Why is it that some people were destined to get served on hand and foot, and the best others could hope for was washing toilets?"

"Nobody was destined for anything. You worked hard, you did well. You think Isaac was born a prince?"

She turns around, flinging the knife in the air. "I work hard," she says. "My son works hard!"

"And you've come a long way from where you started. Shall I remind you of the way you lived when we met you— you and your son in a tiny room with a leaking roof? When we saw you selling flowers on a street corner, your breasts half exposed, it wasn't clear what, exactly, you were selling. But Isaac took one look at you, and your snot-nosed son sitting next to you, picking scabs on his feet, and he said to me, 'Isn't there any way we can take these people in? Didn't you say you need a housekeeper?' Now you tell me. Is this what my husband must pay for?"

Habibeh doesn't answer. She goes on peeling the skin off the chicken, peeling so hard that she takes the meat with it. Again Farnaz wonders if Habibeh is, after all, the one who took her sapphire ring. But she doesn't ask. She looks at Habibeh's stooped back, remembers the time they had taken her and Morteza to their villa up north, when Shirin was still a baby and Parviz was quizzing everyone on history. Throughout the car trip the young Morteza, having discovered girls, insisted on listening to Isaac's tapes of the *Concerto de Aranjuez* on Spanish guitar. "My head is gone with this guitar!" Habibeh complained. "Can't we play something more upbeat?" Morteza shushed his mother. "You don't understand love," he proclaimed. "I don't understand love? How do you think you ended up here, *aghapesar*?" She looked out the car window. "I don't understand love?" she repeated in a low voice. "Love is what sealed my fate as a servant."

TWENTY-SIX

Standing by the statue of Shakespeare under the trees and watching Rachel walk toward him, Parviz realizes how wonderful New York can be—its winter Sundays unfolding in the curves of Central Park. Feeling like he is betraying Zalman, he reminds himself that he has no intention of doing anything dishonorable. Besides, meeting here had been Rachel's idea. A week after leaving her the daisies, he had seen her on the stoop, and as he scrambled to find his keys, she called out to him, "Thank you." She smiled. "They were lovely." That solitary smile managed to assuage all his doubts. As he watched her from below, searching his mind for the right response, she continued, "Come with me to the park one day, and we'll look at more plants." Afterward when she had gone back inside, he stood for some time in the windy afternoon, where, in the circular sound of his neighbors' chimes, he heard his mother's melodic laughter.

"Hello," he says as he reaches for her hand.

She pulls back. "Hello."

"I'm sorry. I forgot about the no contact rule."

It's an unusually warm day for February, the wind carrying a hint of milder days to come, stroking the frozen city with sunlight and filling it with delirium.

"It's strange, to see you here, outside of your neighborhood," he says.

"It's strange for me, too. My father doesn't like me to come out."

They walk quietly for some time and he fights the urge to reach out for her hand.

"These trees," she says, pointing upward, "are American elms. The leaves are all gone now, but look at their beautiful branches underneath—twirling in the air like dancing arms." He looks at the branches and sees them, the naked dancing arms reaching into the sky. "In the summertime," she continues, "when the leaves are lush and green, the trees make a perfect canopy."

It would be lovely to see the world through her eyes, he thinks. To see canopies where he sees leaves, to see dancing limbs where he sees sad branches waiting for the summer months.

They walk westward, past the cyclists and the joggers and the babies dozing in carriages, and he realizes that the people here still live with that sense of permanence he once felt when strolling by the Caspian Sea, past children claiming land with their sand castles and swimmers floating on their backs, trusting their bodies to the waves. It is the kind of trust that comes only from having a place in one's bones, knowing its idiosyncrasies and temperaments like those of a relative.

They arrive in a shaded nook, where trees and overgrown shrubs stand in disarray. "That's the Shakespeare Garden," she says. "It's neglected, but you should see one thing." She walks ahead of him to a tree. "Look. It's a graft of a white mulberry tree planted by Shakespeare at Stratford-on-Avon in 1602. Isn't that something?"

He holds out his hand and places it on the trunk of the mulberry, feeling its ridges. "How come you know all this?"

"I don't know. Plants calm me, so I examine them. I feel they belong to me. I hope to study botany if my father lets me. I haven't had the courage to ask him yet. But my dream is to have a flower shop of my own someday."

"You couldn't have ten children and run a flower shop, could you?"

"No. That's the problem. I have to make a choice. My roots or my passion. But I can't let go of either."

"I have the opposite problem," he says. "Since I've lost my roots, I seem to have also lost my passion. That leaves me with nothing." He leans against the mulberry, the sun on his face. "I wish I could commit something of this city to memory the way you have. Buildings and structures fascinate me, but not because I feel they are mine."

She pulls a leaf from a shrub and brings it to her nose. "You remind me of my boss, Mr. Broukhim. He always says, 'I miss the jasmines and the cypresses.' And I tell him, 'But look at the weeping willows and the oaks. You can love them, too.' He shakes his head. He says, 'The weeping willows are too sad and the oaks are too sturdy, too indifferent to be loved. This country is vast and cold, Rachel,' he says to me, 'like a dark palace made of granite.'"

"Mr. Broukhim is right. This country *is* vast and cold."

"You only think this because you are alone. And because your father is in prison," she adds gently. "I hope you don't mind that I know. My father told me."

That she is privy to his secret pain fills him with relief. "No, I don't mind," he says. Staring into her dark brown eyes, he wishes he could kiss her. He remembers that sweet scent of her winter coat and wonders if that same scent is there today, behind her ears or on her tiny wrists.

"I'm so hungry," she says.

"Me too. But I suppose hot dogs are against the rules." He laughs. "That's all we can get in the park."

"For me, they are. But no one said they should be against your rules, if you don't want them to be. I brought some fruit to hold me over."

They walk to a nearby kiosk. As the vendor prepares his hot dog and she reaches into her bag for her fruit, he is reminded of the divide between them. He does not want to slip into her secure but stringent world, nor does he expect her to slip into his—an unmarked road where visibility is poor.

They walk some more, now in silence. She doesn't point out any more plants, doesn't tell him about their transformations and histories. They walk aimlessly, getting lost inside the park's arteries, eventually aligning themselves with the sun, now lying westward and losing its brilliance.

TWENTY-SEVEN

Isaac stretches his legs, tapping them with his fingers to help his blood circulate. He is glad to have a sink in his room; he rinses his face several times a day and lies back down. He is also glad to have an ant colony, for which he saves his leftover sugar cubes and bread crumbs, distributing them throughout the day and watching the parade of tiny insects carrying the goods. He is not sure how long he has been in solitary. Probably not yet a week since he has neither had a shower nor has he been allowed to take in fresh air. He assumes these to be weekly activities here, as they had been in the communal block, but he may be wrong.

From his basement window, which overlooks a courtyard, he can see feet, and when he gets tired of watching the ants, it is the feet that help him pass the hours. Most are in sneakers, some are in leather boots, some in brown plastic slippers. Some are firm in their step, others drag. Occasionally, when he sees a pair of shoes that he recognizes because of the pattern of a stain or a shaved heel, he counts the number of times the shoes' owner passes back and forth throughout the day. If the number is even, he tells himself that he will get out of prison alive, if it is odd, then he will not. He has fallen on both odd and even numbers enough times to know that they mean nothing, but each time he ends with an odd number he sleeps with a heavy heart and tells himself that it is possible that he missed one of the shoes' passages—he may have been washing his face or studying the ants, who knows?

He lies down, too tired this morning to count the shoes. He hears the steps he has grown accustomed to—someone running up and down the stairs above his cell, with the lightness of a child. He cannot figure out what a child may be doing in a place like this.

After his breakfast of tea and bread the door to his cell opens. "It's time for your shower, Brother," a masked guard says.

Isaac gets up, his joints and muscles hard and unyielding. His lower back is so stiff that it feels numb. He looks into the guard's gray eyes and says, "Brother Hossein?"

"Yes," the guard says. "I have the morning shift on this end."

He follows Hossein down the hallway and into the shower stall. "You have five minutes," Hossein says.

The water is cold. Isaac quickly washes himself, then rinses his shirt and underwear with soap and water in the remaining time. He puts on the wet clothes and comes out. Hossein gives him a lip balm. "Use this," he says.

"Thank you, Brother." Isaac takes the balm, squeezes a drop out of the tube onto his finger and rubs it on his lips, which are cracked and bleeding. He returns the balm.

"Keep it," Hossein says. "Come now. You need some air."

He follows Hossein up several flights of stairs, stopping many times to catch his breath, until they reach a metal door leading to a roof. A dozen benches have been placed here, each one occupied by a prisoner and a guard sitting side by side. The late-morning light is strong, too strong for a man who has grown accustomed to a basement. They walk to a bench and sit.

He feels the clean mountain air on his damp face, smells the soap drying on his skin.

"Brother," Isaac asks. "Why was I brought to solitary?"

"Sometimes people start in solitary then go to the communal block, sometimes it's the other way around. I don't know why."

"Does anyone get out of here alive?"

"Yes," Hossein says. "If you are innocent, you will get out."

"But that isn't always the case, is it? Many innocents die."

"Some innocents die, that's true. And some guilty ones get away. In the end, it balances itself out."

No, it does not *balance itself out*, he wants to say. That my life should be nothing more than an X on one side of an equation to balance the other side is of no comfort to me. He looks at Hossein's callused hands, his stubby fingers ridged at the knuckles, the thick cuticles eating into his nails. He is wringing his hands, looking out into the distance through the holes in his mask.

"What were you doing before you were a prison guard, if I may ask, Brother?"

"I was a mason. I built many homes with these hands. Beautiful homes, with terraces and gardens and porches." He looks down at his hands for a long time, running one finger on the veins of the other, like a man committing a beloved landscape to memory.

"And which do you prefer, masonry or guardianship?"

"Brother, these are different times. There is a time to build things and a time to destroy in order to build again. Perhaps one day I'll be a mason again, but right now this is what I have to do. We must take the weeds out of the soil."

BACK IN HIS cell he lies down. He feels lighter after the shower and the fresh air. Again he hears someone running up and down the stairs above his cell—he knows it is a child because of the speed, that lightness in the step that can only belong to one who has his entire life before him, and believes that this life will be good. He remembers how his own children used to race on the stairs of their house, Parviz sliding down the banister, Shirin yelling, "That's not fair, you are not allowed to slide!" and Farnaz snapping at both of them to stop—someone will end up with a broken head, she said. He enjoyed these sounds—the chaos of a family—even if he himself was only a bystander, reading his paper and sipping his tea in a corner. They were an affirmation of his own existence, proof that he had had enough faith in the world and in himself to have children. Even now, lying here, he is glad that he had once had this faith, like a landscaper who plants an oak tree knowing that it will not be fully grown in his lifetime—but that it will grow.

The door to his cell opens and a guard walks in. "Brother, follow me." He is led down the stairs into an empty room with two chairs and a desk. Mohsen is on the other side. He says, "Brother Amin, we meet again." When Isaac does not respond he continues. "Perhaps we will have better luck this time." He hands Isaac a paper and a pen. "Please write down the story of your life," he says.

"The story of my life?" Isaac hesitates before taking the paper.

"Go on," Mohsen says. "Take all the time you need."

He sits down, holds the pen, which feels foreign in his hand. Something will come to pass very soon with Mohsen, he thinks. If this were a game of poker, this would be the point where Isaac would have to either raise the stakes despite a mediocre hand, or recognize his defeat and fold. He decides to raise the stakes. He will play Mohsen's game. But how can he reduce his entire life to a few lines? It occurs to him that he is writing his own obituary—the sort of scant paragraph he would read in the newspaper and think, There must have been so much more to this man's life.

He starts, "My name is Isaac Amin. I was born in the port city of Khorramshahr, to Hakim and Afshin Amin. I am the eldest of three children. As a young man I worked in an administrative capacity at the oil refinery in Abadan. I studied literature and poetry, then gemology, before beginning my own jewelry business. I had wanted to be a poet but realized that words do not put food on the table. I live in Tehran. I am married, with two children. I hope not to leave this earth without seeing my family again."

He reads the note and wonders if he should have written the last line. Crossing it out now would appear suspicious. He hands the paper to Mohsen.

Mohsen reads it, then says, "So spare, Brother Amin. Surely there was more to your life than this."

"I told you, Brother. I am a simple man."

"How come you have only two siblings? Back then people had many more children, did they not?"

"My parents didn't."

"But you did end up with that troublemaker brother of yours. The bootlegger. You still wish to go on protecting him?"

"Brother, I swear to you I have no idea where he is."

Mohsen keeps on reading. "You had wanted to be a poet? How romantic. How does a poet become such a rich man, that's what I'd like to know."

"Perhaps the same level of idealism is required of both poetry and jewelry making, Brother."

"There is no mention here of any friends or acquaintances. Who were your close friends? People you might have had over for dinner . . ."

"I am an introvert by nature, Brother. I do not have any close friends. I enjoy being with my family, or spending time alone."

"Ah, a specialist in solitary confinement! Then we've

brought you to the right place." He laughs without looking up from the paper. "And of your trips to Israel," he continues, "you write nothing."

"I have also not written of my trips to the many other parts of the world I have been to."

Mohsen walks to a door, which Isaac had not noticed when he first walked in. He opens it. "Brother, I'd like you to listen to something."

At first, he is not sure what the sound is. He thinks it may be a dog howling. After a few minutes, the voices quiet down. He hears footsteps, followed by the shuffling of papers. A pungent odor of sweat and blood spills into the interrogation room. A voice says, "No change of heart?" Another voice, much weaker, says something, but he cannot hear it. Then it comes, the unmistakable sound of leather hitting flesh, and the shrieks of a man, which he had first mistaken for those of a dog. The shrieks grow meeker as the cable grows louder, and with each hit the first voice says, "Speak or breathe your last breath . . ."

Mohsen leaves the door open and walks away, his arms crossed against his chest. He leans over the desk. "You see how much awaits you that you don't know about? Now speak!"

"Brother, what do you want me to tell you? I have nothing to say."

"Tell me about your activities for Israel! And that brother of yours. Where is he?"

Isaac says nothing. Mohsen walks to the door, where the voices have once again quieted down. "Brother Mostafa, your next man is ready for you."

No, no, dear God, please don't. Not this. He feels blood rushing to his head, and a pain in his heart—a tightening. He cannot breathe. *I am having a heart attack.* Perhaps he should. Better to die here than under the cable, with his torturer's voice as his elegy. A masked man grabs his arm and lifts him. He is dragged to the other room and is laid facedown on a wooden plank. His shoes and socks are removed. He feels cables snaking around his ankles and attaching them to two poles. *Dear God, have mercy on me.* So it is really happening. To him, Isaac Amin of Khorramshahr, son of Hakim and Afshin Amin. *My name is Isaac Amin, my name is Isaac Amin. Where are you, my Farnaz? Come and see what they are doing to me. And my little Shirin. Come, look at your father. Come see what has become of him. Come, my Parviz. See your father barefoot and facedown on a plank of wood, about to be beaten like a dog.* The cable slices the air before slicing his feet. It is a jagged pain, unidentifiable, which travels through his nerves to the rest of his body. One, two, three, he counts. Four, five, six, seven. "Will you speak now? No?" Eight, nine, ten. He no longer feels his feet. He keeps counting. Eleven, twelve, thirteen, fourteen. "Still nothing? Repent, you son of a dog!" Fifteen, sixteen, seventeen . . .

Would you like some tea, Amin-agha? Yes, Habibeh, thank you. Shahla and Keyvan are having a dinner party on Thursday night; write it in your calendar. Didn't they just have a dinner party? Yes, well, she is your sister, not mine. Baba-jan, what is the capital of Egypt? Cairo. It's not Alexandria? No, it's not Alexandria. Didn't they burn a huge library in Alexandria? Yes, they did. Who did? First the Romans, then the Christians, then the Caliph of Baghdad. Bah bah, Amin-agha, welcome, welcome! Will it be just the two of you? No, we will be joined by our friends Kourosh and Homa. Very good. Come this way. We have an excellent fesenjan tonight.

A hand shakes his arm. "Brother Amin, wake up."

He opens his eyes. His cell is dark. A guard places a tray by his mattress. "You should eat. If you don't eat you will lose all your strength." The door slams shut.

Isaac sits up, leans against the wall. He cannot feel his feet. He bends and touches the soles; they are all peeled skin and raw meat. A burning sensation travels up his legs. He thinks of Mehdi. He pictures Mehdi in a wheelchair with no legs. He thinks of Ramin. He sees the boy's body, naked, a hole in his forehead, lying in a morgue. He remembers the ill-fated Vartan, sees him in a metallic cubicle not far from Ramin, his long fingers now resting on his gray, swollen body. He takes the bowl on the tray and fills his spoon with rice. He forces it down his throat.

TWENTY-EIGHT

To kill time before her meeting with Isaac's brother, Farnaz walks through the bazaar, running her hands over the silks and chiffons in fabric shops, smelling the spices inside giant sacks, flipping carpets to examine their craftsmanship. She stands across from the silversmith, where last night, during a harried telephone call from a public phone, Javad begged her to see him. She watches the boxes of merchandise being rolled on handcarts, the reds and oranges of the produce being unveiled, the bargaining between vendors and buyers, the money exchanging hands—the hustle of another day unfolding.

He arrives in a tired overcoat, which is missing two buttons. A dense black beard covers his chin. "How nice to see you," he says. "Thank you for coming."

He smells stale—like someone who has lived in too many places in a short amount of time, without the luxury of hot showers and toothbrushes and laundry.

"Good to see you also," she says. "When did you grow this beard? You blend right in with the mullahs."

"Yes." He laughs, caressing his face. His black, humorous eyes have not lost their brilliance. "The idea is to always blend in. That's how you avoid trouble. Come, let's walk."

"So what's happening?" Farnaz says. "Where have you been?"

"Oh, here and there, you know. The friend who told me about Isaac's arrest tells me that the Revolutionary Guards are after me also."

"My God, Javad! They will get us all in the end, won't they? What will you do?"

"I've been staying at different friends' houses around Tehran for over a month now, sleeping at each place for no more than a few nights. I can't keep doing that, and besides, I'm running out of friends." He laughs, caressing his beard again. "So I'm going to a small village up north, where I know a family that has agreed to take me in for a few weeks."

"And then?"

"By then, I'm expecting to receive lots of cash for a transaction . . . I'll use the cash to pay the smugglers who take people across the border to Turkey. I'll be poised right on the border, you know."

"What transaction? Don't get yourself in trouble, Javad-jan."

In a lowered voice he says, "No, no trouble. I'm importing vodka from Russia, and I have people signed up for casefuls. You wouldn't believe how many cases . . ."

"You're a *bootlegger* . . ." She looks around, wondering

if anyone heard what she said, but realizes that their conversation is drowned in the staccato voices of the vendors and haggling buyers. She stops by a shop, looks at the rolls of fabric stacked some thirty feet high, forming colorful walls that stand in sharp contrast to the black-veiled women roaming below. "If they catch you, you'll be executed right off, Javad! What are you getting yourself into?"

"They won't catch me. I'm dealing with real professionals."

"Who are these professionals? The Russian *vory*?"

"Look, I can't really talk about it. But the only thing is, I need a bit of cash to hold me over until the shipment arrives. I was wondering if you could help me."

"How much do you need?"

"About ten thousand."

"Dollars?"

"Of course, what else?" He smiles. "It just so happens that I owe some people some money also."

This is not the first time he has asked for such an amount. His constant requests for loans, which inevitably ended up as gifts, had long become a strain on her relationship with Isaac. "You not only fund his ridiculous schemes, you also bail him out once he is in trouble," she would say, and Isaac, having run out of arguments in defense of his little brother, would answer simply, "The money gives him hope to start over. How can I refuse?" Now it isn't just the amount that troubles her, but the idea of helping him smuggle vodka. "I don't know, Javad," she says. "I don't want to get mixed up in your schemes. If they find out I'm helping you they can make things worse for Isaac."

He stops walking, holds her arm. "Please, if I don't leave

Tehran, they're bound to come after me. And I'll tell you, with my track record, I don't have much of a chance."

By the fruit vendor, where they stand, the sweet-sour smell of pomegranates in their red and golden skins and bowing crowns fills the morning. She looks at him, striped with vertical rays of light, his eyes pleading.

"But if I take out that much cash at once they are bound to get suspicious. And I certainly can't write you a check."

"I've thought of all that. A friend of mine, Shahriar Beheshti, has an antiques shop. You can write a check to him, and he'll give me the money. If anyone asks you what you bought with ten thousand dollars, you tell them you got yourself a miniature painting from the sixteenth century. My friend can even lend one to you if you need to prove you have it."

"Javad, Javad, I don't know. We have so much trouble as it is."

"Please. I have nowhere else to turn. They'll kill me the minute they get their hands on me."

She tries to imagine what Isaac would do in her place. He had come to Javad's rescue time and again, fully knowing that he would never see a dollar back. That she never particularly cared for Javad's complicated schemes and wayward women and continuous demands for money is not the point. Not helping him would mean that he would most likely be killed, and she realizes that that would be something she could not live with, particularly for Isaac's sake.

"All right," she says. They turn into an abandoned alley jutting out of the bazaar where empty crates and bags of trash are stacked one on top of the other. In the moldy air a colony of ants is feasting on a few bruised apples and malformed squashes. She takes out her checkbook. "So who is selling me this ten-thousand-dollar miniature?"

"Thank you, Farnaz. You make it out to Fariba Antiques. When I get to that village I'll send you a letter, under the name Hajji Gholam. When my cash comes I'll send the money to the antiques dealer, who will return it to you. And when I have safely crossed the border, I will write you another letter. Look for the sentence 'The children have grown up and they are looking to settle down.'"

She hands him the check. "Good luck, Javad. May we hear good news."

He takes the check and slips it into his pocket. "You'll see," he says. "One day you and Isaac and the children and I will get together somewhere wonderful, by the Seine in Paris or by the Empire State Building in New York or at the Alhambra in Spain. We'll sit under a tree and drink tea, and we'll say, 'Remember those days?'"

"Javad-jan," she says, "a pond with no water does not need goldfish."

"You have to dream, my Farnaz, otherwise how can you get by?" He straightens his coat, kisses her on the cheek. "Oh, one more thing." He pulls something from his pocket: her missing sapphire ring. "This is yours. I needed collateral against some money I owed. I didn't mention it because I knew I would return it. Here."

"My God, the ring!" She slips it onto her finger. "You didn't think I would notice it was missing, Javad?"

"I knew you would. But I also knew that I would return it. No harm done. All right, I should get going. So long, my Farnaz. Kiss your little Shirin for me. And God willing, I'll see you on some other continent someday!" He turns around and walks away, a bounce in his step.

In his twisted, scam-filled world, Javad has a code of honor, a set of principles about loyalty and respect, and this is what, in the end, endears him to her. She looks at her finger, happy to see the ring—Isaac's first present to her. The weight of the stone on her hand comforts her, and she wonders, briefly, if it's a prophecy of Isaac's return.

She walks back through the bazaar, the alleyway streaked with rays of light streaming through the iron rooftop. How could a life as orderly as hers had been turn into such chaos in such a short time? Imprisoned husband, sickly daughter, disloyal housekeeper, stolen possessions, and now, a fugitive brother-in-law—a marked man on both sides of the Caspian, smuggling vodka into the country, and himself out. And she, linked to him with the check she just handed him, in care of some alleged antiques dealer, from whom she must now pick up a sixteenth-century miniature.

What an illusion, she thinks, the idea of an ordered, ordinary life.

TWENTY-NINE

Isaac stands on one leg. He has lifted the other and placed his foot in the sink, washing out the caked blood from his sole. He does this several times a day, cleaning one foot, then the other, in a time-consuming maneuver that requires great orchestration and willpower.

Since the lashings he has come to realize that his so-called case is not so much a case as it is an endurance test. Nothing has changed here, except for Mohsen's willingness to inflict more pain. Maybe Mehdi was right. Maybe one can tell when the end is near. "You smell it in your interrogator's breath," he had said. "You know he's had it with you."

He lies down. Outside, snowflakes swirl in the wind. He has been here two seasons, almost. In his absence the tea harvest in Gilan ended, the orange and lemon trees in Rasht shed their fruit, the fishermen salted their sturgeon's eggs and produced their caviar. He shuts his eyes. *Six in the morning— the clink of milk bottles outside his door. Seven—the smell of steamed milk, Ceylon tea, and eggs. Eight—leather, paper, and tobacco. Nine—chairs screeching, typewriters buzzing, chatter about the morning traffic. Ten—a gift of freshwater pearls for Farnaz from a Japanese colleague. Eleven—a warm samovar, a new shipment of rubies sparkling on his desk. Twelve—I'm going to lunch now, Amin-agha. One—the sizzle of a steak, Farnaz's hand stretched across the table. Two—a cup of Turkish coffee. Three—a nap on his sofa. Four—the smell of fresh ink on a new contract. Five—chairs screeching, engines starting, the hush of solitude. Six—LEGOs for Parviz, a Barbie for Shirin, an orchid for Farnaz. Seven—the warmth of a cognac before dinner. Eight—the smell of charcoal, the juice of kebab. Nine, ten—a movie. Eleven—bedtime! Twelve—a glass of steamed milk. One—the smell of Farnaz's orange blossom lotion.*

Two, three, four, five—the sound sleep of a man who does not know his hours are numbered.

"Brother Amin, it's time for your lunch."

He opens his eyes. In the dim cell he cannot see the guard's eyes. But it is daytime, and he assumes the man is Hossein. The man kneels down, holds his shoulders, and helps him sit up. "How are you holding up, Brother?" he says.

Isaac rubs his face with his hands.

"Brother," Hossein says. "Try to cry. You'll feel better if you cry."

"I can't. I'm all dried up."

"Well then, try to eat. Tomorrow is your shower day. I will bring you some clean bandages for your feet."

"Thank you."

"Now eat."

●　●　●

BECAUSE OF THE snow and the state of his feet he cannot get fresh air. He sits on his mattress, his feet wrapped with the bandages Hossein brought him—some old cotton underclothes. Hossein sits next to him. He says, "So they did it to you, too. I am sorry. I like you, Brother. You seem to me a decent man, despite the way you lived."

Again Isaac hears the footsteps above his cell. "Brother, am I imagining things," he asks, "or does a child run up and down the stairs all day long?"

"No, you are not imagining. That's Mohsen's little boy."

"Why does he bring his child to this place?"

"Mohsen is very proud of his son. You know, he was in this same prison for many years, and was tortured by Savak. That missing finger? Well, that's not the only torture he underwent. Let's just say he never thought he could have a child."

So that little boy is his miracle child, the badge of his faith. Bringing him to the prison and letting him run free among the prisoners is his way of saying, to himself and to everyone else, What is God's will, no frost can kill.

"He is not a bad man," Hossein says. "You may have trouble believing that after what you've been through. But he is not a bad man."

Isaac looks out the window. All morning he has noticed one distinguishable pair of boots, with a red stain on the left ankle, trudging back and forth in the snow. He thinks it is the fifth time the boots passed by his window; but he could be wrong.

"Well, Brother," Hossein says. "I must go. You have to believe that you will make it. Have faith."

DOESN'T EVERY PERSON who finds himself in dire circumstances believe, deep down, that he will make it, wonders Isaac. Doesn't every man believe that he occupies a special place on this earth and will therefore be spared the cruelest fate? What, precisely, was he supposed to have faith in? That he is more deserving than the others in God's eyes? That a young boy like Ramin could die with a bullet in his head but he, Isaac Amin, will walk free? And is it not ironic that the reason he is in prison is because of his supposed faith in a religion that has become more of a liability to him than a salvation? Why must he bear the burden of this religion, he who has led a secular life, who believed that the chief role of religious holidays was to bring families together? "Why is my name Isaac?" he had once asked his mother, and she had said, "Isaac was the son of Abraham. And he was very special because he was the proof of Abraham's faith in God." He had looked at her as she stood by the stove stirring a stew, a scarf tied around her head to keep her hair out of her face, and said, "But you and Baba and Javad and Shahla, you all have normal names. Why am I the only one with a Jewish name?" She had knelt down beside him. "Because you are extraordinary," she had said.

Mother, do you know that your extraordinary name has cursed me? That I sit here inside a cell not fit for a pig, my feet on their way to gangrene, my eyes on their way to blindness, my body wasted and shriveled? What kind of proof am I?

He sees the red-stained boots pass before him one more time, and he sighs with relief. Six—an even number. He cannot help saying, "Dear God, help me."

THIRTY

At the breakfast table Shirin rests her sleepy head on one hand and plays with her omelet with the other. The radio beeps twice to announce the new hour—7:00 A.M. "This is Tehran, the voice of the Islamic Republic of Iran . . ." They're running late this morning. Farnaz knows this as she cups the eggshells in her hand, piece by piece, to throw them in the trash, drops the frying pan in the sink, and returns the omelet ingredients to their respective homes. She knows it but her body refuses to move any faster. She doesn't tell Shirin to hurry up either. The two of them are defying time this morning, ignoring the inevitable duties that unfurl with its passage: the drive to school, the sad good-bye, the unending daylight hours, the empty dusk, the goodnight kiss, and the knowledge that another day will come and pass like this, without Isaac.

They make it to school, some fifteen minutes late, and as she drives to the antiques shop to pick up the miniature,

Farnaz thinks of the punishment Shirin will no doubt receive
for being late—a sermon about responsibility in front of the
rest of the class, or extra homework for one week—small
humiliations accumulating in her young life. Why then had
she not urged herself and her daughter to move faster, leave
earlier? She doesn't know why. All she knows is that she is
tired. And what's another humiliation, be it for herself or for
her daughter, when there are already so many?

The art dealer, Shahriar Beheshti, with his silver mus-
tache and wool cardigan, greets her warmly. "I was fond of
Javad," he says. "He was a good friend. I was once very ill
and he came to the hospital every day to see me, with pots
of soup and rice and kebab. I'll never forget that. He was
strange, that way. I would trust him with my life but not
with a dollar!"

"Yes, I know what you mean." Farnaz laughs.

"Chances are, Amin-khanoum, you'll never see your ten
thousand."

"I know that, too. And believe me, it wouldn't be the
first time . . . May I take a look around? You have such
beautiful things."

"Please!"

She surveys the shop—the pregnant belly of a sitar leaning against the round metallic face of a medieval shield, carpets and kilims hung along the walls, the footprints of their
previous owners, now dead and buried, imprinted in their
memory. There are French china sets, and Indian silk pillows. Silver tables engraved with figures of Cyrus or Darius
stand in one corner, while in the other, in a glass-enclosed

shelf, are Achaemenian jewels—a gold pendant shaped like a lion, an armlet with griffins—prized relics of an age long gone but to which people cling like proud but destitute heirs to a dead tycoon.

"What riches!" she says. "How do you sleep at night, knowing all this is in your shop?"

"I don't. I leave late at night and come in early in the morning, praying in the interim that my metal gates are doing what they were installed to do. I am a slave to my relics, you see? Plus I worry that the government will come one day and confiscate everything. And I would have to let them take it all."

"This one is incredible. How old is it?" She points at a gourd-shaped jug, verses from the Koran snaking around its neck.

"That dates to the period immediately preceding the Mongol invasion. Sometime between 1200 and 1215."

She considers the sapphire stripes along the white ceramic, the cracks of centuries running like spider veins through the jug's arm. "My husband has a Mongol sword with a gold-leafed handle; it's one of his favorite pieces."

"How is your husband? Javad had told me he was in prison."

"I've had no word from him."

"*Inshallah*—God willing, he will come out safe and sound."

"*Inshallah*. Which brings me to the reason for my visit. Javad had said that you would hold a miniature aside for me, in case the government asks me what I bought with the money. You know, they've already come to search our house once. I don't know how much they are monitoring my activities."

"Yes, that Javad! He is distributing my antiques like halvah! Let me get it for you." He disappears in the back of the shop, where dust particles float in the watery light of late morning. She watches their dance, their random ascent in space, imagines their indifferent landing on the objects below.

He emerges from behind the curtain with a large sheet that he slides on the counter. It is a miniature painting of a palace, one prince slaying another before the eyes of many viziers and courtiers, the scene drenched in sparkling reds, blues, and greens, with gold woven throughout.

"Is it from a book?"

"Yes. It's a leaf from the Tahmasbi *Shahnameh*, Ferdowsi's *Book of Kings*. You know, so many versions of the book have appeared since the tenth century, when Ferdowsi wrote it. This one was compiled in the sixteenth century for the shah Tahmasb. The book originally had more than two hundred and fifty miniatures, all painted by the best artists of the era—Sultan Muhammad, Mirza Ali, Abdolsamad, and the like."

"My son used to perform scenes from the *Shahnameh* for his school play," she says, remembering Parviz practicing his lines, sometimes even answering her in couplets to make her laugh.

"Now schools don't teach the *Shahnameh* anymore. But we should all continue to read it, so we can understand how great our nation once was."

Farnaz looks around the shop. A woman is examining a china set, glancing in their direction every few seconds.

"Be careful," Farnaz whispers. "You never know who's listening."

"Yes, I should be more careful," he says in a low voice. "But I am so tired, Amin-khanoum. Sometimes I just want to scream."

Farnaz nods. She is all too familiar with this illicit rage threatening to unleash itself at the most inappropriate times. "Tell me more about the miniature," she says. "Why was this page torn out?"

"That's the sad part of the story. In 1962 an American collector bought it, and he had the audacity to rip pages out of the book and sell them individually. He sold some to a museum in New York, others to private collectors."

She looks at the orphaned leaf, its counterparts spread around the globe, each adopted by one museum or another, or locked in the cabinet of a European or American collector who picks it up once in a while and looks at it in his dim study, his acquisition filling him with pride not unlike that of a nineteenth-century colonialist in search of a piece of the Orient. "Do you think there is any chance that all the pages will be regrouped one day?"

"No. Many were damaged while in the American's care. As for the rest? What can I say? I suppose anything is possible."

The painting—the thin, precise lines, the red and gold of a courtesan's robe, the indigo mosaic of the floor, where the slain king sits, his sword and shield by his side—

becomes for her the embodiment of loss, and she is pleased to have it, if only for a short time. She will place it in her armoire, between the folded shirts and Isaac's ties, and all the things that used to be.

"You are taken with it," the art dealer says.

"Yes. Very much so."

He walks to the back, pours a glass of tea. Farnaz notices that the other woman has left the shop.

"Some tea, Amin-khanoum?"

"No, thank you. I should get going."

"All right. Just promise me you'll bring back the painting before you leave the country," he says. "Because I know that you, too, will one day leave."

"Of course I'll bring it back! But why do you think I will leave?"

"You could call it sixth sense. I call it statistics."

"You may be right. In any case, thank you. You are very generous for allowing me to keep it."

He stands in the back, the sun on his face, the dust particles floating about him. "No. I am not generous," he says. "I am tired. One less object in the shop is one less worry for me. And I can sense that you will take good care of it."

"I will."

WHEN SHE ARRIVES home Isaac's mother is there, waiting for her. "Afshin-khanoum, how are you? Is everything all right?"

"What shall I say, my Farnaz? Hakim is not well. The doctors say he has only a few months to live." She wipes her eyes with a wrinkled tissue.

"His kidneys?"

"Yes. He is so sick, you wouldn't believe your eyes if you saw him. He is all yellow, and his legs are as swollen as tires." She looks out, shaking her head. "I don't know if I can stand it—to lose both my husband and my son."

"Isaac is not lost," Farnaz says, without quite believing it.

The old woman nods and wipes her eyes.

"This must be so difficult for you, Afshin-khanoum. I wish I could be more helpful to you. But I've been so preoccupied . . ."

"I know, *aziz*! I expect nothing more from you. It's my own daughter I'm upset with. When I called her to tell her about her father, she told me she couldn't talk because she was in the middle of some mess about a bag. A bag, Farnaz! That's what's preoccupying her. Apparently she had given several thousand dollars to some woman who was traveling to Paris so she would buy her a new bag. Well, the woman took the cash and never sent the bag . . ."

Habibeh brings out a tray of tea and pastries. "Shall I pick up Shirin from school today, khanoum?"

"Yes, Habibeh, would you?" Knowing that Habibeh was not the one to have stolen the ring has restored some of her faith in their relationship. She feels guilty, also, for having suspected her in the first place. Since their argument, they have addressed one another with the caution of a bare foot avoiding shards of glass. They have reached a cold truce, each one offering the other a silent apology, but not much more.

The old woman goes on. "I said to Shahla, 'What do you need a new designer bag for? So you can carry it with your Islamic uniform? How can you even think of bags when your father is so sick and your brother is in prison?' You know what she said to me, Farnaz-jan? She said, 'Am I supposed to sit around and mope all day? There is nothing I can do about any of it, is there? Shall I pretend I'm dead, like the rest of you?' This is what she said to me, my own daughter." She strokes the sofa, along the scars. "Look at me, complaining to you, when you have so much trouble yourself. Even your sofas have been torn up. I'm sorry. But I have no one to talk to. Sometimes entire days, even weeks go by before I realize I haven't said a word to anyone."

"Don't be sorry. I'm glad you came to see me."

"I wasted my life, Farnaz-jan. I have a husband who never loved me but whom I'll miss anyway because he's all I've ever known. I have a swindling son and an egotistical daughter. My only redemption is having brought Isaac into this world. And now even he has been taken from me . . ." She looks out the window again, her eyes narrow under the weight of her lids. She slowly dozes off, her head tilted back, her mouth hanging open, as though she were gasping for air.

In the quiet of the afternoon Farnaz watches Isaac's mother and considers the possibility of Baba-Hakim's death. To bury him without Isaac seems unthinkable. She feels sorrow, not for the old man but for Isaac, and she tells herself that should the time come, she will arrange the burial, and pay for it, and pray with the rabbi after the father's passing—as Isaac would.

When Shirin and Habibeh arrive the old woman's face lights up. "Come here, Shirin-jan, I haven't seen you in so long!" Shirin walks over and lets herself be kissed and coddled.

"She is becoming so pretty!" the old woman says, examining Shirin's face. "There is so much of Isaac in this child." She looks again, straight into the child's eyes. "Yes! It's the eyes. They have that look that Isaac had as a boy. How he upset me, with that look. I never knew what he wanted, only that whatever it was, I wasn't giving it to him."

THIRTY-ONE

Everytime she looks at her reflection in the oval mirror, Shirin sees another reflection behind it—her father's raincoat hanging on the coatrack by the entrance. The coat has been there all winter, and she wonders if Habibeh and her mother also see it each time they check themselves in the mirror on their way out of the house. The other hooks have remained empty; no one dares, it seems, to hang anything next to that limp coat.

She tucks the loose strands of hair under her scarf. She feels ugly in her scarf and uniform. Why should a person be forced to go out into the world covered up in dark colors—gray, navy, black—as if prepared for eventual mourning? We all know what the end is, the clothes were saying. So why pretend?

. . .

A FEW CHILDREN are playing soccer on the other side of the courtyard, banging the ball into a metal door every few minutes.

"I knew this would happen," Leila says. "Since I questioned them about the files they won't let me play." She watches the game for some time. After a while she says, "I think it was you."

"What?"

"I think *you* took the files. Did you? Please tell me the truth." She looks at Shirin with pleading eyes. "This morning my father told us that because of the missing files he has been expelled from the Revolutionary Guards. He was so angry that he asked me for a list of all my friends. He's going to investigate himself."

My time is up, Shirin thinks. In the hands of Leila's father there will be a quick conclusion. She feels dizzy and out of breath. Her hand in her pocket searches for something to hold on to. She grabs the three cookies wrapped in a tissue and crushes them inside the pocket.

"Don't worry," Leila says. "I left your name off the list."

Shirin looks down, at her feet nailed to the ground. "Thank you," she says without looking up.

Leila gets up, wipes the dust off her uniform. "I hope I did the right thing. But you were my only real friend. No one came to my house as often as you did. No one had tea and cheese with me, no one offered to carry my mom's fruit crates to the basement. I wouldn't want anything bad to happen to you." Walking away, she says, "We probably shouldn't spend so much time together anymore." She heads to the opposite side of the courtyard, where she stands and watches the soccer game, alone.

I left your name off the list. Shirin plays with the cookies in her pocket, the crumbs—casualties of another bad day—sticking to her hand. She wonders if Leila's father will have to go back to the morgue and stand, as he did before, on the receiving end of the garbage chute.

In the infirmary she drinks Soheila-khanoum's peppermint tea and looks out onto the courtyard, now deserted. Two flies are gliding on the window, happy, she imagines, to find themselves on the warm side of the glass. When she was younger, she would trap flies inside transparent plastic bags and watch them as they suffocated slowly—over three or four days. Each day she would examine their decline like a scientist, taking note of their diminished movement, their lethargy—their final surrender. Was she now being punished for her brutality? She watches Soheila-khanoum putting away vials of medications in a cabinet and wonders how many small cruelties must accumulate over the years to earn a person a dead daughter. Or a dead father.

THIRTY-TWO

His sister answers the phone. "Parviz!" she says.

He unclenches his shoulders as he hears her voice. He has not called home in a while, not only because calls are monitored, but also because of his hope, however faint, that his parents would eventually call him with good news. They hadn't. "How is everything?" he yells over the crackling connection.

"Baba still hasn't returned from his trip. We've had no word."

A faint conversation overlays their own. "But who can understand?" a woman is saying to another. "*Zendeghi hezar charkh dare*—Life has a thousand wheels."

"And the two of you?" Parviz says, wondering if others can hear him. "Are you well?"

"Yes," she says. "We are fine."

He asks her about school, Habibeh, her life, and she says everything is going well. At some point he notices that the conversing women have vanished; whether they hung up or the line was simply diverted, he cannot tell. Before hanging up Shirin sends him a kiss, which makes him hold on to the receiver, the dial tone as flat as the afternoon stretched out before him. He is not scheduled to work today but almost wishes he was. What to do with so many empty hours?

"THE PEACE LILY is easy to care for," Mr. Broukhim is telling a young woman as Parviz walks in. "It thrives in most environments and you don't need to do much for it." The woman rubs the plant's leaves then gingerly pokes the soil. "I don't know," she says. "Every plant I've ever owned has died on me. It's a curse." The old man laughs. "This one," he says, "does not need that much water or light. Like a lover who's easy to please, it makes few demands and brings much pleasure." The woman looks at him with stern eyes. "Mr. Broukhim," she says. "You forget where you are."

"That was close!" Parviz says when she is gone. "I thought she was going to call the cops, or worse, the Rebbe!"

"These pious women are testy, aren't they? No sense of humor. Everything is an insult."

"All the more reason to be careful!"

"Ah, Parviz-jan, if you knew how tired I am of being careful . . . Well, what can I do for you?"

"Is Rachel here?"

"No, she is off today. She switched her days. You're not starting to like this girl, are you?"

"Me? No, no, of course not. She's a friend."

"Good. That's the last thing you need. A religious girl and her entire clan! Because they come as a package, these religious types, Parviz-jan. You know that, right?"

Her personal items—a blue scarf, some hair clips, a telephone book—scattered behind the counter, suggest an intimacy that Parviz knows he will never experience with her. "Yes, I know," he says.

"I am a bitter man, Parviz-jan, so maybe you shouldn't pay attention to me. I have lost so much. My wife not only left me, but robbed me as well. My profession deserted me. I was once one of the best cardiologists in Tehran. I studied in Paris and Geneva. But here they tell me my license is no good. They tell me I have to start all over again—study, take tests—like an eighteen-year-old. I have no energy for all that! In this country, I feel like a ghost. Maybe it's because I am old already. I am at that point in my life where the days ahead of me are fewer than those behind. I envy you, Parviz." He sighs. "I envy your youth." He walks away to greet a customer who asks him for yellow chrysanthemums.

Outside Parviz wonders how he could be anyone's object of envy. His youth is doing little for him, except robbing him of the right to suffer. Pain, he has come to realize, is the domain of the elders, their suffering always more noble and more justified than that of a boy like him, who is expected to find thrills in his new environment and to lock his short past in the cellar, only to retrieve it, years later, like a bottle of wine, and share it in brief sips with dinner guests.

*   *   *

HE WALKS TOWARD the Brooklyn Bridge and then across, continues walking through the city, the skyscrapers casting their long shadows on sidewalks and depriving the pedestrians below of the final minutes of sunlight. New York is a masculine city, he thinks, vertical and with rough edges, with none of the curves of a Paris subway entrance, for example, or the enameled dome of an Isfahan mosque. New York is all steel and glass, economic and functional. It is a city where circles are rare. In his mind he traces halos, rings, wheels of fortune, clocks—all instruments of confinement on the one hand, and hope on the other. Walking along the grid of Manhattan, its numbered streets and parallel avenues, he tells himself that what this city is missing is more roundness. And the people who live here—stacked not only side by side but also on top of one another, always running out of space, time, and breath, paying large sums for slivers of air and settling down in the sky with their cats and dogs—reach upward, continually, without ever returning to themselves.

He walks through the evening, stops at a diner for coffee and eggs, and watches the other patrons, whose number dwindles as the hours progress—families becoming couples and shrinking into loners, who walk in, disheveled, with their newspapers and books, ordering a cheeseburger and fries and pretending that this is exactly how they wish to spend yet another evening.

Around three in the morning, on his way back to the

bridge, he passes through the Fulton Fish Market, watches the delivery vans, the stacked crates, and the fishmongers, their faces covered with soot, warming their hands over small fires that burn inside trash cans, haggling with their customers. The cobblestone streets, bloodstained and slippery, smell of seaports—a familiar smell—reminding him of the port city of Ramsar by the Caspian, not far from his family's beach house. That he is awake at this hour and able to smell the sea pleases him, and he tells himself that to understand the world, and even find in it an occasional reprieve, a person must always alternate his hours of sleep, his road to work, the places he visits, the foods he eats, and even, perhaps, the people he loves.

THIRTY-THREE

A few early risers are at the teahouse, sipping and smoking, some shielding their eyes with sunglasses to cover up the damage of a sleepless night. Farnaz sips her tea, waiting for Keyvan to speak. But he doesn't. He looks tired and thin. He could use a pair of shades, like the others.

"What's on your mind, Keyvan?" she says. "You sounded terrible on the phone."

He throws two sugar cubes on the table like dice, then picks them up again. "Shahla and I are leaving," he says finally.

"What? First Javad, now you . . ."

"Two days ago Shahla was attacked. She was returning from the hairdresser's and she had put on her headscarf very loosely—you know, she didn't want to ruin her hairdo. Some men jeered at her then threw some kind of liquid on her face."

"I can't believe what I'm hearing. Was it acid?"

"I don't know. When she came home her skin was all red. I washed her face with water for a long time, but it didn't help. Now the burning has gotten better, but her skin has patches of red that don't go away. She has tried all sorts of remedies. All day I see her peeling cucumbers, preparing bowls of milk and rose water, dipping sponges in her mixes and massaging her face, but nothing seems to help. And she refuses to see the doctor. I brought him to the house but she locked herself in the bathroom. He stood at the door for two hours, the poor man, trying to coax her to come out. She wouldn't. She was too embarrassed. 'The doctor has known me for so long,' she said to me afterward. 'How can I show him this face?'"

"It might heal still. It may just be irritated."

"Yes. That's what I tell her. But that face. It's all she has. At least that's what she thinks. 'I'm disgusting,' she says to me. 'So go. Find yourself another woman.'" He rubs his eyes with his palms, gently, as if shielding them from light. "After all these years, she still doesn't believe that I actually love her."

The server picks up the empty glasses and replaces them with fresh ones.

"Hajj-Ali," a young man drawls. "You got eggs today? This tea is so good it deserves a sunny-side up."

"Eggs?" The server laughs. "We haven't received eggs in over a month. But maybe in your haze of hashish you've missed the war, Kazem-agha."

A few men chuckle. The lax attitude of the teahouse surprises Farnaz. These men must know one another. Each morning they must force themselves out of bed, their only comfort the prospect of meeting other vagrants. To be sitting here at this hour among them disturbs her. What happened to her morning routine, to her family at the breakfast table, to the sunny-side up in her pan and the milk boiling on her stove?

"I've decided we have to get out of here," Keyvan says. "This country is no good anymore."

"Where will you go? And what about your house? And your belongings?"

"I'm tired, Farnaz. I don't care about the house. Besides, I'm sure they'll come after me, too. Why wouldn't they? They already got Isaac and they're after Javad. With my father's connections to the shah, I'm an even better target."

And what about me, and Isaac? she wants to ask.

"We'll be going to Geneva, where my parents are. There are good doctors there. They may be able to help Shahla."

Yes, Keyvan. Go to Switzerland and fix Shahla's face. And why not? I would do the same if I could. "Good luck," she says. "Give Shahla my best. When will you go?"

"In two weeks. It's all arranged. Friends of mine who escaped a few months ago referred me to a couple of men with a good reputation. We'll be smuggled out through Turkey. Let me give you their information, Farnaz-jan. No doubt you will need it, too, hopefully with Isaac." He jots down a name and telephone number on a piece of paper and hands it to her.

In the back of the teahouse, Hajj-Ali breaks down a sugar cone, the sound of his hammer echoing in the room. The men sipping their tea are quiet for the most part. An advertisement on the radio announces a shoe sale downtown.

"Look at this place," Keyvan says after a long silence. "Half of them are junkies."

"It's been getting worse lately, hasn't it?" she says. "There are more of them now."

They leave some change on the table and walk out. It's a cold day, misty and humid. They stand outside, facing each other, neither of them willing to be the first to walk away.

"Did you bring an umbrella?" he asks. "It may rain." He looks like he may cry.

"Yes, it's in here," she says, pointing to her purse. "Well, good-bye, Keyvan-jan. *Inshallah* we will see each other again soon." She hugs him and walks away. For some time, she senses his eyes on her back, knows that he is watching her as she disappears in the rush-hour clamor of the boulevard.

Walking past the shopkeepers standing in their doorways and killing the morning in gossipy clusters, she remembers Shahla and Keyvan's wedding, that lavish affair at the villa of Keyvan's parents. In her white silk dress Shahla floated among the guests, picking up a sugar-coated almond here and a nougat there, strands of pearls woven into her hair, her dress rippling around her. Her round face, which tended to bloat during her depressive episodes that she referred to as "passing clouds," looked sculpted and radiant, so she walked with her head held high and her back straight, her clavicles forming perfect dashes below her elegant neck, as if to say, Take note of this lovely face. Guests flocked into the garden along the gravel path, greeted the newlyweds, found their seats by the wooden trellises on the side of the house, drank arrack and ate caviar, snapped their fingers to the *santour* and *tombak*, and broke into song. That a palace of the shah and his queen lay a few miles above this villa in the Niavaran hills cast a gilded spell on the evening, so that the guests, pleased with the party for its extravagance and with themselves for being part of it, stayed on until light broke out. And throughout it, Shahla, more preoccupied with the china pattern than with her groom, laughed and danced, pleased to put an end to her quest. "*Noone khaharet too roghane*—Your sister's bread has been dipped in oil," Farnaz whispered to Isaac, to which he said, "Yes, I believe her life's work is finished."

Thinking now of Shahla's disfigured face Farnaz feels a deep pain, not just for Shahla but for the loss of what she had come to represent—shameless extravagance, which others both enjoyed and ridiculed, much as they did their government and their king.

"Amin-khanoum!" a man calls.

She sees the cobbler standing by his shop and smoking a cigarette. "Ali-agha, how are you?"

"Fine, thank God. And you, khanoum? We haven't seen you in a while."

"Yes, well . . ."

"You know, I have a pair of shoes here for your husband. They've been ready since September. He never picked them up. He forgot?"

The cobbler's ignorance of her misfortune is delicious to her. For a while she says nothing, allowing herself to linger in his world, where Isaac has not disappeared but has simply *forgotten* his shoes. "He has been busy," she says, finally. "Let me pick them up while I'm here."

She follows him inside the shop, where rows of shoes hang from their heels on metal rods along the walls. She examines the empty shoes, forlorn under the sheen of their polish, like children in an orphanage dressed up for prospective parents. She spots Isaac's among the others, the shape of his feet still imprinted in the leather's memory. "There," she says, pointing to the familiar pair.

"Eagle eyes," Ali-agha says, reaching for the pair with a pole. He places them on the counter for her approval and she runs her fingers over the leather, flipping them over to inspect the soles.

"Very nice, Ali-agha. Thank you."

He slides them into a bag and hands them to her, and she takes them, like a widow leaving a morgue. She walks home with the bag looped around her wrist, the shoes banging against her thigh, as if kicking her for interrupting their repose.

THIRTY-FOUR

He sees his world in black and white: Filthy snow, a hollow sky, the gray cement of the walls—water stains, like giant ink spills, eating into them—and his own skin, an ashy patina enveloping his body. Even the wounds on his feet, hardened and crusted, have lost their red. He has come to think of color as something fantastic that exists only in his mind—the red of a tomato sliced and salted at the lunch table, the deep blue of a lapis lazuli on Farnaz's finger, the honey hue of his daughter's hair in the sun. As a young man he shunned color, his camera, filled with black-and-white film, swinging around his neck like a dog tag. In the first years of his marriage, he photographed Farnaz everywhere, in parks, in teahouses, in the living room—her young, bare legs on the coffee table, looking into his viewfinder with the exasperated air of a much-too-photographed actress, but pleased, nonetheless, with the attention bestowed on her. The children, too, he photographed in black and white. He preferred the mystery of gray scale to the nakedness of color, believed it to be more substantial, more archival—better suited for memory. Later, as the years passed, he craved color. He switched films and compared grains, and his prints, unlike his life, became more and more saturated, filled, like a canvas, with splashes of longing.

The cell is cold. He walks away from the window and crouches on the floor, wrapping himself with the piece of burlap meant to serve as a blanket. He tries to remove the insects trapped inside, but they are stubborn and stick to the weave. He lets them be. On cloudy days like this he cannot tell the time of day; he believes it must be afternoon, but can a single afternoon be so long?

What was it that the old fortune-teller in Seville had said to him? At Farnaz's insistence he had sat before her deck of cards, his future spread out on the table in the form of knights and castles. "A five of cups," she said in her broken English, then, "*Ay, dios mio, la tarjeta de la muerte también, el número trece*—the death card, señor." The cards—one depicting a stooped man draped in black, the other a skeletal figure in medieval armor on a white horse, terrified him. There were other cards, of magicians and chariots and priestesses, but they seemed inconsequential in the face of those two. He sat still, losing his breath in the small room, the hot Andalusian night weighing down the red velvet curtains and seeping through the arabesques of the railing of the mezzanine, where, upon entering, he had seen a little albino girl surveying the customers below. Even she, he thought, was now privy to his black future.

"Don't worry, señor," the old woman said with garlicky breath. "La tarjeta de muerte does not mean actual death. It is the end of something and the beginning of something new." Behind her, smoke from a lemongrass incense rose all the way up to the mezzanine and the albino girl, who looked at him with her white eyelashes and sneered. "And the grieving man?" the old woman continued. "Yes, he, too, represents the loss of something. But you see his bent figure looking at the empty cup before him? Look carefully and you will see that there are two full golden cups behind him. A door is closing on you, my dear sir. That is all."

Is that all? Remember, my dear Farnaz, how sorry you had been that evening, your face pale even as you laughed and shrugged, saying to me, like a mother to a child, "Such rubbish! These so-called clairvoyants like to scare people. Forget it." But I didn't forget it, and neither did you. Later as we stood in a restaurant by the tapas bar, drowning the oracle of that August night in sangria, you were quiet, and maybe even sad, a little. After all, had you not forced me into the fortune-teller's shop to get back at me for what I had forced you to endure all afternoon? "No, no, I cannot watch animals murdered in this way," you had said all along, but I went ahead and got the tickets anyway, didn't I? As we sat in the stadium, the sun hot and still above us, the matador in his beaded suit parading below and the big, doomed animals pierced with one, two, three, four spears—each spear drawing a louder cheer from the crowd—I looked at you and saw the pain in your face, and still I thought, She'll get over it. Who comes to Seville without watching a good bullfight? So you had gotten even with me, my Farnaz, and you were sorry. So was I.

He opens the Koran that Hossein has brought him, practicing his high school Arabic on a random verse. *Qul aaoothu birabbi alfalaqi, Min sharri ma khalaqa*—"Say, I seek refuge in the Lord of the dawn, From the evil of what He has created." He reads the verse out loud, the sound of his frail, raspy voice foreign to him, but calming him nonetheless. In his middle years he had let go the habit of reading out loud. Rather, he listened. At night he fell asleep to the crackle of the BBC on his shortwave radio, at dawn he awoke to the sound of the morning broadcast and the national anthem. When the children were younger, he listened to his wife reading to them, her fables overtaking his newspaper. Why had he not also read to the children, he who as a young man had hoped to become a storyteller? Why had he come to regard such activities as necessary for the children but superfluous for him—better suited for Farnaz who, as a woman, could afford to be superfluous? Sitting behind his desk at the office, a verse from a favorite poem would sometimes come to him—"I will arise and go now, and go to Innisfree / And a small cabin build there, of clay and wattles made," or "Can drunkenness be linked to piety and good repute? / Where is the preacher's holy monody, where is the lute?" He would welcome these unannounced visits, allow the verse to tickle him like the memory of an adolescent crush, then shoo it away from his mind with the documents before him, waiting to be signed.

Looking out, he sees the snow falling again. He lies

down on his mattress and looks at the flakes caressing the air like gossamer. The prison is calm tonight—no rattle of locks, no footsteps in the courtyard, no sound of a little boy running up and down the stairs above his cell. Even the ants, busy with the sugar cubes he has left for them, seem exact and orderly, as though parading to a hushed symphony they alone can hear. He falls asleep, so comforted by the order of things, that when the familiar rattle approaches his door he is convinced that the sound is rising from his own head, nothing more.

"Brother Amin! Get up."

He opens his eyes and finds three guards before him.

"Follow us," one says. The other two stand above him, each one sliding a hand under his arms and lifting him to his feet.

He tries to speak but his voice won't come. "Where?" he manages to say. "Where? Where?" They drag his body out of the cell and through the dark corridor, lit only by the flashlight of the leading guard. The wounds of his bare feet scraping the concrete floor send currents of pain through his body. He feels a terrible tightness in his chest, his heart contracting like a fist. "Please," he says. "I am not well."

"That does not matter much now," the lead guard says. He unlocks one metal door, then another, and soon Isaac finds himself in the open air, fresh snow falling on his face, a cold wind blowing through the holes of his burlap blanket. The ice on the ground numbs the sores on his feet. It becomes clear to him that his time has run out. He waits for his life to flash before him, but nothing comes, except for a deep, black desire to weep. Even weeping does not come easily.

Dragged to the end of the courtyard, he is told to face the wall and lift both arms in the air. He lifts his tired arms up slowly, and it is at this point that they come, half images of his life blending into one another and passing through him so quickly that he cannot grasp them; only the pain of their loss remains.

"Allah-o-Akbar!" a guard shouts. Isaac hears the sound of boots crushing snow, the pull of a trigger, then the firing of a bullet which bounces against the wall and falls on the snow, followed by another, then another. He stands still, his arms in the air, urine streaming down his leg, afraid to move to the right or left. "That's enough!" a guard yells. When the last bullet bounces off the wall he listens, disbelieving, to the silence around him. "Let this vermin sit in his own shit and recognize what he is up against." He falls on the snow, facing the wall, afraid to face anything but this wall.

Lying on the ice, he thinks of the warm mattress in his cell. Another memorized verse comes to him—"No whiteness lost is so white as the memory of whiteness."

THIRTY-FIVE

Walking in the rain, Shirin watches people's expressions hardening, the women tightening the knots of their headscarves, the men pulling up their coat collars to their ears, the city retreating into itself, clenching its jaw. The taxis, bright orange under the gleam of streetlamps, stop on corners and collect passengers. At a newsstand she reads the headline, "Hundreds of Martyrs Killed in the Shatt-al-Arab."

In school that morning they had discussed the war, the teacher beginning the class by hanging posters of soldiers, some of them children, on the walls. "Which one of you would volunteer?" she had asked, and two girls, out of forty, had cried, "I would! I would!" Leila had raised her hand also, with less certainty than the other two, and said, "Yes. I think I would." When the bell rang the teacher announced that those who had volunteered to go to war—even though the question had been hypothetical—would be excused from homework.

"You would really volunteer?" Shirin had said to Leila after class. She knew that they were not supposed to talk, but the idea of Leila going to war terrified her.

"Yes. If my mother would let me. My father has already told me that he would not refuse. But my mother, she is stubborn."

"My mother says they're using the children to clear the mines."

"So what? Someone has to clear the mines. And it's better to save the grown-ups for the real fighting. You know, they give you your own key when you volunteer."

"A key?"

"A key to paradise. Because if you are killed in combat you are a martyr and you automatically go to paradise."

"If you go to paradise, wouldn't God open the door for you? Why would you need a key?"

"I don't know!" Leila had said, annoyed. "You and I really should not be talking."

WALKING NOW AMONG the chadors and umbrellas, she thinks of the city as something black and permeable, filled with holes through which people fall and disappear. "Tehran, the black city," she repeats to herself. She thinks of the cities she has known and assigns a color to each. Isfahan, the blue city, Paris, the red city, Jerusalem, the ivory city, Venice, the gold city, Jaipur, the pink city. In Jaipur her father had held her hand as they walked past the rose-colored buildings, and he had told her how they had all been painted pink in the nineteenth century for the visit of a British monarch—she cannot remember which one. She had liked the idea of a city changing its color for someone's visit the way people change clothes for a party. In foreign places he seemed to her a different man, lighthearted and playful. At their hotel, once the palace of a maharaja, he told her that the ghost of the Indian prince still roamed the hallways at night, and she let herself be convinced. In the car on the way to the Taj Mahal, he sang along with the radio, even though he did not speak a word of Hindi; when he was at a loss for made-up words, he simulated the sound of a tabla, tapping on the wheel, and she laughed, sitting in the sunlit backseat, watching the colorful saris go by, and the occasional snake charmer wooing his reptile out of its basket. She loved the fact that snake charmers really existed.

"Shirin-jan, what are you doing on the street all alone?" A neighbor stops her.

"I'm just going to buy bread down the street."

"Any word from your father?" she asks.

"No."

"You poor girl," the woman says, straightening her scarf. "Say hello to your mother."

No one opens the door when she arrives home. She looks under the doormat to see if a key has been left for her. It hasn't. She stands by the gate and peeks in at the garden—the accumulated snow, stained yellow with the dog's urine, and the jagged teeth of icicles hanging from the swimming pool's edge. That pool was once clear and blue, and she remembers swimming in it, in the shallow end, while Parviz and his friends dove from the terrace into the water, trying to impress the beautiful Yassi who lounged in her white bikini on a pool chair, her sunglasses crowning her head, her brown legs stretched out long in front of her. Afterward, when they had showered and dressed, they would gather around the kitchen table smelling of soap and chlorine, and eat cherries picked that morning from the garden, just washed and dripping in the sieve. She remembers that lightness that comes after hours of swimming, and the sweetness of the summer's first cherry, eaten under the hum of air conditioners.

The dog runs to her and sticks her muzzle through the gate. Then, getting up on her hind legs and stretching out her large, sculpted body, Suzie reaches for the latch and presses until the lock comes undone. She stands back, watching Shirin enter, wagging her tail.

THIRTY-SIX

What jars him out of sleep is not the sound of the bullet itself, but the thump of the body falling to the ground a second later. Afterward there is always silence. He wonders what they do with the bodies. Most likely they leave them on the ground and pick them up the next morning, like dishes left over after a dinner party.

He lies awake and waits for morning, when the brownish hot water and piece of bread brought to him will remind him that he is still alive. Each time he drifts back into sleep the leaking faucet interrupts him, the drops loud and defiant, so he wakes up and lies still, watching the objects around him—the sink, his shoes, which he has not worn since the lashings, the Koran, still open to the page he last read—all of which slowly merge with the objects of the many rooms he has slept in throughout his life. Drifting in and out of sleep he sees the muslin curtains of his room in Shiraz where he spent so many summers reading and writing, the porcelain pitcher on the night table in the French countryside, the mints left like anonymous letters on his pillow in Geneva, the jade Buddha in Tokyo, the dragon painted on the ceiling in Hong Kong, his bed at home, in which he fell asleep wrapped in his comforter, the hair on his arm brushed by his wife's breath, and the hemp sheets of his boyhood home, rough against his skin, not unlike the burlap blanket covering him now.

He wonders if something of him remains in those rooms, if a curtain pulled open so many years ago to reveal a sunny provincial day still holds his fingerprints in its folds, as if to say, Isaac Amin was here. He understands now the scribbles on monuments and sidewalks, even in toilet stalls—a name and a date inscribed for future visitors, a sorry attempt to communicate with people of another era, to say to them, I once was. He remembers how on a summer stroll along the promontory of a southwestern French town, once a Victorian resort, he had seen such an engraving—*Jacques 1896*—and the sadness he had felt on seeing it. He saw this Jacques with his walking stick and tailcoat, breathing in the cool Atlantic wind, discussing with friends topics of his day—Debussy's *Prelude to the Afternoon of a Faun*, or the Dreyfus Affair—before returning to his hotel for afternoon tea. And as he stood in the sun, looking at the autographed rock, Isaac felt jealous suddenly of those who would stroll on the same promenade centuries after him.

When the door opens, it is still dark. He sits up on the mattress. *Has the time come?* Two guards walk in. "Brother, follow us," one says. He is led down the stairs to the same room where he last saw his interrogator. Mohsen sits behind the same desk, tapping his nine fingers on the table. The stump of the tenth moves up and down. "Brother, Brother," Mohsen says. "We've seen so much of each other. Surely you must be getting tired of me, as I am getting tired of you." He points to the chair facing him. "Sit."

His file has swollen, scores of papers jutting from it.

"What can you say in your defense?"

"I say what I said before. That I am innocent. But I will also say this: that I followed the wrong path in life. I pursued material wealth, which in the end brought me nothing."

"Nothing? Look at your villas, and your carpets, and your paintings, and all the other things you've amassed. You call that nothing? And the trips you took, and the cars you drove. I could go on and on." He shuts the file and looks up. "Me, I have nothing. I live in one room with my wife and my son. We have one kilim under our feet and we roll out our mattresses at night to sleep. We have no oven, but a portable gas stove. For two years my son wore the same shoes because I couldn't buy him a new pair. In the end I had to cut the front, so his feet could grow."

"Yes, but look at me now, and look at you. I sit here before you, my fate in your hands. My daughter, with her closet full of shoes, has no idea where her father is. Can the shoes help her? And can the cars save me? 'The power of Abū Lahab will perish, and he will perish. His wealth and his gains will not exempt him,'" he quotes from the Koran, reciting verses he has memorized.

Having spent long hours with the Koran—the only

book they had allowed him to read—he had memorized much of the text, and as he lay awake on his mattress one night, the verses buzzing in his head, it occurred to him that a display of his newfound learning may help him. Wouldn't reciting a few well-chosen verses demonstrate his wish to repent? It could, he also knew, backfire, making him look like a desperate opportunist trying to earn himself a few points. Playing and replaying in his mind his next interrogation—which he believed would be his last—he had come to the conclusion that with a man like Mohsen, one had to take risks.

Mohsen nods. "Well said, Brother!" he says. "I see that you have been using your time wisely." He looks down at his hand, at the space where his finger should have been. "I did the same thing when I was in prison. I read. Those were difficult years, but the Koran gave me hope." He places his elbows on the table and leans forward. "You know that I bring my boy here every day?" he asks.

"Yes. I hear a boy run up and down the stairs above my cell. Brother Hossein told me he is your son."

"I was not supposed to have any children. Not after what I went through. You know, Brother, I once sat in a chair very similar to the one you are in now. So now that the tables have turned, why should I have mercy on you?"

"Because I have nothing to do with the people who caused you pain."

"But you do! You looked the other way, and that's enough to make you an accomplice."

"Yes, you are right about that. I was blind, and I recognize that now. Please, Brother. If you say you once sat in my chair, then you must know my fear, and more than that, my dismay at never seeing my family again. You are a father, and I am sure you understand this."

"I not only know your fear, but I smell it. I am afraid I have gotten addicted to it." He gets up, his chair letting out a loud screech against the concrete floor. He paces the room several times. "You're a tough case," he says finally. "Your file is clean. We did not find any evidence of spying for the Zionists. And yet, the way you lived condemns you . . ."

"Brother, I can change my ways. And to prove my sincerity, perhaps I can sustain the cause of the revolution with a generous donation."

Mohsen stops pacing. "Yes? How generous, Brother Amin?"

"As generous as necessary."

"Brother Amin, I have received similar offers before. None were satisfactory. I need a more specific answer."

"My entire savings."

IN THE CELL a guard forces Isaac's feet into his shoes, the leather unable to expand enough to accommodate the swelling. He leaves the laces untied and taps him on the back. "Hurry, let's go."

The soles of his feet pleated like a fan at the bottom of the shoes, Isaac limps as fast as he can to keep up. In the hallway a masked guard rushes to him, and says, in a voice that he recognizes as Hossein's, "Brother Amin! Are you being released?"

"Let's go!" the other guard yells. He pulls a black handkerchief from his pocket and ties it around Isaac's eyes, then nudges his rifle into his lower back. "Move!"

He is taken up the stairs and through a metal gate, then dragged across the courtyard—the same path he traveled the night of Ramin's and Vartan's executions. Another gate rattles open and he is shoved inside a car. Seated by the window, he realizes that the handkerchief, hastily tied, has left him a sliver of vision, and looking down he sees his own deformed feet, then the black boots of the guard, next to him. Near his feet is a plastic bag filled with gold watches and jewelry.

They drive away in the early morning. Through the blindfold he can feel a bright light and he knows it will be a sunny day. A cool wind blows on his face from a crack in the window, and as the car makes its way down the mountain he sees patches of green peeking through snow, and the ridged trunks of trees firm in the ground. Lightness overtakes him. As the road disappears under the car's wheels he replays his conversation with Mohsen. Quoting from the Koran had been a good idea. It had shifted the tone of the interrogation, turning it into a conversation. "You're much smarter than I am, Amin-agha," Ramin had said. "Me, I'm a bad liar."

Am I smart then, Isaac wonders, or just a good liar? Maybe one is not possible without the other. Was Ramin a fool, or just fatally honest? And what about the contribution that I am about to make to this revolution? How will my money be used? To build more prisons, to buy more bullets? In buying back my own life, will I facilitate the death of others?

He senses the city approaching. Through the exhaust fumes of the morning rush hour he smells bread rising in coal ovens, raw meat just brought in from slaughterhouses, fish hauled overnight from port cities, boxes of produce unloaded on fruit stands. The nervous honks of cars excite him, and he sits back and listens to the sounds of feet on sidewalks, buses going by, shops opening, children on their way to school. He imagines his wife at the kitchen table, drinking her tea and reading the paper.

A man has a right to want to live.

"WHERE IS YOUR bank?" the driver asks.

"The bank is near my office. But we must first go to my home to pick up a piece of identification. I assume you know my address."

"Don't you have your driver's license?"

"My wallet was never returned to me, Brother."

When his blindfold is removed he sees his own street, unchanged. The guard seated next to him is biting his lips, his mouth contorting to the left and right as his teeth mutilate the thin layer of skin inside. Isaac feels a rush in his stomach as the car slowly drives up, the numbers on the plaques above the iron gates getting closer and closer to his.

Here is the blue paisley curtain of the Sabatis' kitchen, there is the red bicycle of the Ghorbanis' little girl; they kept it on the porch even though the girl had long ago been sent to relatives in London. He wonders if his own wife and daughter have already left for school. He wishes now that he had asked the guards for a few extra minutes to wash and groom himself; the thought did not occur to him at the prison.

As they approach his house he imagines it as he left it— his newspapers on the coffee table, the cool blue bedspread of his room, his green pajama pants hanging on the bedpost, his daughter's clogs in the living room, tripping someone. When they arrive the gate is open, so the car rolls in with ease, and parks behind Farnaz's car. She is home, he thinks, his heart lightening, like a boy brought to his mother at the end of a long, cruel day.

The dog howls, and as Isaac exits the car and walks to the house she runs to him, barking with both joy and violence. "Make it shut up!" the guard says, his rifle pointed at her. Isaac embraces her and she rests her muzzle on his shoulder, tickling his ear with her warm, wet breath. The door opens. In front of him, firm and familiar, are Farnaz's feet in her black pumps. She kneels down and helps him get up. "Isaac!" She says. "My God! It's really you."

He holds her hands. For the first time since his arrest he feels tears forming in his eyes. He fights them back, knowing that once they come, he won't be able to stop. Farnaz, already crying, brings his hand to her mouth and kisses it, right between two knuckles, the spot that, strangely, he too had kissed in prison.

"Save the hugs for later!" the guard says. "We're not done here."

Farnaz lets go and steps aside. Isaac enters the foyer, where the smell of laundry detergent and freshly brewed tea remind him of the life that he may yet live. He climbs the stairs with great pain, leaning on the banister and slowly pulling himself forward. The guard follows close behind and Farnaz, by Isaac's side, stares at his feet, holding back her questions.

In his study he finds that nothing is where he left it. Files and papers have disappeared. "My passport, Farnaz-jan, where is it?"

"The passports were confiscated," she says.

"I need some kind of identification for the bank."

Farnaz opens drawers and closes them, her hands unsteady. "I'll get you your birth certificate. But I'm not sure where it is."

"Brother," Isaac says to the guard. "I am sorry for delaying you. It must be here somewhere."

"I don't have all day," snaps the guard. He walks around the room, his rifle pointed upward, and examines the books on the shelves, the photographs, the sword collection on the wall. "Where did you get these?" he says, pointing at the swords with his rifle.

"I collected them, Brother, over the years. From different places," Isaac says.

"You like swords?"

"I like the workmanship."

"The workmanship? How about the functionality? You don't like that?"

"I never tested it," he says, forcing a laugh.

The guard moves in on a sword, runs his free hand over the gold engravings on the handle. "Take it down."

"Brother . . . These are just for decoration. I mean . . ."

"Take it down!"

Farnaz lifts her pale face, the deep lines around her eyes visible in the harsh light of morning. She has aged in his absence. Isaac removes the sword, which has left a half-moon imprint on the wall, like a smile. "Look at all the engravings on the handle, Brother," he says, distracting the guard as long as he can. "This one dates from the period of Genghis Khan."

The guard rests his rifle between his legs and holds out his hands, palms upward, like a pilgrim awaiting blessing. Isaac carefully places the sword into them, and steps back, allowing the guard to lose himself in the object. He looks at Farnaz and she shakes her head. "It's gone," she mouths, and looks back down again.

Why is it that every towel, every sock, every piece of underwear, is always in its place, but something as crucial as his birth certificate is lost? He feels something akin to rage rising in him, but realizes that what he feels is not potent enough to be called rage; it is a loneliness, a hardened sense that no one can come through for him, not even his wife.

The guard rests the sword's glistening tip on Farnaz's neck, pressing lightly. "Find the damn certificate, Sister!" he yells in her ear. Her body is stiff under the blade. Isaac stretches out his arm across the desk and holds her hand. "Please, Brother, just another minute," he says to the guard.

To her he says, "Think, Farnaz. When was the last time you saw it?"

"The day they came to search the house. I had left it here," she points at an open drawer. "And then, wait!" She lets go of Isaac's hand and walks to a corner, where stacks of files and papers are piled up high. "They emptied the drawers, and didn't put everything back. The rest they put here." She collapses the pile onto the floor and rummages through the paper rubble. Lost birth certificate—further proof, Isaac thinks, of his arbitrary existence.

"Here!" she says finally. "Here."

"Good, let's go. We've wasted enough time." The guard takes the rifle in one hand and the sword in the other.

"Brother, the sword," Isaac says. "You forgot to put it down."

"No, I didn't forget. I'm taking it."

"But . . . my dear Brother, this isn't really a weapon, it's just an antique. You know that, right?"

"Let's go! Just a few hours ago you didn't know whether you were going to live or die. Now you're arguing with me about a sword? Let me tell you something." He leans forward and whispers in Isaac's ear, "Don't relish your freedom just yet. You go free when I tell you you're free. Understand?"

THE MARBLE FLOOR of the bank, just scrubbed for the morning rush of customers, calms him. Sandwiched between the driver and the guard, he walks to the desk of Fariborz Jamshidi, his old friend.

"May I help you?"

"Fariborz, it's me. Isaac Amin."

The man stares at Isaac with furrowed eyebrows. "Isaac? Isaac Amin? What happened—" He examines the guard then the driver, then Isaac again. "What can I do for you, sir?"

"I would like to withdraw my savings, all in cash." Isaac endorses the withdrawal form and places it on the desk, along with his birth certificate. The banker stares at the documents, his hands flat on his desk. He does not take them.

"You heard the man, Brother!" says the guard.

"Yes, right away." Fariborz takes the papers and retreats in the back, where several other bankers have already gathered, surveying the scene. Isaac knows them all—Keyhani and Farmanian, and the young, flirtatious girl, Golnaz. He nods, forcing a smile, but they all look away, except for the girl, who smiles back.

His banker returns with five bulging canvas bags, which he places by the guard's feet.

"Good," the guard says, his eyes gleaming the way they had back at the house, as he held the gilded sword.

OUTSIDE, THE SUN now bright in the sky, Isaac stands back as the guards throw the bags into the trunk. There it goes, his life's hard work, his long hours at the office, the missed school plays, the late dinners, the promise to his children that they would never know the meaning of envy, the promise to himself that he would never become like his father.

"Aren't you getting in the car?" the guard says.

"Aren't we done?" A chill runs through his body. Is it possible that they will still kill him after robbing him?

"Yes, you are free now, Brother. But don't you want a ride back to your home?"

"No. I'll manage from here."

"As you wish." The guard rests his hand on the car handle. "Congratulations, Brother Amin. You are one lucky man."

From the sidewalk Isaac watches the car drive away from him. People pass him to the left and right and he realizes that he is blocking the entrance to the bank. He steps aside. He looks again at his feet bulging out of the shoes, pulls up his pants, now many sizes too large. The stains on his clothes are much more visible here in daylight than they had been in the dim light of his cell. He searches his pockets for a coin to call Farnaz, but he has nothing. He remembers how as a boy he would stand in front of the movie theater, his hand-me-down pants too large and his pockets empty, and wait for Ahmad-agha, who would pass by the theater yelling "*Shahre Farang*—Foreign City!" On his back the old man would carry an ornate metal box, inside of which were three-dimensional images of distant places—of a medieval castle in England or a Parisian café on a summer afternoon—places far away from the bare street in which he stood. This peek into a foreign land had a small price of a few cents, but Ahmad-agha always let Isaac look in for free. "One day, Ahmad-agha," he would tell the old man, "I'll send you a real postcard from a place like this." To which the old man would say, "*Inshallah*, my boy! And better yet, take me with you!"

THIRTY-SEVEN

He smells of sweat, and blood, and of something else, an acrid smell, like a disinfectant—formaldehyde or ammonia. He cries for a long time. "It's all finished now," Farnaz repeats in his ear. "You're safe." But he can't control himself. She leads him to the bathroom and runs a hot bath. "No, no baths," he says. "My skin . . . I have cigarette burns, and my feet . . . No baths. Just a quick shower."

Bent over the sink, he avoids his reflection in the mirror but glances at it periodically, like a motorist peeking at the gruesome remains of a roadside accident. He walks to the toilet and sits, fully clothed. Farnaz lingers, curious to see what they have done to him, but realizes that he won't disrobe in front of her. "That's it, Farnaz-jan," he says. "I don't need anything else."

. . .

AT THE KITCHEN table he is quiet. "That shower felt good," he says after a while. "We didn't have real soap there."

She wonders why he did not shave. The six-month-old beard, bushy and white, makes him look like an old man. His hair, wet and streaked with the traces of the comb, has thinned noticeably, revealing a peeling scalp. She serves him rice and kebab, and as she rests the plate in front of him, he shuts his eyes, breathing in the meaty vapors rising from his food. He smiles at her. "I can't believe I am sitting here with you, eating this food."

"And neither can I."

He eats quickly, stopping only for occasional sips of water.

"Be careful," she says. "Don't eat too fast. Your body may not be able to take it."

"Yes, I know. But it's so good!"

After a while she asks, "What did they accuse you of?"

"Of being a Zionist spy."

"A spy? How absurd!"

"Yes."

Outside, the lunch hour clamor of children at the nearby school fills the street. The wooden wheels of the knife sharpener's cart roll by. "Bring down your knives," the old vendor yells with his hoarse voice. "Sharpen your knives!"

"Spring is approaching," she says. "All the vendors and menders are out again. Just the other day the quilt mender passed by. I'll have to call him in one of these days."

He nods, looking down, chewing more slowly now.

"So you went with them to the bank?" she asks.

"Yes."

"How much did you give them?"

"Everything."

"Everything?"

"Yes, everything!" He looks up, but not at her. "Should I not have done it? Is my life not worth it?"

"Of course it is. Of course it's worth it! I'm sorry. I shouldn't have asked. Not now. I asked only because something terrible happened while you were gone. Morteza and the other employees looted your office. There is nothing left. No office, no employees, no equipment, no stones."

"Really? Morteza?" He moves his spoon back and forth along the side of his plate. "Well, at least we still have the Swiss accounts. There is enough there for a good, decent life."

They stay at the table for a while, neither of them touching the food or saying a word. So much silence to be stirred, she thinks.

"Isaac, you may find me ill-equipped for your pain," she says. "But I want you to know that your absence was very difficult for me. I suffered also. Maybe not like you. But I did."

"I know." He lets go of the spoon and looks up. Even his eyes seem to have thinned, if such a thing is possible. "The whole time I was there I thought of you and the children. I talked to you and embraced you and lived among you. At night I held the idea of your body in my arms, smelled your lotion on my mattress. Now that I am here, I feel like a dead man resurrected." He gets up and kisses her forehead, then limps across the kitchen floor. "I think I will go and lie down. You were right about the food. I'm not feeling well."

She clears the table, hearing all the while his slow, painful progress to the bedroom. Outside, melting snow drips from rooftops, making it seem like it's snowing all over again. So many times she had fantasized about Isaac's return, but none of her mind's creations resembled this tired afternoon, where a cold light moves on half-empty plates, and she finds herself alone in the kitchen, separated from him by the walls and endless corridors of the house.

When she lies down next to him on the bed, he is already asleep, a pained snore emerging from his half-open mouth. His eyelids flutter over their gray, hollow sockets. Looking at his beard closely, she sees the blisters under the hair and understands why he had not shaved. His arms sag, the skin loose and wrinkled over the bones, resembling the arms of old men who spend entire afternoons in teahouses throwing dice onto the backgammon board, testing their luck as they wait out their final years. She unrolls his sock and discovers his swollen foot, one toe bluish, the soles marked by unhealed lacerations. Looking at the foot she realizes that she will never know what happened to him— even after he has described it all down to the last detail.

She lies back down and holds his limp hand. She remembers that summer they first met in Shiraz, how one time she went back with him to his apartment and sat next to him on his sun-flooded bed, the windows wide open, the breeze tickling the curtains, the sun bright and high in the sky, approving their languor. Time did not press them

then. He recited a poem and they laughed at his dramatiza-
tion. With the ceiling fan circling above them like a whirling
dervish, they spoke of the future, that vast medley of constellations whose brightest stars, they believed, would become
theirs. Later that summer, when she mentioned Isaac to her
family on a weekend trip to Tehran, the reaction was luke-
warm. "We know the Amins," her mother said. "The father
is no good. And who doesn't know about the syphilis he
gave his poor wife?" Like a salesman, Farnaz sat with them
in the garden and told them how hardworking Isaac was,
how literate, how kind. "One can shut the town gates but
not people's mouths," her aunt said, taking bird bites out of
the piece of bitter chocolate that she took nightly with her
Turkish coffee. "And what will people say? That a daughter
of ours has married one of the Amin children? Such shame!"
Her mother nodded, in agreement with her sister. "We did
not raise a daughter so we could hand her over to wolves,"
she said in that absolute manner of hers that made any dis-
senter reconsider his position, if not out of persuasion, then
out of fear. Her father, who had been reclining in his chair,
flipping his worry beads and sipping his arrack, said, "The
Amins were once a noble family. This boy's great-great-
grandfather was a reputed rabbi in Mashhad. His great-
grandfather had amassed a fortune importing silk from
India. It was his grandfather who ruined the family name,
after he married that crazy girl from Kashan. He spent all his
money on her fancy and later on her folly. He even sent her
to a sanitarium in Switzerland, back in the days when only
the king had set foot in Europe." "Yes," her aunt chimed in.

"Such beauty, that girl! People still speak of her green eyes and black hair. But they say she had an unlucky face, the kind of face you should avoid on the New Year."

It was eventually agreed that Isaac's roots were actually noble, that his family name had suffered a few bad harvests, and that he would be the one to resurrect the Amins' old glory. And so he had. What no one had predicted was that he would also lose it.

THIRTY-EIGHT

Habibeh chops off a fish's head and slides it into the overflowing trash can, but it slips and falls on the floor, the eye gazing upward. "Help us prepare this dinner for your father. Aren't you happy he is home?"

Shirin has not yet seen her father, or rather, he has not yet seen her. "Your father has come back," was all her mother said when Shirin returned from school that afternoon. Once upstairs she added, "He is resting now. He is very tired." Walking past her parents' bedroom she saw his horizontal body framed by the doorway, a bushy white beard on his chin. He seemed small on the bed, the way she imagines a child would look in an adult coffin. He looked at her through half-open eyes, but he did not seem to see her.

A car honks outside. "It's Abbas!" Habibeh calls from the kitchen. "Come, khanoum, come!"

Minutes later, in the garden, Abbas the gardener is crouching over a lamb, a knife in his hand. He pulls back the animal's head with one hand, and with the other slices its throat. Blood gushes out, flowing over his bare hand and forming a small puddle near the pool. The lamb falls. *"Allah-o-Akbar!"* Abbas says. "Thank God for Amin-agha's return! May he live in good health!" He wipes the sweat beads above his mouth with a handkerchief, the knife hanging from his coat sleeve like an extension of his arm.

The smell of blood fills the garden. Shirin tucks her nose into her shirt collar and stands aside as Abbas hoses the ground. Night is falling, the streetlamps coming on one after the other, casting a funereal light on the dead animal. The dog runs up and down the staircase, agitated.

Why do people thank God with blood, she wonders. For as long as she can remember, Habibeh and Abbas, who could not afford to buy a whole lamb themselves, urged her parents to do it for them and have it sacrificed, so that they could thank God properly, as their religion demands. While her parents would oblige them, her mother would refuse to watch the killing, and would forbid Shirin to witness it also. But today her mother had stood there and watched, without flinching, without saying a word—not even to Shirin.

In the kitchen, the cooking resumes and half an hour later Abbas appears with a tray of meat, cut up into large pieces of rib, thigh, shank, and intestine.

"Look at this meat!" Habibeh says.

"May God accept our gratitude," Abbas says. "I packed up the rest and put it in the freezer downstairs, Farnaz-khanoum."

"Thank you, Abbas. You and Habibeh should take some

for your families. And we'll distribute whatever is left to neighbors tomorrow. *Inshallah*, God will accept our offering."

The lights go out, the city going black. The refrigerator's hum comes to a halt. Only the blue flames flicker under the pots. "They're bombing Tehran again!" Habibeh says. "The Iraqis are bombing Tehran!"

"It could just be another blackout," Abbas says. "If they were bombing we would have heard the sirens by now."

As they scramble for candles, a soft glow appears in the doorway. Behind it is her father, his face lit up from below, the white of his beard stark in the night. Abbas, who had received no warning of his altered appearance, gasps, whispering, "*Bismillah*—In the name of the Lord!"

"Hello, Abbas-agha," her father says from the doorway. "I scared you . . ."

"Amin-agha! No, I didn't . . ." He walks to him and shakes his hand. "Welcome back! We just sacrificed a lamb in your honor. May you have nothing but good days before you."

In the candlelight her father resembles a Dutch painting—Rembrandt's *Old Jew Seated*—whose reproduction he had kept above his desk for years. Looking at the old man painted in so many shades of brown—at his gaunt, aged hands and his downcast eyes—Shirin had once said to him, "This painting is so sad, Baba. Why do you keep it here?"

"One day," he had said, "you will understand it. And then you will find it beautiful."

He walks to her now and kisses her forehead. "My Shirin," he says. "I didn't think I would see you again." His lips feel chapped against her skin. She sits without moving, letting herself be kissed. She wraps her arms around his waist and brings her head to his stomach, but feeling the protruding bones of his ribs against her cheek, she lets go. She looks at the floor, at his injured feet.

"Did you sleep well, Amin-agha?" Habibeh says.

"Yes. But when the lights went out I thought I was back in prison."

"I keep telling them the Iraqis are about to bomb us, but they don't believe me."

He pulls out a chair and sits, with some difficulty. "If they bomb, they bomb." He smiles. "There isn't much any of us can do about it."

"Very well," Habibeh grumbles. "If we are going to get blown up, at least let's do it on a full stomach." She shuts the curtains and pulls out several heavy white candles.

"Why these candles?" her mother says. "Don't we have others?"

"No, we finished the others during the last blackout. What's wrong with these?"

"These . . . These I light on holidays to commemorate the dead."

"If Iraqi bombs fall on our heads, we'll need these to commemorate ourselves, khanoum-jan."

THE THREE OF them pass the bread and the salad and the salt, smiling at one another occasionally. Shirin tries to think of something to say, but she cannot come up with anything. Her parents don't talk either. *What was prison like*, she would like to ask. *Were you alone, or did you have cellmates? Were people cruel to you? What happened to your feet?*

"Are you happy to be back, Baba?" she finally says.

He breaks off a piece of bread. "Yes, very," he says.

Then why do you look so thin, so sad—so old? She finally understands that painting.

BY THE MEAL'S end some candles continue to burn calmly while others flicker wildly, casting stormy reflections on the opposite wall before guttering out. Her mother had once said that if a candle goes wild it means that the person in whose memory it has been lit did not leave this earth peacefully, that the person is still searching for harmony in the other world. Shirin wonders whose spirit is trapped in the flickering candles. Mr. Politics? His wife, Homa? Her father's cellmates? Are there enough candles in the world to account for all those who have not left peacefully?

THIRTY-NINE

Rachel bursts through the door, flushed and out of breath. "It's Mameh! Her water broke. The twins are on their way."

Zalman taps the counter with his firm, freckled hands. "*A shtik naches*—A great joy!" Turning to Parviz he says, "Close the shop for me, will you, son? I probably won't be back tonight."

"Yes, of course. Good luck to you!" He watches the Mendelsons hurry out of the shop into the scattered light of the afternoon, now nearing its end. Since that day in Central Park, he has been alone with Rachel only once. Returning home from a late class, he had seen her outside, struggling to dump large trash bags into garbage cans. He offered to help and she let him. "You guys need your own landfill," he joked. She didn't laugh. She explained, apologetically, that her parents were entertaining three emissary couples and their families. Snow had just begun falling, the night clean and still. It occurred to him that with a house full of guests, her absence would go unnoticed. "Let's go for a walk," he said. She looked around, swirling his proposition in her head, and before she could come up with the excuse of not having her coat, he took off his and draped it on her shoulders.

They walked in the hush of fresh snow. The silence calmed him. Occasionally she would glance at her watch and look back with a worried look, but she kept on walking forward. Guilt was brewing in him but he suppressed it; he had not felt this good in a very long time. She stopped at the house with wind chimes, hesitating. "Come," he insisted, holding out his hand. To his amazement, she reached out and took it. Her hand inside his filled him with longing. He had never thought that a mere hand could stir so much.

The street, deserted, was growing white. The neighborhood had vanished in the fog. Street lamps lit up the way, and as he looked at her face in the hazy golden light, he leaned forward and kissed her. Her lips, stiff and reprimanding, softened.

Afterward she hastened back and nearly slipped. He tried to break her fall but she pushed him away gently, holding on to a wet lamppost instead. His apologies, he knew, would come later. But for now, the kiss, like the snow, was still fresh, and he let it linger. He walked behind her slowly, restoring her solitude and watching the white space grow between them. He decided that despite her distress, he would remain happy, at least for one night. There would be plenty of time later for shovels and salt.

Since that night, now nearly three weeks ago, she has refused to speak to him, except to let him know that she had not gotten into trouble: the next morning she had told her parents that she had gone to bed early, and they had believed her. He stands by the shop window, looks out into the dusk. The twins will no doubt arrive in the night, when insomniacs will be talking themselves to sleep and the sick will be numbing their pain with drugs, waiting for those first, pale hours of daylight that will reassure them that they have made it to a new day. Parviz himself had been born hours after midnight, on a moonless winter night as his mother often liked to remind him. And so he wonders if the Mendelson twins, born like him in the night, will be prone to fits of sorrow.

He returns to his stool and steams the remaining hours away. A heavyset woman walks in as he is about to close up. "Where's Zalman?" she says sharply, as though she were offended to find Parviz there instead of the owner.

"His wife is giving birth."

"Ah, the twins!" she says, her face lighting up.

"Yes. What can I do for you?"

"I'd like to buy a hat for my grandson Herzel. He is going to Los Angeles as an emissary. He is about your age, you know. Already married and off to Los Angeles!"

"That's wonderful."

"Yes, we are all so proud of him. Well, let me get you his measurements." She opens her purse and pulls out crinkled papers, two orange medication bottles, and some used tissues. "What a mess," she apologizes. She picks up one of the papers. "Here."

Parviz retreats to the back, where rows of black hats stare at him with the dark, purposeful eyes of their future owners. Not finding the exact size of the grandson—this accomplished boy of eighteen who has already found himself a wife and is on his way to save the Jews of Los Angeles—he goes down to the basement, where he knows Zalman keeps all the unusual sizes. The hat he wants is resting on a wooden chest, which Parviz had never noticed before. The chest is weathered, chipped around the edges, a broken brass lock dangling from its side. Curious, he opens it, and finds a heap of letters inside, with the careful, scripted handwriting of a different time. He shuts the chest and takes the hat.

"Here," he says, proud of his excavation.

She pays for the hat and reshuffles her life back into her purse. "Goodnight!" she says. "Mazel tov to Rivka and Zalman. God willing, everything will go well."

By the time she leaves the sun has set. Lights are coming on in living rooms, where families are gathering, fitting their day inside a single dinner hour before retreating for the evening, so much left unsaid. He thinks of Rivka Mendelson forcing her twins out into the night, offering her husband two more reasons to be happy. Tonight, he knows, the lights in the Mendelson household will be off, and their usual chaos, which Parviz would overhear from his basement apartment, will be absent. They are all in a hospital somewhere, pacing outside the delivery room, calling family, praying.

He returns to the shop basement and walks straight to the wooden trunk. The yellow-edged letters are scattered inside in no particular order. He opens a few envelopes and finds greeting cards, for this or that holiday. From others he pulls photographs of Hassids in their black suits and hats. In one envelope he finds a letter and a single photograph of a young woman in a long floral-print dress. On the back are the words *To Zalman, love, Nadia. Marrakech, July 1960.* He flips the photograph and stares at the girl, seated on a chair in a garden, her legs crossed, playing what seems to be an oud. She is not beautiful, exactly—her face is too round and her neck too sturdy—but she has humor in her blue-gray eyes.

He unfolds the letter enclosed with the photograph:

October 5, 1960

In the name of G-d.

Zalman,

You have disappointed me. I ask that you leave Morocco at once and return home. I did not waste away so many years in Siberia so a son of mine would marry a Muslim girl. You are in Morocco to help our religion, not to dilute it. And what will you do next? Slide down the chimney as Santa Claus? Haven't we been persecuted enough as it is? Shall we exterminate ourselves voluntarily now?

You do not have what it takes to be an emissary, as you have shown yourself to be too open to temptation. Please pack up and return home immediately. You belong in Crown Heights.

Your father.

So Zalman had once loved but had let go, his father's suffering condemning him to a geographical prison. *You belong in Crown Heights.* Parviz wonders how long it had taken Mr. Mendelson to forget about Nadia. Maybe, to this day, Zalman slips down to the basement once in a while to look at the fading photograph. Tonight, when holding his new infants, will he forget Nadia, or, on the contrary, will he recognize in them something of her—the blue-gray of the eyes, so common in newborns? The prospect of not forgetting fills Parviz with dread.

Feeling uneasy, as though he had interrupted a grave, he shrouds the letter in its envelope. Guilt overwhelms him, and he wonders if he has already become for Rachel what Nadia has been for Zalman—a sad transgression. He hears footsteps upstairs so he shoves the envelope back in the trunk. "Mr. Mendelson?" he yells. "Is that you?"

The steps grow louder but there is no response. "Hello?"

Mr. Broukhim walks down the stairs. "Are you all right, Parviz? I was walking home and saw that the lights were on but no one was manning the shop. I got worried."

"Oh, I forgot to lock the front door," Parviz says. "Yes, I'm fine. Zalman is at the hospital. His wife is giving birth."

"You mean giving birth *again.*" Mr. Broukhim smiles. "What are you doing here so late?"

Parviz shuffles some hats on a shelf. "Just cleaning up a little . . ."

"Did you have dinner? Come eat with me."

He has grown so accustomed to eating alone that the idea of sharing a meal intimidates him. "Thank you, but I better go home. I . . ."

"You what? Come eat with me. I'm alone, like you."

They lock up. Two snowstorms have hit the city since the kiss, leaving behind their gray, slushy remains along the sidewalks. Mr. Broukhim's studio apartment is on the second floor of a brownstone, a few blocks down. His dog greets them enthusiastically when they arrive, his wide mouth stretched ear to ear, as though he were smiling.

"That's a friendly dog," Parviz says.

"Yes. He's wonderful. He is a Samoyed. I call him Samad-agha. If only people could be this sweet—Well, sit down. I'll start cooking."

The apartment is clean, with spare furnishings—a sofa, a coffee table, a twin bed, a shelf with a couple of books, a small rug with a Persian motif, clearly machine-made. On the windowsill is a single framed photograph of a dark-haired girl with mischievous eyes.

"That's my daughter, Marjan," Mr. Broukhim calls out from the kitchenette. "She's studying at Princeton. She loves it. She wants to be a doctor, a cardiologist, like me. Well, I should say, like I once *was*." He takes an open box of pasta from the counter and spills the contents into a pot of boiling water. "I hope you like spaghetti, which I make with my special sauce—tomato à la vodka." He smiles, picking up a bottle of Smirnoff and pouring a good cup into another pot. "There won't be any *ghorme sabsi* here."

"It's better than *my* special sauce—ketchup," Parviz says. He plays with the dog, the smell of warm butter and tomato sauce filling him with an unexpected joy.

"Bon appetit!" Mr. Broukhim says, placing the cooked

pasta on the table. He uncorks a bottle of wine and pours two glasses. "I can do without a lot of things," he says. "But I need my wine. This is a fine Bordeaux. Enjoy!"

Sitting across from Mr. Broukhim, Parviz realizes how lonely he has been all this time. How wonderful, he thinks, to sit at a table with someone and share a meal. The dog sniffs his way to their feet, wagging his curled tail, happy. Its creamy-white coat has shed throughout the apartment in round tufts, like snowballs.

"Is the food all right?" Mr. Broukhim asks. "I know it's not La Grenouille. But I try. You know, I've had a rough time. I came to this country thinking I had already lost everything I could possibly lose—my home, my profession, my life. But that was just the beginning. Little did I know what I had coming. The day my wife told me she wanted a divorce I actually laughed. I thought she was joking." He pours himself a second glass of wine. "It's the same for you, I imagine. You came here, having left everything behind. Then you hear your father is in prison. You don't mind that I know, right? Rachel told me."

News of misfortune travels. Parviz has come to accept this as an unavoidable part of life, like cockroaches, clogged drains, landfills. Hadn't he heard from Zalman about Mr. Broukhim's ruinous divorce? "I don't mind," he says. "I try to keep going also. But there are days when I wonder how much I have left in me. I am tired."

"At your age, you are tired? You have so many years ahead of you!"

"That's the thing, Mr. Broukhim. Fatigue has nothing

to do with age." As he says this, exhaustion washes over him. His head feels heavy, weighing on his tense shoulders. He wonders if the wine is getting to him. His stomach churns, suddenly, as the incident with Rachel reappears in his mind. He recalls the look she had after the kiss—first of exaltation, then of shame. He realizes that his anxiety is caused not only by the embarrassment he caused her, but also by the belief, however irrational, that having tainted her sanctity, he has also spoiled his prayer for his father's safe return. She had, after all, been his liaison to God.

Mr. Broukhim wipes his mouth then turns on the stereo, slipping in a cassette of a classical Persian ensemble. "The singer in this group was my cousin," he says. "They killed him last year." He dims the light, sits back on the sofa, and smokes hashish, his eyes moist.

In his moonlit corner by the window, Parviz listens to the reed flute and sitar accompanying the deep, precise voice of Mr. Broukhim's cousin singing ghazals. From time to time he looks at Marjan's photograph and envies her lightness, her apparent lack of gravity. How could someone his age love her new life here? Does she not miss her house, her street, her friends? Sitting here, in the melancholy smallness of the studio, the executed singer's voice filling the room, Parviz remembers, suddenly, how in the summertime his whole family would bring mattresses onto the terrace and sleep under scores of stars, a vast, black night surrounding them. Or how, during holidays at the beach house, he and the neighboring teenagers would sit by the sea around a campfire, grilling kebab and singing until dawn. How could these things be replaced—forgotten? When the music ends he feels a gnawing pain magnifying in his head, so he gets up and says good-bye.

HOURS LATER, DEEP in sleep, dreaming that he is stranded on a boat with Zalman somewhere in Vladivostok, he hears the shrill ring of the telephone, a sound that has become unfamiliar to him. Speaking into the receiver, only half conscious, he hears a faint voice—his father's. *Parviz-jan, can you hear me?* the voice repeats.

"Baba-jan, is that you? Yes, I can hear you!"

"I just returned from my trip. I wanted to let you know that."

"Yes? Was it a difficult trip?"

"Yes, well . . ." The line breaks off, letting through fragments of words drowned in static. " . . . I am back . . . but you know . . ."

"Good. That's great."

"And you? Are you well?"

"Yes, Baba-jan, yes."

"I woke you up, no?"

"No, it's all right! I was up."

"Go, go back to sleep. I just . . . Be well, my Parviz."

"You, too, Baba."

He holds on to the receiver, the dead tone soon followed by a repetitive beep and a mechanical voice urging him to hang up. "Good, that's great," was all Parviz had managed to say. He sits in the dark, the phone on his lap. His father sounded old, and depleted, as though the very act of speaking had diminished him. He is becoming an old man, Parviz thinks, and I remain a boy. Who will care for whom, then?

He lies awake, stares at the red lava lamp on the table next to him, the crescents—anemic blood cells—swimming inside it. "My father is alive," he repeats in the dark, disbelieving.

He wishes he could share the news with someone, but aside from Zalman and Rachel, both at the hospital, he doesn't know anyone who would care enough about him to appreciate being woken up at two in the morning. He considers calling Mr. Broukhim, but reminds himself that with all the wine and hashish, Mr. Broukhim no doubt has a throbbing headache.

FORTY

His desk is the only object in the office left untouched. His files are scattered everywhere, the calendar still open to the date of his arrest, the scribbled appointments now infused with the knowledge that they would never be met. Even the glass of tea is where he left it, filled now with greenish layers of fungus. Everything else, including the furniture, the stonecutting equipment, and the jewels, is gone.

But he is not finished. He thanks God now for the banks dotting the Rhône in Geneva, where he had had the wisdom to wire money over the years, knowing, as many before him had known, that a Jew should not leave all his eggs in one basket, even if that basket happens to be his own beloved country. He also has several stones stashed in the bank's vault; luckily his banker had been clever enough not to mention these to the Revolutionary Guards when they seized Isaac's savings. He makes an inventory of the stones in his head: two emeralds from Colombia, dozens of rubies from India, five sapphires from Burma, and five diamonds from South Africa, one of which—a pure, perfect, stone—he had hoped to transform into his career's masterwork.

He sits on an empty box behind his desk, his pants cinched with a belt, the extra fabric strangled in pleats. Of his sixteen employees, only Farhad, his best stonecutter, had taken his call and offered to come in. He wonders why he even bothered to ask the man to come; there is nothing to cut here. He picks up the receiver—the telephone on his desk is the only one they spared—but doesn't know whom else to call. He hangs up. Above him the ceiling creaks. He dismisses the sound as an illusion, an echo of Mohsen's little boy running above his cell. But the steps continue, interspersed with the squeak of the closet door he had intended to oil for sometime. He walks through the empty corridors and goes upstairs, where he finds Morteza sitting on the floor, a heap of papers in front of him.

"I see you haven't missed a day of work, Morteza."

"Amin-agha! You're free!"

"Yes. Apparently not many around here thought it possible. I'm surprised your mother didn't tell you."

"I haven't talked to my mother for some time." Morteza scans the empty room with his bearded, narrow face. "I, for one, was sure you would be released. That's what I kept telling the others, but you know how it is."

"Yes. And what might you be doing here now?"

"Now? I was trying to figure out what was taken from you Amin-agha. I wanted to keep a record for you."

"I am not an imbecile, Morteza. I know what took place here. My wife told me everything. You are a thief."

"Me, a thief? How can you say that, Amin-agha?"

"Then show me this so-called record that you are keeping for me."

"Well, I just got started," Morteza mumbles.

"Look, I am tired. I have no strength left for such games. Whatever you stole is now yours. We both know that. There are no courts for me turn to. At least have the decency to look me in the face and admit that you are a crook."

"I would not talk this way if I were you, Amin-agha" Morteza says. He gets off the floor, pulls out a cigarette from his pocket, and lights it with deliberate indolence. "You see," he says, exhaling and approaching Isaac. "I have a document in my pocket that could make a lot of trouble for you."

"What document?"

"The past has a way of coming back to haunt us, doesn't it, Amin-agha?"

"What document?" Isaac demands. He feels dizzy as he watches Morteza prance in front of him. Is it possible that this third-rate impostor will have him sent back to prison?

Morteza pulls out a faded, crinkled paper from his pocket and unfolds it. He reads, "Sale of one ruby and diamond pendant to the empress and . . ." He looks up, speaking now with an affected accent: "Shall I read the attached note from her majesty? Here it is: 'Thank you, Mr. Amin, for your impeccable workmanship. Iran is proud to have an artisan such as yourself. You have a light hand, which I am sure will make countless women feel like empresses in their own right.'"

One of the first pieces Issac ever designed was this pendant for the empress. He was cocky then, and young. Having served two years in Paris as an apprentice to a jeweler, he had returned to Tehran, locked himself in his dark studio for five months, cutting and polishing stones, combining them to form a pendant inspired by a Chinese temple. Stunned by his own creation, he had delivered the necklace to the shah's palace personally, with a note, "For Her Majesty's Consideration," and she had actually replied, the very next day, through a small, severe man in a black suit and dark sunglasses, who showed up at his apartment and handed him an envelope filled with dollars, along with the handwritten note. How distant it all seems to him now. That period of his life, which he spent in his Tehran studio, discovering the brilliance of stones, now sparkles in his mind like the red, radiant ruby he had offered the empress. "That was so long ago!" he says. "It means nothing now."

"But that's what made your reputation, was it not? Didn't all the women with cash in their pockets flock to you after that, thinking if he is good enough for the queen, he must be good enough for me? This paper establishes your link with the shah. And you know what that means."

"Give me that letter."

Morteza folds the letter and puts it back in his pocket. "This piece of paper, my dear Amin-agha, is your death certificate. Why should I give it up so easily? You're lucky I didn't find it sooner."

"You've already stolen all my jewels, Morteza. They are worth millions. You know that. What else could you possibly want?"

Morteza bites his lower lip—just like his mother, Isaac thinks—and plays with the tip of the letter protruding from his pocket. "I want the diamond," he says finally. "The one you brought back from Antwerp. Where is it? I looked everywhere."

"No, Morteza," Isaac says, his steady voice belying his fear. "I'll give you any other stone, except that." An image of Ramin holding a cockroach in his fist sends a sudden shiver through his body. "What has gotten into you?" he continues. "We are friends, after all. Your mother has lived with us for twenty years. You are like my own son—"

"No. Not *lived* with you. She has slaved for you. And I am not like your own son. You never treated me like your precious Parviz."

"Such nonsense!" He walks to the window, opens it to let in the clean light. He does not want to give up that diamond, not simply because of its value, which is not negligible, but also because all his adult life he had searched for a flawless stone, one that could assure him of the possibility of perfection. Precious stones were accidental secretions of the earth—of volcanic eruptions and sedimentation—yet nearly all of them possessed a perfect internal order, called crystalline state—manifested by a regular arrangement of atoms repeated one hundred million times per centimeter. But even in this perfect world of gemstones other hierarchies existed—classifications according to hardness, cleavage, color, luster. Thus a diamond, the hardest stone, could also have "bad cleavage," meaning that it would break easily, or could contain fractures, which would interrupt the paths of light rays and reduce its luster. The diamond he had found was a pure, colorless, eight-carat stone, classified as exceptional white.

He remembers meeting his broker, Yacov Yankevich, a Hassidic Jew, in a dim house in Antwerp, on a clear day, not unlike this one, the wooden shutters wide open, the flawless diamond placed on a blue velvet cloth before him. "It's a rare one," Yankevich said. "You won't be sorry." Walking back to the main square, the stone in his briefcase, he thought about creating another pendant for the empress, or for the shah's sister—a woman with considerable influence on her brother—or perhaps even for a foreign dignitary. But as he reached the café where Farnaz sat with her espresso, waiting for him in her sundress, her shoulders rubbed that morning with sunscreen lotion, smelling of the ocean and the many summers they would yet spend together, he wondered if this diamond should be for her. Many summers later, when he still had not morphed the stone, it occurred to him that perhaps he did not deem anyone worthy of its perfection.

"I'll give you another diamond, also of very high quality," he says. "And a sapphire."

"Stubborn Jew! Bargaining all the way to your grave! I want the diamond, or this little piece of paper will be sent to the office of Imam Khomeini."

Isaac looks at Morteza's tall, fidgety body. He is just a boy, really. Just a few months ago he was fetching tea, filing papers, typing letters. "Listen to me, you little snitch," Isaac says. "I am on better terms with the office of Imam Khomeini than you may imagine. After all, I've just become one of their biggest contributors. All it would take to get *you* in trouble would be a phone call from me, informing them of all the additional items that I would have liked to donate to the cause of the revolution had they not been stolen by a small-time thief called Morteza. Do you understand me? So hand me that piece of paper and get out of here!"

Morteza shifts his weight from one leg to the other, as though considering the gravity of the threat. He crosses his arms, bites his lower lip, looking down, at the heap of papers on the floor. He runs out, finally, the letter in his pocket.

Isaac considers running after him, but he can hardly walk, let alone run. He stands by the window, waits for Morteza's stomping steps to die down. He watches him as he makes his way down the quiet street—one more person exiting his life. He thinks of the first day he had brought Morteza to the office, remembers the eagerness with which the boy took notes and answered the phone, and the satisfaction he himself had felt at taking in a boy with small prospects but ambitious goals, the kind of boy who made no secret of his appreciation, thanking him for the smallest charity—a free meal, a ticket to the movies—gratitude he knew he would never receive from his own children. How does such affection turn into such hatred? Do people cease loving someone when their perception of themselves changes? Did Morteza once care for me, he wonders, because he needed me? And now that he no longer needs me, is he really willing to have me killed with that letter? But I am the same man. I am still Isaac Amin. I have not changed.

He feels a heavy pain in his heart and does not know

what to do with it. The last time he had felt a pain like this, on the day he learned of Kourosh's execution, he had released it in the grinding sound of the stonecutting machines and the buzzing activity around him. But today, in the bareness of his office, the pain lies heavy in his chest, becoming a burning, unfamiliar mass. He walks into the sleepy afternoon. His street has thinned out, the neighboring businesses closed or barely functioning. Like his livelihood, his city has been liquidated, and he knows now that he must leave it at once.

FORTY-ONE

Isaac brings the scissors to his chin and clips off his beard, the white, coarse hairs falling into the sink. He glides the razor along his jaw, working his way around the cigarette blisters—two pink, wrinkled circles on his right cheek. Let the world see them, he thinks, these unsightly reminders of pain. As the last patch of hair disappears, his bony, naked reflection stares back at him from the foggy bathroom mirror. He recoils at the transformation of a once handsome man: two craters have formed on each side of his face where his chin and jaw intersect, and his brown eyes seem lost inside deep, gray sockets. His head—his entire body, in fact—has shrunk, suggesting the skeletal frame under his ashy skin.

He stands for some time in front of his closet, his clothes—costumes of his previous life—now foreign to him. Despite the rising spring temperatures he chooses a heavy sweater to add mass to his diminished torso. He forces his feet into his shoes; the foot lashings, he decides, are not to become public knowledge. Thinking back on that episode, of himself lying facedown on a plank of wood and getting beaten, he does not remember the pain—only the shame.

Sitting on her side of the bed, Farnaz is slipping her legs into dark stockings, lifting each leg in the air with pointed toes like a dancer. She is wearing nothing but a brassiere and underwear, her back still guitar-shaped, her spine like well-adjusted strings, asking to be caressed. He leans across the bed, managing no more than a kiss on her shoulder, which she acknowledges by placing her hand where his lips had been.

They say little on the way to his parents' house. The smell of jasmine seeps into the car through the lowered windows.

"I've been meaning to tell you something," Isaac says. "I saw Vartan Sofoyan in prison."

"Really? I saw him . . ." she says, then pauses in midsentence. "When I went to look for you. Did you talk to him?"

"Yes, we ended up in the same block." He considers telling her about his death, but decides not to. "I got to know him," he says instead. "I found him to be a gentle soul."

"Yes," she smiles. "He is, I think."

The other thing he has not told her about is Morteza's threat. He knows that if the Revolutionary Guards come back for him because of that letter from the empress, he won't be spared. What would be the point in telling her?

"I'm going to call Keyvan's men today," he says. "We need to start arranging everything."

Farnaz looks out the window, nodding. "I hid their number in a book. I'll look for it when we get home."

"When did you say Habibeh is going to see her mother?"

"In August. For two weeks."

"We need to sell the house and close the deal while she's away. Any price we can get. We should also try to sell small items, like antiques, maybe even jewelry. Things that she won't notice."

She nods again, her eyes invisible under her sunglasses. He thinks she may be crying, but prefers not to know for sure. Knowing would require that he console her—something he is no longer capable of.

"ISAAC?" HIS FATHER says from his bed, lifting his head for an instant before letting it fall back down on his pillow. "Is that really you?"

"Yes, Baba-jan, it's me." He watches his father's body, shriveled in places and swollen in others, looks for his hand under the blanket and holds it, feeling with his fingers the cool, wrinkled skin. The smell of urine permeates the air.

"Let me look at you," his father says, coughing. "What did they do to you, son? I didn't think I would see you again. And this would be a bad thing. To lose all my children without saying good-bye. You know, your brother and sister both left without a word. From Javad I expected no more. But Shahla, too?"

"I'm sure it wasn't intentional Baba-Hakim," Farnaz

says. "She was too ashamed to go out. She wouldn't even see the doctor."

"Eh," the old man says, dismissing the excuse with a sweep of the arm. "Too ashamed? Doesn't she know her parents will die here soon? And who doesn't have something to be ashamed of these days? Look at me! And Isaac! He doesn't look so good, either."

Isaac wonders if shaving had been a good idea. Why did he decide to expose himself like this, especially in front of his father? "Where is mother?" he asks.

"I don't know. Probably cleaning. She disinfects all the rooms, day and night, rubbing all the furniture with alcohol."

On the old man's night table, next to a small bottle of whiskey, is a framed photograph of Isaac as a boy of nine or ten, leaning against the palm tree in front of their home in Khorramshahr.

"Your mother found this recently while cleaning some closets and I asked her to put it here." He smiles, toothless. "You may find the gesture overly sentimental. I suppose I'm getting sentimental in my old age."

Seeing his own photograph by his father's bed unsettles him; throughout his childhood his father had not shown such interest in him. Why now, he wants to ask, now that everyone is preparing for a departure of one sort or another?

"You were a beautiful child," Farnaz says.

"Yes, beautiful," the old man says. "But moody. And reckless, too. One time he nearly set fire to the house . . ."

Not this story again, Isaac thinks. Of his entire childhood this was the episode that his father seemed to remember best, the one that he recounted most often.

"He had built himself a little cabin outside the house with wooden logs," his father goes on, as though he were telling the story for the first time. "And he did everything in that cabin: he slept there, he did his homework there, he even cooked there. Well, the cabin caught fire one day and the whole house was about to burn down. From that day on his mother forced him to live with the rest of us. Me? I didn't care one way or the other."

He sees the house now, that two-room tenement at the end of an unpaved street, the wash hanging on lines, the teal-colored walls bubbled from humidity. For the first five years of his life he slept in one room and his parents in the other. As the family grew, their space did not expand; rather, he had to minimize himself to make room for newcomers, an obligation that turned his mother's syphilis and subsequent barrenness into a secret celebration. He recalls sleeping with Javad and Shahla in one bed, and the choreography needed to pass the night—the three of them simultaneously turning to the left or right like a troupe of showgirls. On summer nights, their bodies clammy from humidity, they would shrink themselves even more to avoid contact.

"Say a poem for me, Isaac," the old man says.

"A poem? What poem?"

"I don't know. Any poem. In those days you knew hundreds of them by heart. How you used to get on my nerves with your poems! Now I have time for a verse or two while I wait for God to come and take me."

"Be not too sure of your crown," Isaac starts. "You who thought / That virtue was easy and recompense yours."

His father shuts his eyes. He dozes off, his head falling to the side, his mouth a harmless organ with no teeth, hanging open.

Isaac continues reciting the poem though he knows his father is no longer listening. "From the monastery to the wine-tavern doors / The way is nought." He stands over the bed and looks around the room, at his father's dentures sitting in a glass of water, the gums pink and lifelike; at the wallpaper with an iris motif, stained yellow and peeling; at the photograph of his father's mother as a young woman, before she had gone to a sanitarium in Switzerland; and at the wool house robe she had sent him from her retreat in the Alps, explaining through a brief handwritten note that all the male patients, the ones who were not entirely mad, owned a robe like this for their rest periods. From the day he received it, when Isaac was just six or seven, his father would put on the robe as soon as he would get home. He would wear it even in the summertime, when he would sit by an open window and fan himself with a magazine, beads of sweat bubbling on his forehead. Isaac found him stubborn then, and irrational—a child refusing to take off his carnival costume when the party is long over. Much of his interaction with his father was like this: an unspoken war, a mutual dislike, broken only occasionally, when his father would come home with a deflated ball he had found on the street, or an amputated doll—crippled presents but presents nonetheless, which made Isaac and the others run to him and kiss his hand. But for every act of kindness came multiple punishments—being beaten with a belt for not returning the milk to the icebox, having to spend the night alone outside the house for having laughed too loudly. His rage without warning turned the children and their mother, like inhabitants of a fault line, into fidgety human beings.

He remembers how, for his twelfth birthday, his father had promised to take him to see a theater troupe from Tehran. He had come home late, as usual, reeking of arrack. By the time they arrived the doors had been shut, the audience inside erupting into cheers and applause. And the usher, a man his father had wronged one way or another—as he had most people who entered his life—refused to let them in. While his father cursed the man and yelled, Isaac receded into the cheers behind the closed door, the grand spectacle unfolding on the other side, away from him.

Looking now at his father, he sees not the despot he had known but an injured old man, softened by illness, still mourning the loss of his mother, who was taken from him when he was just a boy. He looks at the mother in the photograph: The stunning girl with the green eyes and black hair who went crazy. Of her middle and old age spent in Switzerland there are no photographs, and so no one knows how her face and body gave in to time. She had grown old in exile, anonymously, breathing in the cold, crisp air of the Alps, so unlike the hot, humid air of her Abadan.

Isaac thinks of his own imminent departure. He, too, will grow old in exile, breathing the unfamiliar, inhospitable air of another country. And of his final years perhaps nothing will remain. Decades from now, when a descendant who does not yet exist will stumble upon a photograph of him, seated at a teahouse or walking along the Caspian, he will ask, "Who is this man?" And people will squint at the old photograph and say, "Oh, him? That's Isaac Amin, the man who polished his way out of misery but in the end lost it all."

FORTY-TWO

Reclining against the wall and hugging one knee, the boyish man sits on the floor and sips his tea, closing his eyes every now and then, as though he were just succumbing to a narcotic. His partner, a balding man about a decade his senior, sits next to him with a stiff back and nervous eyes.

"So you say you have no passports?" the older one says.

"Our passports were confiscated when the Revolutionary Guards searched the house," Isaac says. "But our daughter's passport still exists, and I can make a family passport out of that."

"Good! That will speed things up. Use bleach to erase the names and dates." Sipping his tea he says, "We've taken many people across the border, *sarkar*. But you will need God as your partner throughout this adventure."

Isaac enjoys not being called "Brother." Hearing the word *sarkar*—a friendly way to refer to someone as "boss," pleases him. "Yes, I've called on God many times already this past year," he replies. "I hope he'll continue to answer."

The young man places his tea on the carpet and extends his bent leg. "Well, bring God along if he makes you feel better," he says as he smiles, "though of course he'll have to pay a fare like everyone else. But more importantly, remember this: You'll need to wear warm clothes, in many layers, because the mountains are freezing at night. You'll need to be well-rested, because we have a long way to go, and we can't have people slowing down or falling asleep on us. Stopping on the way is not an option. Besides, it will be dark, and if you don't keep up with the group you'll get lost. And you'll need cash in case we get caught. The border police on both sides are vigilant but easily bought. Of course, there are no guarantees. Some of them are more zealous than greedy."

Isaac looks at Farnaz, sitting on the floor and pulling an undone thread from the lining of her navy uniform. In the furtive atmosphere of the smugglers' apartment, where the curtains are closed and tapestry-covered pillows line the walls, she has let her scarf slip down to her neck, maybe in anticipation of freedom. "How often do you get caught, Mansoor-agha?" she says.

"Not often. Twice in the past two years. The first time it was with one of the shah's generals, the second time with a family of eight. The family was let go, with some cash of course, but with the general it got ugly. When they found out who he was, they shot him on the spot."

"And you?"

"Us? We pay a fine and they let us go. If we happen to

be transporting some valuable goods, we give them a whiff of that also. We're repeat business for them, so they look the other way. It's the passengers they're after. But don't worry, Amin-khanoum," he says, reaching for the samovar and re-plenishing his tea. "Like I said, it's not often." He pulls out a cigarette from his shirt pocket, then removes the whole pack and throws it in Isaac's direction. "Help yourselves. It clears the head. There are matches on the table next to you." He reclines again, cigarette in mouth. "So let me explain the route again. You will arrange a ride from Tehran to Tabriz, where you'll have lunch. Make it a hearty lunch because you'll need your energy. In the afternoon our people will meet you at a designated place and you'll ride with them to a village near the border. We'll pick you up from there and the rest, well, the rest is a surprise."

"A surprise? I've had enough of those this year, Man-soor-agha," Isaac says. "What do you mean by 'surprise'?"

"I'd rather not get into details now, *sarkar*. Suppose you get arrested again between now and when we leave. I cannot have you revealing any details. All you need to know beyond what we've told you is that the road is fairly safe, and most people make it. As you know, your sister and her husband got through just fine."

"*Fairly* safe?"

"You may be used to things being precise, Amin-agha. In your business you measure stones by carats and look at them under magnifiers. Our business is the opposite. Everything is approximate. Nothing can be predicted. There are so many factors: the weather, the people patrolling the border on any given night, encounters with snakes and foxes, the Turkish police on the other side—I could go on and on . . ."

Settling back into his old life is no longer possible, but forging ahead requires courage Isaac is not sure he has. And what about his wife and daughter? Should a man deliver his family to the mountains like that? "And the fee?" he asks.

"Thirty-five thousand dollars per person for the two of you, forty thousand if you want better accommodations, which means that we would take care of you personally all the way. For the little girl the fee would be forty-five thousand, if you want us to guarantee that should something happen to both of you we would arrange for her to join relatives somewhere."

"Her brother is in New York."

"Then that's where we would send her. You'll have to give us his telephone number beforehand."

The thought of his daughter, orphaned and dependent on two smugglers somewhere in Turkey, makes his heart lurch with fear. Farnaz flashes him the same terrified look she had when the guard had held the sword to her throat and she couldn't find the birth certificate.

"How do we know you'll really send her to her brother?" she says. "What prevents you, two men with admittedly questionable ethics, from trafficking her?"

"Nothing would prevent us," the young one says, exhaling his cigarette smoke in the stuffy room. "Just as nothing would prevent us from taking off with your money and leaving you stranded. In these matters you have to follow your heart. If you feel you can trust us, then you should do it. If you don't, then of course, you shouldn't."

"The chances of something happening to both of you are very slim," the older smuggler says. "I wouldn't worry too much about it."

"Very well, we'll think about it and get back to you," Isaac says. "And should we decide to go ahead, when would the trip take place?"

"September," the young one says. "In the summertime traffic is high because of the warmer weather. But the chances of getting caught are higher as well. In September the traffic is lighter but the weather is still tolerable." Then, looking down at Isaac's shoes he says, "Besides, you need to let those feet of yours heal. You can barely put your weight on them. I know what they do to people's feet in prison, Amin-agha. There are no secrets here. But we can't have someone in your condition on this trip. Make sure you take care of yourself by then."

Isaac looks down at his shoes, overstretched to accommodate his swollen feet. Was it not enough that his wife had been pestering him to see a doctor, frightening him with the grisly consequences of neglected wounds? That his humiliation should be visible to the world makes him want to go home, lie in his bed, and cover his body with a blanket—out of sight. "All right, Mansoor-agha," he says. "We'll be in touch."

"Yes, *sarkar*. Think about it, but don't think too much. If you think too much you'll end up doing nothing."

. . .

OUTSIDE HE REACHES for Farnaz's hand and they walk together in silence. They pass by a one-legged man in a wheelchair, who reminds Isaac of Mehdi. On the windowsills of the neighboring homes are oval trays of grass, announcing the arrival of *Nowruz*, the Persian New Year.

"Look, it's the New Year already," Farnaz says. "People are growing their grass. And we forgot to grow ours."

"It's not too late. If we get the seeds today we'll still have it in time. Would you like that?"

"Yes," she says. "I'd like it very much. We should celebrate it here one last time."

So she wishes to go ahead with the trip. She has insinuated it without coming out and saying as much. He does not press her further; he too believes that they should go.

"And the mirror," he says, "we'll put it in the middle of the table this time, not at the edge!"

"No, not the edge." She laughs.

He had been the one who had placed the mirror on the ceremonial table that previous year, along with the rest of the ritual items—the goldfish, the painted eggs, the grass. They had just arrived at their beach house, where they liked to spend the holidays, and he remembers the scent of humid cedar rising from the wooden beams of the ceiling and fusing with the smell of cooking—which would begin as a single note of caramelizing onions and would expand as the hours progressed, becoming an orchestra of scents—of meats, spices, and herbs. He recalls too the curtains moving with the breeze, the distant breath of the waves, and the open windows forming an invisible artery through the neighborhood, the sounds of clinking dishes and laughter traveling from one house to the next. But when the lights went out—another blackout, so frequent in the early days of the war—he hurried in the dark to the dining room console for a candle, knocking against the mirror along the way. For an instant, he stood completely still, knowing that one black, silent second separated him from that devastating sound of shattering glass. The sound brought with it his fretful wife, who knelt to the floor in her white dress and picked up the broken pieces, mumbling, "Oh, but it's bad luck! A broken mirror on the New Year is such bad luck!" He had knelt beside her, telling her that it's just glass, nothing more, that it's all just a silly superstition, but she shook her head, saying it's not a superstition, it's a fact. Her doggedness irritated him, but not because he found her conviction ridiculous. On the contrary, he, too, believed in the silly superstition, and wished that someone could convince him otherwise.

THE WARMTH OF her hand comforts him now, and he tells himself that maybe things will turn out all right: they will leave the country and start over in a new place, together with the children, in a matchbox apartment in a Manhattan high-rise or in an anonymous clapboard house in an American suburb, where people will mispronounce their names and where they will eventually stop correcting them, laughing instead at the botched words.

At night he lays out his tools on the dining room table:

bleach, cotton balls, toothpicks, a fountain pen, paper, and the passport. He places some cotton on a toothpick, dips it in bleach, and erases his daughter's name, letter by letter, then her birth date—the day, the month, the year. The ink dissolves, as though the birth had never occurred. He practices the handwriting of the official who issued the passport, the curl of his As, the length of his Ms, then writes his own name, his wife's, and his daughter's. Tomorrow they will have a family picture taken, to replace his daughter's photograph, taken a few years earlier, when her front baby tooth had just fallen out. He remembers that tooth and imagines how she must have placed it under her pillow, anticipating the tooth fairy. But the fall of the tooth having coincided with the fall of the shah, he and Farnaz had forgotten all about it. He sees her now, lifting the pillow the following morning and finding the tooth still wrapped in its tissue, where she left it.

Later, in bed, he asks Farnaz if she had, by any chance, left a present under Shirin's pillow when her front tooth had fallen.

"What tooth?" Farnaz says in her sleep.

"Her front tooth, the first one that fell."

"I don't remember," she mumbles. Then turning to him, she says. "No. I'm sure I didn't."

He lies awake, sorry that for his daughter—as it had been for him when he was a boy—a fallen tooth was just a fallen tooth; there were no fairies.

FORTY-THREE

In the car, on the way to the Caspian, where they will spend the week-long spring vacation, her parents tell her of their planned departure. It has all been arranged with smugglers, the same ones that Shahla and Keyvan used. They will leave in September via the border of Turkey. But you can't tell anyone, her father says, not even your friends.

There are no friends left, Baba, so no need to worry.

Sitting in the back, groggy still at this early morning hour, Shirin watches the road shift color from gray to yellow, becoming a pale gold as the morning hours pass. Her mother peels fruit, the red gingham kitchen towel on her lap, infusing the car with the smell of citrus. Music plays on the tape player, a pop song whose singer has long fled.

"I still don't think this trip is such a good idea, Isaac," her mother says, handing him an orange slice. "We should keep a low profile."

"We *are* keeping a low profile," he says. "We're going

about our lives as if everything were normal. Shirin is on vacation, and we're going to our beach house as we always do. Besides, is it written on our foreheads that we are planning an escape?"

Planning an escape. What kind of escape, Shirin wonders—like Papillon, Louis XVI and Marie Antoinette, or something more leisurely and altogether bucolic, like the Trapp family? And what if Leila's father finds out about the files between now and September? Will all three of them get arrested this time and get sent to prison? Do children go to prison? If they go to war, why not prison?

Looking out the window, she realizes that they will never travel on this road again. Miles of asphalt disappear under their wheels, bringing them closer to the sea and to the end of their lives here. Yet it is not sadness she feels, but an emptiness, a certain guilt even, for not feeling sad enough. A departure like this, so definite, should devastate her. But it doesn't. She tries to memorize her surroundings—the ridges on the rocks, the color of the sun as it illuminates the road, the stretches of sea coming in and out of view according to the curves of the road—knowing that someday she will miss them. But there are too many details to remember, too much to record in a single viewing, and she wishes now that she had paid more attention back when she believed that, like the mountain, and the sun, and the sea, she would always be there.

Sheets hang on washlines in the garden of their beach house. A black Jeep is parked outside. "What's this?" her father says as he gets out of the car. He walks to the door and tries to open it, but his key won't work. A bearded man opens the door.

"Good afternoon, Brother." She hears her father through the open windows of the car. "This is my house. May I ask what you are doing in it?"

The man shrugs. "It's now my house."

"*Your* house? Who gave it to you? I didn't sell it, and I certainly didn't donate it."

"The government gave it to me. You already have a house. Why do you need another one?"

"Brother, what kind of a question is that?"

"A serious one. I serve the revolution, and I didn't have a decent house. You serve only yourself, and you have two houses. It makes perfect sense that, like you, I should have a comfortable house. You understand?" He looks over at the car, squinting his eyes to better see Shirin and her mother. "Now if you are not happy, all of us, your wife and daughter included, can hop in my Jeep and pay a visit to the Revolutionary Guards."

Her father walks back to the car, shaking his head and mumbling something. "Well!" he says, slamming the door and turning on the engine. "Looks like we'll be renting this year!" He laughs bitterly as he puts the car in reverse and pulls out of the driveway. "You have two houses so I took one!" he says. "Ha-ha! Just like that! Can you believe it?" He presses on the gas, making the wheels screech forward, not once looking back at his confiscated property. "We will find ourselves a cottage on the beach, and no one will prevent us from enjoying our holiday. After all, they can't confiscate the sea, can they?" He laughs again, a violent laughter, making him pull to the side of the road to let it pass. When he calms down he wipes his tears and drives on, slowly now, craning his neck to the right and left as he looks for a " To Rent" sign. And there, at the edge of the sea, he finds it, a white house with blue shutters and muslin curtains that sway in the wind, a hammock swinging between two trees in the garden, and a terrace looking out on the water. "Ladies," he says. "I'm going to call this house's owner and settle the rent. And then I'm going to take a long, uninterrupted nap in that hammock. Don't wake me," he sighs, "unless it's to feed me." He gets out of the car and breathes the salty air. "Isaac!" he says as he slams the door and bangs his fist against the car's roof. "Live long enough and you will witness it all!"

Here is her father, Shirin thinks, the narrator of his own ghazal, invoking himself at the end, his hands in the air.

FORTY-FOUR

A festive spirit fills the Mendelson household for many days and nights. On the seventh day following the birth of the twins, both boys, *Gottze dank*, scores of well-wishers stream into the brownstone to witness the circumcision of the infants. From his basement window Parviz watches the passing legs, paying special attention to one pair in stockings—thin, almost boyish—whose owner, he knows, is Rachel, because of the low-heeled pumps with the bows he has seen her wear before. He puts on a clean shirt and goes upstairs.

The house overflows with guests, the men in their black suits and hats gathered in the living room, filling their plates from a long buffet table, the women in the dining room and kitchen, preparing more food for the men and helping themselves to healthy portions. He spots Zalman in a corner, laughing with a group of men. Since the incident with Rachel, his guilt amplifies whenever he is in Zalman's presence. But he tries to act as natural as he can. "Mr. Mendelson," he says, "Congratulations!"

"Parviz, you came!"

"How is Rivka? I don't see her."

"She is a bit tired. She's lying down. That's why we're not celebrating at the synagogue. It was a difficult delivery. The little devils didn't want to come out! Did you eat? Shall I fix you a plate?"

"Don't trouble yourself. I'll get something in a minute." But Zalman heads for the buffet table and Parviz has no choice but to follow. "I have good news of my own. My father was released from prison. I heard from him the same night your twins were born."

"Really?" He stops and turns around, his eyes wide. "Mazel tov! And you didn't tell us anything?"

"Well, you've been so busy with the babies. And since the shop has been closed . . ."

"What a beautiful day," Zalman says. "So filled with blessing!" He fills a plate with salads, salmon, bagels. "Here, my boy. Eat!"

Music comes on, a joyful European Jewish tune that sends the men dancing in a circle, their arms locked around one another, their feet kicking the air in tandem. On the other side a few women dance also, holding hands, their long colorful skirts creating a kaleidoscope as they swirl around the room. In the corner, next to a bookshelf of heavy brown volumes with Hebrew lettering is Rachel. In her blue dress, her hands behind her, she surveys the dancing women and glances, every now and then, at the men's section. She notices Parviz and looks away, then walks to the circle of dancing women, breaks it off by unlocking two hands and closes it again with her own, and spins with the others, becoming, like them, no more than a spiraling strip of color.

Later, for the ceremony, she stands at the threshold of the living room, her feet still in the dining room but her torso bending forward into the men's section. Parviz plays and replays the kiss—the snow, the street, her hand, their lips. Zalman and a younger, slimmer version of himself, a brother, Parviz realizes, walk to the rabbi, each carrying one of the swaddled infants on a white pillow, while Rivka, looking pale, waits for them, leaning on the wall behind the rabbi. The twins, oblivious to the procedure they are about to undergo, sleep soundly. In a few moments, Parviz knows, their shrill cries will fill the room, drowning the rabbi's prayers and the congregation's "Amens." He thinks of photographs he had seen of himself as an infant, carried in much the same way on a pillow by his own father, and imagines how his father, too, must have undergone the same thing, each generation welcoming the next with an irreversible scar—a covenant with God, yes, but perhaps also a covenant with pain, instilling in the newborn—still in his milky, talcum-dusted present—the notion of suffering, both past and future.

Afterward the twins, exhausted from their ordeal, are taken to a bedroom along with their mother. The others disperse, regaining their previous posts by the buffet table or on sofas. Red wine flows freely among the guests, a sweet, innocent wine that Parviz first mistakes for grape juice, drinking it in large quantities until someone calls out to him, "Take it easy on the wine, my boy, or we'll have to carry you out of here on a white pillow like the twins!"

"Wine? This? Oh well!" he says, refilling his cup, as do the others, laughing now, clinking their glasses in the air and yelling "*L'chaim*—To life!" Rachel stays in the doorway, surveying this room then the other. He eyes her through his wineglass and she looks at him finally, and smiles.

"You are fond of my Rachel," Zalman says, tapping his back.

"Mr. Mendelson! You scared me," he says, the wine nearly spilling out of his glass. "Me? No, I'm not fond, I mean yes, of course, since she is your daughter, but no . . ." He feels his face getting hot. He breaks into a sweat.

"Relax! She is a pretty girl. I may be her father, but I'm not blind."

Parviz hides his blushing face behind his wineglass. "Yes, I'm fond of your Rachel," he mutters.

"You shouldn't be," he says, without his earlier cheerfulness. "Unless you are willing to live a life of Hassidus, of observing orthodox practices. My Rachel," he says, looking across the room with sad, worried eyes, "is already confused. She has her heart in both worlds, here and outside. I don't want to introduce any temptations to her."

"But shouldn't she be the one to decide?" Parviz says, trying to temper the nervousness in his voice. "You can't force spirituality on someone."

"You can. I am proof of it. I once almost renounced it all for a girl because I was young and was thinking only of my own happiness."

"Whose happiness should you be concerned with then, if not your own?"

"Ah, but you see, that's the difference between your world and mine. I look at myself not as an individual, but as piece of a whole, as a brick in the house. A few broken bricks and the whole house falls down. I may have sacrificed a temporary happiness, but look at what I've accomplished. I have eight children, counting the twins, God bless them, and I'll probably have at least another two before I throw in the towel. If my children each have ten children of their own, and their children do the same, in three generations little old Zalman standing here before you will have brought one thousand decent, observant Jews into the world! Now isn't that something?"

"Well, yes." Parviz smiles. "If you look at it that way."

"That's the only way for us to make up for the extermination of our people, Parviz, you see? We have to resist temptation."

"But I'm a Jew also, Mr. Mendelson. Would it be so terrible for Rachel to end up with me?"

"You're a Jew, yes. But let me speak frankly here. If the two of you marry, the chances of her giving up Hassidic practices are much higher than you taking them on. So slowly your union, as innocent as it may seem, will dilute the religion, watering it down so much that in three or four generations what was once heavy cream will only be skim milk. You understand?"

"Yes, I understand. I think."

"Good! Now if you really, honestly, believe that you

want to become a Hassid, then come and see me. But please, don't think you can become religious for a girl. That sort of thing doesn't last."

Zalman is right about that. As much as Parviz has come to like the Mendelsons, he does not have the drive, nor the desire, to lead a life similar to theirs. And unlike Zalman, he cannot live according to a global calculus, counting his offspring like a census bureau. He realizes that he cannot plan his future; he can only remain open to it.

He walks out on the porch and leans forward on the railing, watching the five o'clock sun cast its brilliant rays on the produce stand on the corner. The reds of the tomatoes and the yellows of the bananas calm him. The days are getting longer, and will continue to do so until June, when second by second, they will shorten, an insidious evaporation that will make itself noticeable sometime in late October, when someone will look out a window at the five o'clock dusk and sigh, "Winter is coming! Turn on the lights!" So it will always be—the warm days of spring and summer giving way to the bleak nights of fall and winter, when anticipation for brighter days will begin all over again. In time, he realizes, his own darkness, like the winter he just lived, will lighten. Standing here and enjoying the remaining minutes until sunset, Parviz thinks of how this same sun, some eight hours ago, cast a similar light for his father, as he took his tea in the garden, or went for a long walk, as he liked to do before dinner.

FORTY-FIVE

Any moment now, Isaac knows, his father will die. Afterward, he will have to stand above the body and look at it, knowing that whatever it was that he once expected from it—love, or maybe even the initiation of an embrace—won't come after all.

"Isaac," his mother says. "Why are you sitting on the ground, *aziz*? It's dirty!"

"It's all right. It's cooler here than inside."

She wipes her forehead with a tissue. "I wish it would rain already."

In the garden of his parents' home, where cypresses offer him some relief from the heat wave that has been choking the city for two weeks, he watches the cigarette smoke exit his nostrils and slowly merge with the oppressive air. He looks at her, at his diminutive mother, wrinkled like a dried apricot. "Come with us in September," he says. "What are you going to do here, all by yourself?"

"Me? You think I have life left in me for a trip like that?"

"But how can I leave you here all alone?"

"You have a family to think of. And besides, how much time do you think I have left?" She runs her fingers through his hair, the way she did when he was a boy. "We should go inside, Isaac-jan," she says. "I have a feeling it won't be much longer now."

He puts out his cigarette and gets up, his muscles stiff and tired. He wonders if *he* has life left in him for a trip like that.

The room smells like disease. He walks to his father's bedside and holds his hand.

"This is it," his father says.

"Don't give up hope yet, Baba-jan."

"Hope?" He laughs weakly. "What hope? It's finished." He repositions his body with great effort, his arms shaking as he tries to move his torso upward, but fails. "So much pain!" he says.

"Do you need something? A glass of water, maybe?"

"No. And where would it go, this water, since I can't pump anything out? I'll explode!" He tries to laugh.

Isaac forces a smile. Since the end has been determined, it is the waiting that seems intolerable to him, each interminable minute infused with the possibility of death, yet passing uneventfully.

"The doctor was here this morning," his father mumbles. "He asked me . . . what is your name and what year is it. I answered. I still have my head, you see? Then he said, 'The Caspian, what is it?' And I looked at him, for a long time. I knew . . . I just couldn't find . . . 'Water,' I said. 'It's water.'

And he said, 'Yes, it's water. It's called a sea.' A sea, Isaac! I couldn't remember the word!" In his agitation he lets go of Isaac's hand and slowly lifts his arm, twice tapping the air before letting it rest again by his side. "All your life . . . you think of this . . . You ask yourself . . . 'Will I die in my bed . . . or in some freak accident?' But no matter . . . you never know what it's like until it starts . . . It's terrible . . . this thing."

"Calm down, Hakim," Afshin says. "You're getting yourself all excited."

"They say a calm overtakes you as you're about to go. But it's not true, it's just not true . . ."

And with that he goes. Afshin leaves the room in tears and Isaac stands there alone, watching the body, frozen now in a gesture of protest—the palms facing upward, the fingers slightly curled, the brow furrowed. Like an undesirable diamond, Isaac thinks, his father had been hard but had "bad cleavage." He broke easily.

THEY BURY HAKIM Amin on the last day of August in the Jewish cemetery in Tehran, next to his father, the heartbroken siphon of the family fortune, his grandfather, the silk merchant, and his great-grandfather, the rabbi from Mashhad. Aside from the rabbi performing the services, only Isaac, his mother, and Farnaz are present at the funeral. Isaac watches the casket being lowered into the ground and the earth covering it, bit by bit, until it can no longer be seen.

His father will be the last of the Amins to rest here.

FORTY-SIX

A letter arrives, from a certain "Jacques Amande," post-marked Paris:

> Hello! Just a quick note to let you know that I am well. Hajji Gholam sends his regards; he says he is sorry he wasn't able to contact you sooner. The children have grown up and have settled down. As for me, I am in my little apartment in Paris, in the Montmartre district, overlooking the Sacré Coeur church. It is small, but lovely. Hope to meet again in the future.
>
> Regards, Jacques.

Farnaz reads the letter twice before running to the bedroom, where Isaac is placing a handful of gemstones in a pouch. "Isaac! A letter from Javad. He is in Paris! He has an apartment in Montmartre."

"That devil!" Isaac laughs. "No doubt he got himself an apartment there to be close to the cabarets. Ah, that little devil," he says again, and his face opens up, a hint of playfulness returning to his eyes. "We're next, Farnaz-jan! We're next."

"Yes, we're next." The escape assembly line—people waiting their turn to cross the border and settle like dust on the world map. "If we leave this country without taking care of our belongings, who in Geneva or Paris or Timbuktu will understand who we once were?" Shahla had asked once, and perhaps she was right, after all. Even if they make it across the border, Farnaz wonders, what will become of them on the other side?

"Mostafa is bringing the rest of the payment for the house this afternoon," Isaac says.

"He'd better. He's getting this house at a bargain, that opportunist!"

"You should be happy we've even managed to sell it in such a short time."

"Yes, I'm happy. But the house is worth at least five times the price you settled on."

He throws the pouch on the bed. "The price I settled on? You think I had a choice? We are leaving, Farnaz. What part of that don't you understand? We are leaving in two weeks. You should be happy we got a buyer at all. Those smugglers, they're calling me every day, asking me for the money. And I tell them, it's coming, it's coming!"

"All right! You don't need to yell."

"But I do!" he says, walking to the bathroom and

splashing his face with water. "I do need to yell, because I can't take it anymore!" Hunched over the sink, he looks at his wet face in the mirror. "I don't have much left in me," he says, calmer now. "If it weren't for you and the children, I would probably just stay and wait out my final years with my mother."

"What final years? What has gotten into you? You're not even sixty!"

"I will be. In a couple of years."

"You have many years ahead of you, so stop talking like an old man." She sits on the bed and opens the pouch, freeing the stones on the blue satin bedspread, against which they sparkle. She runs her hand over them, their hard, still-unpolished edges pricking her skin. "You think I really want to go?"

"So now you don't want to go? You're the one who kept insisting, remember? What are you saying?"

"I'm saying what you're saying. That I don't want to go, but that I will go, because I have no other choice. Somehow I don't have the right to say that, do I? Coming from me it sounds like ingratitude. But I am tired also, and like you, I've lost much." She pushes back the stones and lies down on the bed. The heat persists despite the air conditioners working at full capacity. She watches him, still hunched over the sink, looking down. She realizes that her husband will from now on have the monopoly on grief, for the simple, inarguable fact that he has been in prison, that he has faced death, many times over, and has seen and heard others die. Her own unhappiness, negligible next to his, will have to be suppressed if they are to continue their lives together, because there is simply not enough space between them for that much sorrow. She hears him crying now, the way he had the night he heard of Kourosh Nassiri's execution. She lies on the bed and listens, without interrupting him.

She leaves the house, knowing that when she returns, it will no longer be theirs. She drives for a long time, her hands shaky on the wheel, the sun on the windshield, blinding her. Everyone's story must come to an end, she knows, but to prepare for the end, as they have—to liquidate one's belongings and sign over the deed to one's house—is not unlike selecting a casket, lying in it voluntarily, and shutting it from inside.

She stops the car to run one final errand: returning the sixteenth-century miniature to Javad's friend. The thought of spending some time in the shop surrounded by antiques comforts her, and she tells herself that if Shahriar Beheshti is not busy she'll stay for a while and have a cup of tea with him. But when she arrives, she finds the store empty and shut. She walks up and down the street, looking for it, mistrusting her memory of the exact location.

"Are you looking for Beheshti?" a carpet seller smoking outside his shop calls out.

"Yes. He closed?"

"You mean he *was* closed," the man says, walking toward her. In a lowered voice he continues, "They came after him too, khanoum. They seized everything, all his antiques, the poor man. And when he started protesting, they blindfolded him and took him away in a van."

She peers inside the shop through the glass. Nothing is left but dusty shelves, and a glass filled with turbid tea on the counter, along with a half-eaten sandwich, surrounded now by ants—Shahriar Beheshti's final lunch. "Looks like they got him recently."

"Yes, just last week."

She thanks the man and walks away, the painting still tucked under her arm. She decides to take it with her on the trip. Like them, the antiques dealer may one day cross the border, and show up in America, where he may look for them, or in Paris, where he may run into Javad at a sidewalk café. She would return it to him then, and he would hold it—this painted sheet that will no doubt become as dear to him as a lost child—the only item to remind him of times past.

FORTY-SEVEN

Isaac sips his tea at the kitchen table. Sunrise is still hours away. This morning he washed and dressed as usual, leaving his pajamas on the bedpost, his towel on the rack behind the bathroom door, his razor on the sink. Farnaz insisted on making the bed. "Why bother with the bed?" he told her.

"I don't know," she said, fluffing and tucking. "Habit."

He reviews his checklist one more time: passport, cash, aspirin, bandage, rubbing alcohol, gauze, the pouch of stones, and the diamond. Farnaz would take care of the clothes: extra underwear, one pair of pants, and one sweater for each. Her jewelry, whatever they had not sold, she would wear under her clothes; Shirin would do the same.

Habibeh appears in the doorway, her eyes puffy and bloodshot. "Amin-agha?"

"Habibeh! You are supposed to be with your mother!" His heart races as he watches her approach him. Had she known about their escape all along? Is Morteza downstairs with Revolutionary Guards, waiting to take him back to prison? "We thought you left yesterday. What are you doing here?"

"I came back last night."

"Last night? We didn't hear you. Why didn't you say anything? Habibeh, what is this? What are you—"

"Amin-agha" she says in a lowered voice. "Calm down. I came back because I had to take care of something."

For the first time he sees in her face something menacing and ominous. Is it the gap between her yellowing teeth? The mole on her cheek? Will this woman bring him to his end?

"A few days ago Abbas was working in the garden," Habibeh continues, "and he found some files buried there."

He scans the kitchen counter and spots the meat knife— its straight, glimmering blade and curved tip. Would he be able to use it if he had to? He steps back slowly, to bring himself within reach of it. I am not going back to prison, he thinks.

"Amin-agha, are you listening to me?"

"Yes, yes. But I'm not sure I'm following."

"I'm telling you that Abbas found some very strange files buried in the garden. In *your* garden."

"What files? What are you talking about?"

"I'm not sure. They seem to be files of accused people, people that the government is looking for." She pauses, then hands him a muddy piece of paper. "One of the files was for your brother. Look."

He reads, *Javad Amin, 54. Charge: smuggling vodka into the country, an advocate of indecency.* Under it is a log of the many attempts to arrest him. Isaac wonders if he should believe what he is reading. How difficult would it be, after all, for someone like Morteza to fabricate a piece of paper like this? "Did Morteza put you up to this?" he says.

"No agha, no! You have to believe me. My son and I are hardly speaking. For a while I admired him. I thought he understood more than I did. But in fact he knows nothing. I realized this after he turned in his own cousin to the revolutionaries, on account of her being a communist. Now the poor girl is in prison, no one knows where. This revolution is destroying families." She wipes a few tears, then looks at him, defiant. "I swear on the prophet Ali that the files were there," she continues. "Abbas and I didn't tell you or Farnaz-khanoum because we could see how crazed you were already. And since we didn't know what to do with them, we left them in the boiler room. It seemed to be the safest place, safer than the garden. But last night, Amin-agha, after I left and was already on the bus, I found myself breaking into a sweat, in a way that has never happened to me before. You see, I know you're not going on vacation to the Caspian today, as you said you were. I know you're leaving, for good."

"Of course we're going on vacation! You're imagining things, Habibeh."

She looks down, a quiver in her voice. "No, no. You don't have to pretend anymore. Not with me. I've known it for weeks now. And last night, on the bus, I got so scared. I thought, what if someone, maybe the new owner of this house, finds these files and alerts the authorities? All sorts of thoughts passed through my mind, Amin-agha! I thought maybe they'd catch you on your trip. So I came back and

I burned the files during the night in that abandoned alley near the baker. I kept your brother's file just so I could show you. But I'll destroy that one too. I promise."

He feels dizzy as he looks down at the paper again. He does not know what to believe anymore. "Who would put something like that in our garden?" he mutters.

"Agha, I have no idea. And I have to tell you something else: Morteza wanted to send to the authorities some letter that the empress had written you. Do you know about this letter?"

"Yes."

"We got into a big fight over it. Finally I stole it from his pocket when he was napping and tore it up."

"Habibeh . . . thank you."

"No, Amin-agha. You don't need to thank me. You don't know how hard it is for me to see you go." She wipes her tears with her sleeve. "I said some nasty things to khanoum some time ago. But you were my family—you, Farnaz-khanoum, and the children." She looks out the window, then at the clock on the wall, about to strike five. "All right. I'll go see if khanoum needs any help."

The news about the files and the letter unsettles him. How many people were plotting against him, Isaac wonders, and how many were helping him—all without his knowledge? He finishes his tea, leaving the empty glass in the sink as usual, and as he is about to walk away he glances at it, at this hourglass-shaped *kamar barik* that he bought with Farnaz soon after their marriage. He realizes that he just drank from it for the last time.

Downstairs he starts the car to warm it for Farnaz and Shirin. Last night the temperature dropped considerably and the sky clouded, without bringing any rain. They opened the windows and welcomed the cool air as they sewed cash into the lining of their travel bags, slid bank notes into the belly of a transistor radio, and stitched the diamond, wrapped in fabric, to Shirin's underwear. But the cooler air has now turned into an inhospitable chill, and as Isaac looks out at the mountain, slowly revealing itself in the morning's first light, he tries not to think of the wintry draft moving through its folds and tunnels. At the northwest tip of the country, from which they are to exit—along the border of Turkey and not far from that of Armenia—the terrain, Isaac knows, is harsh, more erratic than the landscape visible through his window, the Ararat mountains falling into plains and becoming mountains again, the cold rising insidiously with the altitude, bringing with it dry, rugged winds that pierce the bones even through layers of wool.

Habibeh holds up a Koran and makes them pass under it for good luck. "You are doing the right thing," she says, "to leave this country. No one has ever seen the eye of an ant, the feet of a snake, or the charity of a mullah!" The dog barks as they get in the car, protesting their departure. Isaac hugs her one last time, memorizing her musky scent. As they drive away Habibeh splashes a bucket of water on the back of the car—also for good luck—and Isaac watches her shrinking reflection in his rearview mirror, the empty bucket and the somber dog by her side.

They drive in silence through the streets of Tehran, just

now coming to life—people on their way to work, tea brewing in the samovars of teahouses for the daily stream of idlers, who will come, as they do every day, to pass away the hours. Once on the highway they pass the incongruent suburbs, into which the city has spilled over the years, and drive on through miles of plains. The smoke of factory chimneys clouds the sky.

Just a week ago was the anniversary of his arrest. Isaac had remembered it, of course, his stomach churning as the clock's hands were about to reach half past noon—the exact hour of his captors' appearance in his office. But he did not make a fuss about it, and neither did anyone else. "They got me exactly a year ago" he said that night to Farnaz as he brushed his teeth, the words coming out of him like an afterthought, and she, preparing a box of family photographs to be shipped to Parviz in New York, said, "Yes, I know. I've been thinking about it all day. What a year!" He understood, as she did, no doubt, that any sense of relief at what they had survived would be premature, considering the trip still to be completed.

Passing through the town of Qazvin, the seat of power of the Seljuk dynasty in the eleventh century, and three centuries later, that of the Safavids, he sees the square with its loggia of colonnades and thinks of the countless hands that had governed the country, some generous, others despotic— all ephemeral. And they had all left their marks throughout the land, colossal remnants of brick and stone, like those built by the Achaemenids in Persepolis, or ornate monuments of ceramic, whose turquoise domes towered over cities— Shiraz, Isfahan, Qom. It was in the shadow of these past glories that the country now lived.

"Before Isfahan, Qazvin was the capital of the Safavids, Shirin-jan," he says to his daughter, cramming one final history lesson into her aborted repertoire. He watches her in the rearview mirror as she opens her sleepy eyes and looks out the window, then slumps back into her seat.

In Tabriz they stop for lunch, as instructed. He dips his bread in yogurt, feels under his teeth the crunch of the cucumbers diced in it. He remembers now their weekend lunches, when they would forgo the restaurant and eat in, setting up the table in the garden—the yellow striped tablecloth a canvas for the kebabs that would arrive from the kitchen, preceded by their sizzle and trailed by their steam like trains of a bygone era. There would be yogurt, creamy and unpasteurized, bought in pots from a village in the north, Beluga caviar from Bandar-e Anzali, rice from Mazandaran, fish grilled at the last minute, melon from Qazvin, tea from Lahijan, peaches from the neighbor's garden, cherries from their own.

"Who can eat now?" Farnaz says. "I feel sick."

"Try, Farnaz-jan. We have a long day ahead of us. Try to think that tomorrow at this time we will be free."

She looks at him, then at the mildewed vinyl tablecloth, her elbow on the table and her chin in her palm. "Yes," she says. "I'd like to think that. But I'm still very uneasy about the fact that Habibeh was there this morning. And those files. What was she talking about? And that letter! You never told me about your altercation with Morteza. Why didn't you tell me?"

"What would have been the point? Now you know."

"What else haven't you told me, Isaac?"

The pianist's voice echoes in his head again, how he had called out Isaac's name in the dark. One day I will tell her about you, Isaac thinks. Not today.

They abandon their car near the restaurant and walk to the Blue Mosque, where they are to meet two men in a black car. Farnaz glances one last time at her Beetle, which they chose for this trip because they believed it would be less conspicuous than Isaac's Jaguar.

"Stop looking back," he says. "You'll turn into a pillar of salt."

The men arrive, all beard and hair, and motion to Isaac to get in.

"Mansoor-agha sent you?" Isaac says.

"Yes, get in. Fast!"

They slide into the backseat, the car taking off before Isaac has a chance to shut the door.

"We must move quickly," the driver says. "Remember this all along your trip. You cannot linger anywhere, because you may leave a trace, and these sons of dogs will smell you. Where did you leave your car?"

"We abandoned it on the street. But I replaced the license plate with the fake one Mansoor-agha gave us."

"Good." The driver watches Isaac in the rearview mirror with black, distrusting eyes. "You're going to be all right," he says.

They drive for hours, through towns and villages no longer familiar to him, and he watches their inhabitants going about their day—a woman in red slippers bent over a pail of dirty wash, three boys playing soccer on an unpaved road, kicking up the dust under their feet, a shepherd leading a flock of goats, the bells around their necks clinking. The two smugglers are not garrulous. They must make this trip several times a week, Isaac assumes, and so they have little interest in their trip or their passengers. From time to time they signal checkpoints to one another, but not much more. Farnaz and Shirin are quiet also.

As night deepens, Isaac traces the stars like a child connecting the dots, searching for a shape, as he once did in Shiraz, when he would recite to Farnaz the names of constellations—Andromeda, Aquila, Lyra—words he liked to say even if the shapes they suggested existed in his mind only. She would laugh, and say, "Tell me about Lyra," and he would speak to her of Orpheus and his lyre, and how they were both thrown into the river, floating their way to Lesbos.

They arrive at a rugged road and the car comes to a halt. "Quickly! Quickly!" the driver says. "You must switch from this car to the pickup."

Isaac grabs Shirin by the waist and glides her small, compliant body out of the car; Farnaz runs out of the other side. From afar he sees people seated in the back of the truck.

"The lady and the little girl go in the front," the truck's driver says when he sees them. "You, in the back!"

He climbs in the back, where he carves for himself a spot to sit. He is surrounded by some fifteen pairs of feet—all male, except for those of a young, pregnant woman wearing sneakers with sheer flesh-colored stockings; on her left foot, under the stocking, the filigree of a gold anklet is visible thanks to the driver's flashlight. "Excuse me," he tells the driver, who stands below, directing more people to the truck. "This young woman . . . she is pregnant. Maybe she can sit in the front with my wife."

"No time for this," the driver says, helping an old man climb into the back. "You mind your own business. Your family got the front seat because of the extra cash you paid. What do you think?" He gets in the truck, accelerating with a trained, furious foot.

Despite the darkness Isaac feels the other passengers' eyes on him. Again he has been singled out, as he had in prison. Why is it, he wonders, that wealth must always be accompanied by guilt, if not shame? Had he not worked hard for it, and had it not, in the end, saved his life? Had it not ensured his family's comfort, as it does now—his wife and daughter the only ones of the group seated safely inside the truck? Why the constant indignation at a man who dares to live well? Does living well imply selfishness? Was he—Isaac Amin—a selfish man?

The truck wobbles forward, stones bursting under the tires and hitting the sides of the vehicle. The night is cold, the wind made more piercing by the truck's speed. From time to time the woman's foot, extended because of her pregnant stomach, touches his right calf, but she does not seem to notice. He lets it be, the small, jeweled foot stirring in him a certain instinct—fatherly, he thinks—but perhaps simply masculine.

The truck comes to a stop. They are told to dismount

and walk to a stone house on a hill. Inside a few people are seated on the floor, filling their plates from platters of rice and potato stew. The two smugglers from Tehran are there also. "Amin-agha! Good, you made it," the young one says, rising and wiping his mouth.

"Mansoor-agha, what's all this?"

"A quick meal before we set off. Sit. Eat."

"What do you mean 'eat'? I'd like to get going."

"You'll see what I mean when we'll be walking through the mountain at three in the morning in the bitter cold. This is not to entertain you, believe me. You must eat if you want to withstand the trip."

Isaac examines his fellow passengers: the pregnant woman; three young men with round faces and dark, pensive eyes—brothers, no doubt; a few middle-aged men; an older man wearing a fedora; a young, quiet boy of sixteen or seventeen, who reminds him of Ramin Ameri; and a man about his own age, with salt-and-pepper hair, dressed in a white suit. Isaac sits next to him.

The man offers Isaac a plate from a stack near him. "Your first time?" he says.

"Yes, first and last, I hope," Isaac says, taken aback by the question.

"It's good to hope. But one can never be sure. Me? It's my third time."

"You got caught twice? And here you are again. You're strong-willed."

"No. Just desperate."

"What happened when you got caught?"

"Money bought my freedom. Actually, my father's money, God bless his soul." The man has the lean, elegant build of an aristocrat and the face of a poet, capable of irony, but too injured to use it. The white suit, not the most convincing camouflage, must not help his chances, Isaac thinks. The man's penchant for tragedy is endangering the whole group.

Afterward they are told to relieve themselves in the woods and they stream out of the house like schoolchildren, taking turns, two or three at a time. Farnaz, Shirin, and the pregnant woman head out together. Isaac walks out with the man in white. Urgent urine, his own and the man's, drills into the ground.

"So why do you think you got caught twice?" Isaac says, thinking again of the white suit.

"Some people are born with bad luck. I may be one of them. The things I touch turn to dust. I squandered my father's money. I studied music in the best schools in Europe, but I turned out to be a third-rate pianist."

You're lucky to have been a third-rate pianist, Isaac thinks. Had you been first-rate, you would have been dead.

"Now that music is banned altogether," the man continues, "there is nothing left for me in this country. This white suit, it's from my wedding band days. I wear it to remind myself of my failures, so that I may start fresh in a new country. It's ridiculous, at my age, to dream of starting over, isn't it?"

Unsure of what to say, Isaac drops the subject. When they reach the house he sees rows of horses parked outside.

"You said nothing about horses, Mansoor-agha," Farnaz is saying to the young smuggler.

"Come, get on the horse, Farnaz-khanoum," he says. "Don't worry. I saved you the best one."

Isaac watches his frazzled wife being led away and feels responsible, somehow, for her distress. He holds Shirin's hand and stands in line. A large, uncooperative horse is brought to him, and he is told to mount it, with his daughter. The horse fidgets, refusing his passengers, turning right, then left, then in circles, and stops, finally accepting his fate.

The group sets off, each horse guided by a villager. Stones and gravel roll under the horses' hooves. He holds his daughter's cold hands, wrapped around his waist, and taps them gently from time to time to keep her awake. He hums to her, a little song that he would sing when he would drop her off at school, "*Ressidim-o, ressidim. Dame kouhi ressidim*—We have arrived, we have arrived, we have arrived at the foot of a mountain." The night is brisk and black, revealing little. He looks for his wife among the moving shapes, but sees nothing. He trusts she is there, on her small horse, looking for him also. The only visible shape is a pale dot far ahead of him, which he knows is the man in white. Why hadn't the smugglers made him cover up? This seems typical of his country—the fondness for drama, exhibited by the man, and the lack of attention to detail, demonstrated by the smugglers. And me, Isaac asks himself, why didn't I protest? He wonders if, by renouncing his old life, he has also surrendered his old self: he is no longer the one in charge.

Hours later the horses are brought to a halt and they

dismount in a field of wild vegetation. With his stiff back he walks through the stalks, as tall as he, holding Shirin's hand, looking for Farnaz. The joy he feels at finding her reminds him of what happiness is.

They walk for hours in the dark. In the distance patrol lights glimmer, spinning like a carousel. "That's Turkey, over there," Mansoor says from time to time. "We must follow the lights." But the lights don't seem to be getting any closer, and Isaac wonders if they will really make it across by dawn. He holds his wife's rigid hand, and watches his daughter, a few meters ahead of him, holding Mansoor-agha's hand. They tread quietly through the unmarked path. From time to time people whisper to one another and count heads, making sure no one has been lost. The pregnant woman trails the group.

Isaac thinks of the cities ahead of him—Ankara, Istanbul, Geneva, New York—and of the cities behind him—Tehran, where his home stands, empty now of life; Ramsar by the Caspian, its air filled with fog; Isfahan, with its domes of blue; Yazd, where brick alleys shelter its inhabitants from the daytime heat and nighttime freeze of the desert, and where the undying flame of the Zoroastrians burns in a small urn of oil; and his beloved Shiraz, the city of his youthful summers, where he discovered both poetry and Farnaz, and where, along the mausoleums of the medieval poets Hāfez and Sa'di, he recited verses, finding his future in them. Occasionally passersby would see him with his books and ask him for a Hāfez oracle, and Isaac, who in his younger days believed in such divination, would oblige them: "What's on your mind?" He would ask, and people would say, "my sick mother, my dying father, my dreadful job, my poverty, my dead-end marriage." It was usually the dejected who sought divination. He would open the divan of Hāfez for them, and the first verse that would catch their eye was believed to hold in its letters the answer to their question: "The wheel of fortune is a marvelous thing: / What next proud head to the lowly dust will it bring?" or "Not all the sum of earthly happiness / Is worth the bowed head of a moment's pain." Come September he would pack his bags and head back north to Tehran, knowing that in eight months he would return. The Septembers of Shiraz, unlike this September, held in them the promise of return.

They arrive at a Turkish village at dawn. The runaways trickle into a makeshift house—a bare room, really. They find a spot on the floor, keeping silent and to themselves. Isaac smiles at the man in white, covered now with mud and grime. The man nods and smiles back, holding up his right thumb. *It's ridiculous, at my age, to dream of starting over.* But the promise of milk and honey keeps us going, doesn't it? The pregnant woman arrives last, holding on to her stomach. People get up and make room for her; space is all they have to offer. Sitting in the bare room with his wife and child, Isaac thinks of his mother, now on the other side of the border, alone.

A few hours later a truck carries them from the village to Ankara, where they wait for a bus to Istanbul. It's a cool, sunny morning, white linen floating outside the houses' windows. A woman across the street dusts her carpet by her window, another waters her anemones. Here, too, Isaac thinks, people carry on with their lives, as they no doubt do in the neighboring town, and the town after. Here, too, people want hot coffee, cool breezes, clean sheets, good love.

He will soon have to arrange for a fake entry stamp on their passport and visas for Switzerland and America. In Geneva, their first stop, he will visit his banker to retrieve the remnants of his life's work, and no doubt visit Shahla and Keyvan, who by now must have settled into a small apartment somewhere, maybe overlooking the Saint Pierre cathedral, or Lake Leman, which will distract them with its annual springtime regatta. Once in New York, they will plan, together with Parviz, for the weeks, months, years ahead.

But for now he looks at his wife, with whom he has shared an education in grief, and at his daughter, who is falling asleep standing up. Later in Istanbul they will sit by the Bosporus, squirting lemon on their grilled fish, remembering the Caspian and imagining all the waters that await them, elsewhere.

ACKNOWLEDGMENTS

I want to thank Lee Boudreaux, whose sensibility, expertise, and thoughtfulness make her the kind of editor I always dreamed I would one day have; Daniel Halpern for his vote of confidence; and the entire staff at Ecco for their enthusiasm and tremendous efforts. I am also grateful to David McCormick, who has been not only an excellent agent but also a good friend, P. J. Mark for taking this book to nearly all corners of the world, and Alison Smith for making the first introduction.

I will forever be indebted to my dear friend, Joy Jacobson, for reading every draft and offering her invaluable comments (and for bringing me tea and fruit while I wrote) and to Hilary Jacobs for restoring my faith in the possibility of goodness. Many thanks to Lucy Rosenthal, whose early encouragement drove me to pick up the pen (those morning workshops in the hills of Umbria have left behind an indelible imprint) and to Melvin Bukiet, Joan Silber, and Sheila Kohler, who offered me their generous advice as I began this book.

I am grateful to the Corporation of Yaddo for granting me a month of uninterrupted silence, Sean Kennedy for letting me use her house as a retreat, and Diana Mason for her incessant generosity. Thanks also to the photographer Abbas, whose powerful images of Iran offered me great inspiration, to Simin Habibian for her book, *1001 Persian-English Proverbs*, and to the many political prisoners whose candid accounts provided me with the painful details of imprisonment and torture: specifically, I am indebted to Hassan Darvish, Monireh Baradaran, and my own dear father, Simon Sofer.

Many thanks to Tanya, Prudy, and Marc for their continuous encouragement, Stephanie and Andrew for their kindness and enthusiasm, and Maya and Ellie for helping me dust off my memories of childhood. Thanks also to Shahrzad for her heartfelt support, to Sophie, who was there for me when it mattered most, and to Olivier, who shared my life as I wrote this book and filled my days with humor and lightness. Finally, I want to thank my brothers, Joseph and Alfred, who throughout the years have offered me so much comfort and affection, my loving sister, Orly, with whom I have shared both terrible grief and great joy, and above all my parents, Simon Sofer and Farah Abdullah-Shlomo Sofer, whose boundless love continues to sustain me.

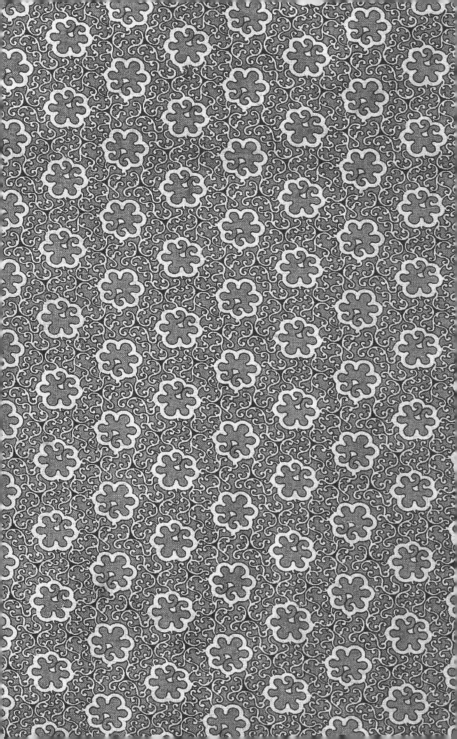

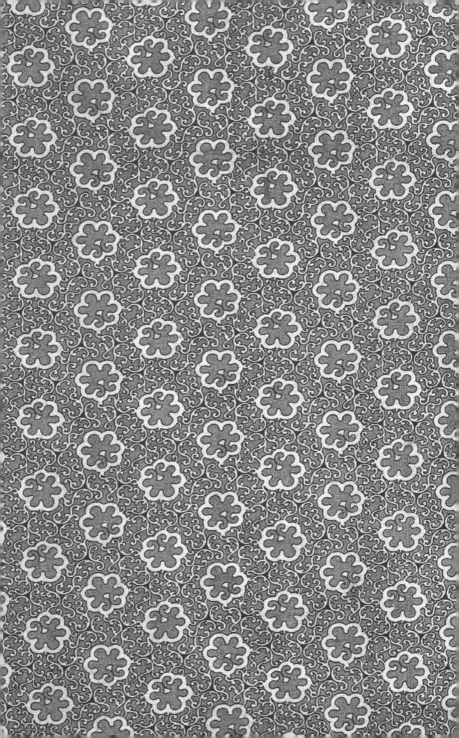